Carol Arens delights in tossing fictional characters into hot water, watching them steam, and then giving them a happily-ever-after. When she's not writing she enjoys spending time with her family, beach-camping or lounging about in a mountain cabin. At home, she enjoys playing with her grandchildren and gardening. During rare spare moments you will find her snuggled up with a good book. Carol enjoys hearing from readers at carolarens@yahoo.com or on Facebook.

Also by Carol Arens

'A Kiss Under the Mistletoe'
in *A Victorian Family Christmas*
The Viscount's Christmas Proposal
Meeting Her Promised Viscount
The Gentleman's Cinderella Bride
Marriage Charade with the Heir
The Truth Behind the Governess

The Rivenhall Weddings miniseries

Inherited as the Gentleman's Bride
In Search of a Viscountess
A Family for the Reclusive Baron

Discover more at millsandboon.co.uk.

THE LADY'S CONVENIENT HUSBAND

Carol Arens

MILLS & BOON

First published in Great Britain 2025
by Mills & Boon, an imprint of HarperCollins*Publishers* Ltd,
1 London Bridge Street, London, SE1 9GF

www.harpercollins.co.uk

HarperCollins*Publishers*, Macken House, 39/40 Mayor Street Upper,
Dublin 1, D01 C9W8, Ireland

ISBN: 978-0-263-34540-7

10/25

FSC
www.fsc.org
MIX
Paper | Supporting responsible forestry
FSC™ C007454

This book contains FSC™ certified paper
and other controlled sources to ensure responsible forest management.

For more information visit www.harpercollins.co.uk/green.

Printed and Bound in the UK using 100% Renewable Electricity
at CPI Group (UK) Ltd, Croydon, CR0 4YY

Dedicated to the ladies of Canoga Park High School
Class of 1966 and friendships that last a lifetime.

Chapter One

Winter 1887, Montana, The Crooked R Ranch

The first sign of the wicked thing coming happened on the last sunset of the year. Folks from neighbouring ranches commented on the unnatural purple-yellow light hovering over the horizon that evening. Boone Rawlins hadn't paid it much mind at the time. Even if he had known it as an omen of disaster, there was nothing he could have done to get out of its way.

Now, days later, all anyone could do was hunker down and pray they'd survive the blizzard bearing down upon the land.

The ranch house was solid because Boone had gone to the effort of harvesting the thickest, most durable logs he could find to build it. He'd sweated in the heat and ached all night after he built it. But now he was thankful that he'd gone to the effort because the thick logs had held sturdy throughout the first day and night of the blizzard.

Living in Montana all his life, Boone had seen plenty of storms. But never one like this, where nature seemed alive and raging and almost intentionally hostile.

As much as he felt the need to check on the cattle, he could not risk going outside. It would be a useless thing to do and far too dangerous with the temperatures being glacial. Even if he didn't freeze, he'd be blinded by snow swirling around his head as thick as a bee swarm.

The herd would live or die in the elements and there was nothing to be done about it.

Die was what he reckoned. The poor beasts had gone into the blizzard weakened from hunger because of an earlier thaw followed quickly by a freeze. The grass the herd ate was now covered in a layer of ice. Even if the herd managed to live through the cold, they would likely starve.

The horses had better odds, having the shelter of the barn and the feed he'd put in their troughs only hours before the blizzard hit.

For all that he was thankful to be sitting in his chair in front of a great warm fire, it did not keep him from biting his tongue to keep from spewing useless curses.

It might be days before he knew if he was financially ruined, and his neighbours with him.

Wind howled under the eaves with an unsettling moan…as if a graveyard had let loose of its ghosts.

His belly gave a sickening turn thinking of all the

death happening beyond his front door. It was unlikely that any living thing caught out there would survive.

Even people…especially them.

The smell of baking biscuits filled the parlour. It was a good, homely scent but it set his stomach on edge. Could be it was guilt for being safe inside when some were not.

'Are we going with the angels, Uncle Boone?'

The sound of Marigold's voice jerked his attention away from the snow piling up the window and over to the kitchen doorway.

He dug for a smile and, seeing biscuit crumbs dotting the child's mouth, it wasn't so hard to find one. He only wished her lips were not trembling.

Sweet baby must be terrified. She would be remembering her father and how last November he had died from exposure in a similar storm. The memory was never far from his own mind, even on days when the weather was easy.

At only four years old, Marigold had lost her only living parent and Boone had lost his business partner. He swallowed hard to keep tears from welling in his eyes. There was a time for indulging in grief and this was not it. The child who called him Uncle needed him to be strong and confident.

Boone reached his hand towards her and flexed his fingers. Marigold raced forwards and scrambled onto his lap. He wrapped his arms about her and kissed the top of her head with its dark wavy hair.

At the heart of it, Marigold was akin to his own child. He'd been the one to soothe her newborn cries when the angels took her sweet mother, Guadalupe. He'd rocked her through the night for the following three months while Grant was too weak with grief to be a father. Her first baby smile had been directed towards him.

'There are angels here for certain, little darlin'. But to keep us safe, not take us away. Don't you be afraid.'

He made sure to sound unwavering. To express his faith in the strength of the log house and the presiding angels hovering in protection.

Montana could be a breath of Heaven. But it was as harsh as Hades when it wasn't. There was danger in every season if a person was not watchful.

Not only were there were grizzlies, cougars and snakes to be wary of, but there were also the gentle streams that turned tumultuous without warning when thunderstorms happened higher up in the mountains.

From a tender age, Boone had been instructed on how to live on this land. His father had taught him that being caught off guard could be fatal. If a person was to survive he needed to be as much a part of the land as a bird or a tree was. A man's duty was to be prepared for the turns nature took, for his own sake and the sakes of those who depended upon him.

Yet, there were three graves on the hill several hundred yards from the house to remind him that no matter how prepared a man was, it might not be enough to save those he was responsible for. Life could be snatched away from one breath to the next, in a blink or a heartbeat.

A blizzard could get a person so turned around that they could freeze to death only feet from their front door. That is what had happened to Grant and some others Boone had heard of.

Boone's partner, Baron Grant Greycliff from England, used to say he didn't fit in with London society. For all that he'd tried to, Grant hadn't completely fit in in Montana either. He had never respected the land as a man should and now Marigold was an orphan.

'You are shivering, Marigold.'

Not from cold he thought. There was enough firewood stacked inside to last until the spring thaw if it came to it.

'The wind is scary,' Marigold said shakily.

'It's only a sound, little darlin'. No reason to be afraid of it. We are snug as can be inside.' He grinned at her and winked. Hopefully, his playful attitude would make her feel safer.

'Leaves are afraid. Wind blows them out of trees and we never see them again.'

'Yes, that's true…but let me look at you.' Boone lifted her chin with his thumb, gave her a frown. 'Hmmm, your eyes do look green all of a sudden. And your hair…now that I see it close up, it looks green, too. I wonder if you are becoming a leaf?'

Marigold blinked chocolate brown eyes at him.

'Senora Martinez,' he called towards the kitchen where whatever the cook was making enveloped the house with delicious scents of spice and stewing beef. 'Come and have a look at our girl. Tell me if you think she is becoming a leaf.'

Senora Martinez peeked out of the kitchen, brows arched in her round, wrinkled face. Bustling across the room, she wiped her hands on her apron. Petunia, a large hairy dog made up of a few unknown breeds, trotted after her sniffing hopefully at her apron pocket.

Senora Martinez withdrew a hunk of cheese and fed it to the dog.

'Oh, si…perhaps it is true.' The cook cocked her head and clicked her tongue.

'I'm not a leaf! I'm a girl!'

'And that is what you must remember.' Boone tapped the child on her little round nose. 'You are a girl and the wind is not going to blow you away. I will not let it.'

He had not meant to let three graves mark the top of the hill either but there they were.

No matter the cost, there would not be another.

Even as he silently vowed it, he understood that matters of life and death were not in his hands…not ultimately. If it were true, his wife's smile would not just be a memory. Susanna would be smiling at him from the chair beside his.

April 1, 1887

Boone guided his fretful horse up the hill towards the three gravestones without looking to his right or his left. If he did he would see the bodies of his cattle rotting in the spring thaw.

There was nothing he could do about breathing, though. The stench was suffocating.

The results of the storms of '86 and '87 had come to be known as the Great Die Up. Every one of his neighbours had fallen victim to it. Thousands of acres around him were filled with a nightmare of decomposing cattle and broken dreams.

Dismounting his horse, he looped the reins around the top rail of the fence surrounding the small graveyard.

He went to Susanna's grave first. He knelt down, took off his hat and set it on the grass. Memories of her played in his mind. Enough time had passed that there was more joy than sorrow in remembering. Still his eyes were damp.

'I had to sell the ranch,' he told her. Somewhere, she would be listening. Even if it was not from this very spot. 'All our neighbours have sold out too. There is nothing left. I made enough money from everything to begin again someplace else. Someplace safer to bring up a child.'

He glanced to the left, at the grave of Marigold's mother. 'Guadalupe, I promise I will raise your daughter to be as fine a woman as you were on this earth. I have always loved Marigold as if she were my own. But I reckon you know that already.'

He shifted his gaze to the grave next to Guadalupe's.

'There was nothing I could do to save our ranch, Grant. I hope you cannot see what our place has become.'

A hell of death and stench was all that was left of their dream. Their bit of heaven was no longer a fit place to live.

'Even back when you left me your house in London in your will, I never expected to see the place. But I'm taking Marigold there. It seems fitting for her to know where her father came from. With her being the only one left of your family line, I'll make sure she knows. We won't be there long though. With what I made from the sale of the Crooked R, I purchased a ranch…or a farm is what they call it in England…in Oxfordshire. I don't think you will mind, but I'll sell the house in London to buy cattle for the farm. I'll carry on with what we planned. Your little girl is legally mine now that the lawyer got that settled. But she'll up safer on the farm than in London, I think.'

Safer than here for certain, with no bears, wolves or rattle snakes. Life was bound to be gentler in England. Nearly as gentle as his parents' orange groves in California, where his parents moved when his father's aches and his mother's pains had sent them to an easier climate.

It had been a hard, sorry time for Boone when his parents went away. He had no other family but them. The same had been true for Grant. It is one of the things that had bound them.

Now, seeing how things had come to ruin, he was relieved his parents had gone to live in California.

There was a letter in his saddlebag from his mother urging him to go and join them there where, at this time of year, the air was scented with blossoms. While he had waited out a blizzard, his parents had been harvesting oranges…golden sunshine they claimed.

'I wrote her back, Grant. Turned her down,' he said as though his late partner had heard the thoughts he had not spoken aloud.

Grant knew how deep Boone's love for ranching was. How the land and the beeves were his breath and his heartbeat.

'I will start our dream over again but this time in England.'

That's about all he had to say to Marigold's parents. But there was still Susanna. He'd expected to have a lifetime's worth of things to say to her. But now it was only goodbye. Although he had uttered a soul-ripping goodbye after she took her last breath, he had continued to come and speak to her at her grave site since.

Now here he was to say goodbye for the last time.

He touched the letters on the gravestone and traced the grooves that etched her name.

'I've got to go,' he whispered. He closed his eyes,

felt his throat cramp with tears. 'I know you already have and now I must. I hope you do not mind.'

A breeze touched his hair like gentle fingers stroking it... Susanna's gentle fingers. And the oddest thing was that, for that instant, the air did not stink of death but instead of flowers.

When he opened his eyes he spotted something he had not noticed before. A crocus flower was pushing up from the dirt beside his hat. He plucked it from the soil and put it in his pocket not bothering to breathe in its scent. Crocuses had no scent.

He was as certain of this as he was of the sunshine warming his back, the floral scent he had just smelled had been his wife saying goodbye and urging him to move on with his life.

Moving on was something he knew he had to do even though kneeling there saying goodbye felt as if he were losing her all over again.

'I love you too,' he murmured.

Rising, he found that he was smiling in spite of the ache clutching his soul.

He had his memories of this ranch, of the people he had loved here. Those remembrances would always be with him.

Now it was time to move on. To take Marigold across the ocean to the place of her father's birth.

They would settle on their farm and come to love it like they had loved the Crooked R. In time, it would become home.

May 1, 1887, Mayfair, England

The sentiment 'Absence makes the heart grow fonder' was written by someone long ago but Ambrin believed it to be flawed.

Whack! Whack! She sliced a carrot more vigorously than was called for and then dumped it into a stew pot.

Perhaps she was wicked to feel embittered at being abandoned… But a proper brother would send regular correspondence to express his affection and send funds to support the home he was responsible for.

There were only the two of them after all. No other sisters, brothers or cousins. The Greycliffs were not terribly fertile. Unless her brother wed and produced an heir it was the end of the family line.

There was no one to keep Greycliff solvent except the baron. There was no long-lost relative who would come to her aid and save the family home.

Grant had promised to come home within two years. He had vowed it on his honour as her brother and she believed that a vow made should have been a vow kept.

Five years was far too long for a baron to withdraw from society. It was past time for him to come home and lift the burden of keeping the baronetcy solvent from her shoulders.

The money Grant had left for her to carry on was intended to last for two years but was now stretched too thin for anything but bare subsistence and was running out. Ambrin could not recall the last time she had indulged in anything resembling a luxury.

Worse than that, it was becoming more and more difficult to keep up the appearance of prosperity to others. She would not be able to carry on much longer without society discovering the title was all but bankrupt. She could only hope that no one noticed that she had been forced to let all but two of the house staff go.

What an embarrassment it would be if the truth had become known. Gossip rags would blather on about it with glee. Her chances of making a respectable match would be greatly hindered, if not altogether eliminated. Day by day she had become more certain that a prosperous marriage was the only thing that would save the day.

If Grant suddenly and miraculously stood before her, she would give him the sharp end of her tongue and then turn her back and not speak to him for a week.

Although that in no way meant that she did not love him. Growing up she had discovered that it was quite possible to love a person and want to throttle them in the same moment. The truth was, after she throttled him, she would be quite grateful to have him home.

She put the lid on the pot to let the stew simmer. Cooking was a skill she would never have imagined she would be called upon to learn. And, not to boast, but she was not awful at it.

One did what one must. Unless one was a baron with

a foolish dream he felt entitled to explore while leaving his only sibling to carry on with his responsibilities.

Had her brother no thought that she might have a dream of her own? A dream that did not include acting like a maid in her own home?

A flash of lightning prickled the clouds beyond the window bleaching the kitchen in brilliant, shocking white. How many seconds before thunder shook the windows? Ambrin covered her ears, her fingers trembling.

Whenever lightning flashed and thunder rolled, she became a little girl again, lost in the countryside and abandoned by the one who was supposed to watch out for her. On that awful day, Grant had run for the home their family had been visiting and left her behind. Too frightened to follow, she had cowered in the woods under a wet, scratchy hedge. Lightning had struck a tree close to her while the earth rumbled and her hair stood out from her head. Explosive thunder had left her unable to hear for a few moments. In that instant Ambrin had been convinced that death had reached its bright, sketchy fingers out for her.

For all that she counted upon Grant, her brother was not someone she could depend on. She would bear the scars of his abandonment forever. At least when it came to storms.

Footsteps tapped in the hallway. Millie Burton, her aged housekeeper, hurried into the kitchen with her skirts streaming about her short, plump frame.

'My dear, come into the parlour at once. It won't sound as loud.'

'The stew is ready to be served, I shall—'

Another flash of lightning brightened the room. Thunder crashed, closer this time.

A bull snorted in her face.

No, that was then. She blinked away the vision of the big wet nose. And yet no matter how much she willed herself not to tremble, she could not manage.

Over the years during her brother's absence she had become a bolder person…independent even. But in this moment, she was not.

'Let me dish up for us this time. And we will eat in the parlour, where there are not as many windows as there are in the dining room. The storm will not seem as bad. We shall be ever so cozy.'

'Yes, thank you, Millie. Perhaps it will help.'

Five years ago, she would not have taken meals with the house staff, nor would she have called them by their first names. Such a thing would be unheard of.

Now however, if she did not dine with them, she would be dining alone. Besides, she was quite fond of the housekeeper and butler, Millie's brother, Frederick Haver. Somehow, along the way, they had become more like an aunt and an uncle to her.

Taking heart, Ambrin reminded herself that the lightning would soon pass. She entered the parlour where Frederick sat in his chair, clearly waiting on his meal. He arched his wrinkled brow expectantly.

'Dinner will be out shortly. Your sister is serving us tonight,' Ambrin told Frederick while she picked up the fireplace poker and bent to poke the logs. Flames leapt and the wood crackled.

'I wonder if you know how much we appreciate you, my dear miss. We are past an age to be of much help. If you turned us out I do not know what would become of us.'

'Turn you out? After all your years of service to this family? Do not even think of it. I am grateful for you both. I cannot imagine how I would get by without you.'

In the moment, Millie came into the parlour carrying a stack of trays with three steaming bowls balanced on top.

She served her brother first.

Frederick smiled warmly at Millie. His eyes twinkled.

Not for the first time, Ambrin envied their close relationship. Even if Grant were here, she wondered if they would be as devoted to one another.

With her brother always in pursuit of some dream or another, he rarely gave her a thought...as his lengthy absence would attest to.

'What you will do is marry of course. Frederick and I will not be here forever and you do not wish to live in this big house alone.'

Ambrin dearly loved her family home. Every door and window, each familiar creak and groan of the floor, but living here by herself did seem a dreary prospect.

They were right, of course, there was nothing for it but to marry of necessity…or more precisely, desperation. They could not go on as they were. Oh, but the very idea made her heart droop. Since the time she had her first romantic crush on the grocer's delivery boy, Ambrin had set her heart on a love match.

Mother and father had one. Millie too, before she was left a young widow and came to work at Greycliff House.

Perhaps if she could hold on for a little bit longer, Grant would walk through the front door and things would return to the way they had been. If she could only get by for another week, or month…surely not another year…but if she could, she might escape a marriage of convenience and make her love match.

'My glory but that rain is coming down hard!' Frederick let his soup spoon pause halfway between the bowl and his mouth to say so. 'Loud as I've ever heard it.'

'That may be,' Millie declared, then handed Ambrin her bowl. 'But it will move out quickly and with no harm done. Wait and see. Tomorrow the garden will be all a dazzle.'

Millie settled into her chair. 'Isn't this lovely?'

Lovely? If Ambrin could somehow not hear the thunder and the rain it might be. She really did need to master this anxiety.

'Warm stew, good company…nothing could be finer,' Ambrin declared in an attempt to convince herself that a bolt of lightning was not going to pierce the ceiling.

That it was not going to hit the window and blaze through the house. Nor was a huge, smelly bull going to lumber through the parlour.

Impending doom was not sitting on her shoulder.

That was what she was thinking when the front door suddenly blew open.

Wind whooshed a smattering of leaves inside. They were wet and made smacking sounds when the gust pushed them across the hallway floor. From where she sat she had a clear view of the doorway and the darkness beyond.

A blaze of lightning revealed the black silhouette of a man.

Heaven save them!

The dark figure was large and had a broad stance. His hat dipped low over his brow. She had an eerie sensation that a character from one of her brother's American dime novels had come to life to threaten them all.

She leapt to her feet, grabbing the fireplace poker as she rose. Her bowl thudded on the floor. Maybe she was just having a fearful vision because of the violent weather, she thought, although the metal of the poker in her fist felt hard, warm from the flames and quite real.

This moment was no vision.

There truly was an encroacher standing in her hallway. She firmed her stance, brandished the poker at him.

'Get out or I shall stab you!' Why, oh why, did her voice have to quiver? If it came to it and she lunged at him, he would only snatch the weapon from her.

Rather than charge at her, the man reached behind him and closed the door on the rain and wind.

Lamplight from the parlour shone dimly into the hallway, revealing the villain to be every bit as large as she'd feared. What had not crossed her mind was that he would be handsome, too.

Not that it mattered in the least. Well-formed or ill-favoured she knew she should expel him from her home at once.

'Go upstairs,' she called over her shoulder to Millie and Frederick.

Frederick was the only one to move and that was to stand beside her. He took a boxer's stance, his bony fists circling.

Hopefully the old man's challenge did not inflame the villain.

So far he had not advanced towards the parlour but rather glanced behind him and nodded.

Drat, oh, drat! He must have an accomplice.

Perhaps they should all retreat upstairs and wave franticly out of a chamber window to signal a passing constable.

Chapter Two

Moments previously, Boone had carried Marigold up the front steps of his new home. He'd wrapped her in his coat in an attempt to keep her dry but it hadn't done much good since the coat was already soaked by a downpour of relentless rain.

The house ought to have been vacant. Yet smoke rose out of the chimney and, caught by the wind, skimmed across the rooftop.

Concerned about what trouble he would find on the other side of the door, he had placed Marigold behind him and ordered Petunia to guard her.

Trouble turned out to be a small woman waving a fireplace poker at him and an old man punching the air with his fists.

Not much of a threat, he reckoned, so he glanced behind him and nodded for Marigold to come out.

'Good evening, ma'am.' He addressed the woman since she seemed to be the leader of the squatters.

He walked forward slowly, keeping Marigold's small

hand clutched in his. Petunia trotted beside them wagging her tail in anticipation of making new friends. As far as Boone could tell, the dog was going to be disappointed.

Not sure what to say next, he simply watched the woman. Would she attack him with the poker or have a reasonable conversation with him?

The lady was very easy to look at and that was a fact. A man could forget she meant him harm if he gazed too long at those wide pretty eyes, which were almost but not quite brown. More like the colour of autumn honey.

She had a strong, yet feminine, face. She must have come by that independent tilt of her chin by living a hard life.

He'd never had to seek shelter in a place that didn't belong to him but he supposed it would take a toll on a person. Especially when she had the care of a pair of elderly folks.

How long had they been in his home and how long was it going to be before he could get them out?

Not until the rain let up and England sure did seem to be a rainy place.

At least they had laid a fire in the hearth, which had already warmed the room. A delicious aroma filled the place, too. He hadn't smelled anything so mouthwatering since his last meal with Senora Martinez.

The squatters looked defensive of the place so he

figured they must have been here for long enough that they felt they had a right to live in his house.

'I don't mean you any harm, ma'am. You may put the weapon down.'

'Once you and that vicious beast leave the premises I will do exactly that.' The woman danced forward, lunging at him in her dainty shoes.

'Ambrin, dear, I do not think the dog is vicious. Look how it is wagging its tail,' the older woman pointed out.

'For mercy's sake, Millie, the man is wearing a gun on his hip. Even if the dog does not attack, we could be shot.'

'Don't be silly. No one shoots a person while holding the hand of a little girl,' the older gentleman said, dropping his defensive stance.

'Uncle Boone only shoots dangerous critters. Like rattlesnakes,' Marigold pointed out.

The woman narrowed those amber coloured eyes on him. 'I assure you, if it is snakes you are hunting, you will not find them here.'

The situation didn't call for a smile but he couldn't hold back a grin. Anger made the woman look even prettier, with her cheeks red and blotchy.

For the life of him, though, he couldn't figure why she would be angry. It was his home she had invaded, not the other way around.

Petunia took the moment to trot over to the bowl and lick up whatever had spilled on the floor.

'I am so, so, hungry, Uncle Boone.'

'Whatever you've got cooking smells mighty good. Under the circumstances, I reckon it's not too much to ask if Marigold might have something to eat.'

'Under the circumstances?' The lady exclaimed, her eyes blinking sparks.

'There are no circumstances in which a child ought to go hungry.' The older woman bustled forwards, cupped Marigold's cheeks in her plump, wrinkled hands. 'Aren't you the sweetest thing?'

'Yes, ma'am. It's what my pa used to say before he went with the angels.'

The poker sagged in the younger woman's fingers. She nibbled her bottom lip while looking at Marigold.

'Very well, then. Place your weapon in the umbrella stand beside the door.'

It seemed safe enough so he did as he was told.

The older lady shot the younger a frown. 'Ambrin Malcomb, it is not like you to behave so uncharitably. We must entertain strangers, must we not?'

'There is a vast difference between a common stranger and an armed intruder breaking into the house.'

Malcomb? The name rolled over in his brain a few times before he took in the import of what the old woman said.

Boone could not have been more stunned had he accidently discharged his gun into his gut.

'Just goes to show,' the younger woman mumbled while walking stiff-backed out of the room. 'Storms always bring ill tidings.'

Millie was correct. They must entertain strangers and there was plenty of stew in the pot. She had meant for it to last for tomorrow's meal as well but she would not deny a child a meal…and she supposed the man must eat as well.

Perhaps hunger is what had driven them into her home. Once they were fed, they would leave.

She dished up a bowl for the child and one for the man.

Coming back to the parlour she found them sitting side by side on the stone hearth with the dog stretched out at their feet. The child leaned her shoulder against the man's arm. As impossible as it seemed, the man did indeed appear to be an American cowboy…with steam curling up from his clothes.

She handed them each a bowl of stew, not fully convinced that what she was seeing was real, that the storm had not induced a vision. After all, her mind had conjured up a great smelly bull a short time ago.

Crackling flames and rain pinging the window were the only sounds in the room while the man and the little girl ate.

And no wonder for the silence. What sort of a conversation did one have with someone who rudely invaded her home? Someone who was accompanied by an adorable child and an aggressive looking beast named Petunia... Ambrin simply had no words.

The child sighed contentedly while petting the dog with the tip of her shoe.

The cowboy did not seem satisfied by his meal. No, indeed, he had not stopped scrutinising her from under his hat brim.

The fact that he had compelling eyes, so handsome and expressive that she found it hard to look anywhere else, did not put her at ease. Not even a whit.

Under the circumstances, she should not even have noticed his eyes. Let alone admired how they reflected the colour of the sky on a cloudless morning.

For pity's sake, that was the last thing she should have noticed about the trespasser.

There was but one thing to do and that was stare right back at him, being ever so careful not to expose how compelling she thought his gaze was. That might have made the man mistakenly believe she admired him in a certain way, when she did not admire him at all.

Why, oh, why was there a big cowboy and his huge wet dog in her parlour? Why was a sweet looking little girl eating stew on her hearth?

It seemed hard to believe they had simply been seeking a meal or even seeking shelter from the storm.

Such things did not happen in Mayfair.

The cowboy set his bowl on the floor, slid it in front of the dog.

'Ma'am.' He removed his hat, turning it slowly in his fingers.

If she did not know better she would take his gaze as being sad…regretful even.

But surely the fellow had no reason to be either. Here he sat, warming by the fire. His appetite had been satisfied with tomorrow's dinner. Even his dog had been fed.

The reason he was fidgeting with his hat and looking downcast must be because he was thinking about what he would do when she sent him on his way.

Yes, the child was adorable and the man had a face of the sort she had fanaticised about when she still entertained dreams of a love match, but the three of them must be on their way. The sooner the better.

His hatband was evidence enough to remind her that he was not anything like the gentlemen she had entertained in her mind. Never once had her ideal fellow worn a hat with a band fashioned from…yes, quite clearly it was…snakeskin. No doubt some unfortunate reptile he had shot with the very gun stashed in the umbrella stand.

'May I have a private word?' he asked.

She glanced about, hoping he meant her butler or her housekeeper but he was looking directly at her.

'I rather think a private word is unnecessary.' They had never met so how could it be?

'It's necessary, ma'am.' He scrubbed one large, calloused looking hand through his hair, looking at her with moody eyes. 'I wish it wasn't.'

The woman's last name was Malcomb?

It took him a minute or two of breathing deep and slow not to cuss out a dead man. Grant had never mentioned a wife, if that is what this woman was. If she was, it would make Grant's marriage to Guadalupe invalid. Then what did that make Marigold?

Even if she was not Grant's wife, she was someone named Malcomb and she clearly believed this was her home. A great mansion of a home to which he held the deed…and meant to sell.

'Ma'am.' He nodded to the older woman who was the only one to have smiled at him since his arrival. 'Would you mind taking Marigold to the kitchen? I imagine she would enjoy a treat if you have one at hand.'

'She would!' Marigold declared, then slid off the hearth.

'Come along then, my sweet,' the old woman said with an indulgent nod at Marigold and then raised a questioning brow at Boone. 'You come too, Frederick. You look as if you could use some pudding.'

Good, she understood things were going to be said that a five-year-old did not need to hear. Nor did anyone else except the woman sharing his late partner's name.

'Well, what is it?' the lady uttered with a snap in her voice as sharp as the crackling logs he sat in in front of.

Boone rose from the hearth and motioned for her to sit down in a chair near the warming flames.

'I shall stand, sir,' she declared, her eyes round from staring at his hatband.

He couldn't force her to sit so he stood closer to her. He reckoned she'd rather not be this close to him but he was about to deliver shattering news and did not wish to shout it.

Had he known she existed, he would have written to her as soon as Grant passed. When Grant had claimed he left his life in London behind for good, how could Boone have imagined he meant the people in his life, too?

His partner had always been one to act and then consider the consequences later, but this was beyond belief. If this woman... Ambrin Malcomb, was Grant's wife, his late partner was insane as well as irresponsible.

To leave a woman like her behind? To marry another? He was so angry in the moment that the bond he shared with his partner splintered some.

Here he sat with devastating news to deliver and not even knowing who he was delivering it to. Since her last name was Malcomb she was some sort of kin, which meant he was about to bring her sorrow.

'Are you Mrs Malcomb... Grant's wife?'

'Well, no... I am not.' Her face drained of colour.

Her eyes grew wary, as if she sensed some wicked news coming. 'Do you know my brother?'

His sister, then. Better than wife, he supposed, but curse it, she would still be depending upon Grant.

Brother's protected their unwed sisters. Devotion to family demanded it.

And yet it looked as if when Grant came to America, got his ranch and had a new family, he forgot his obligation in London. He must have done some serious forgetting since he had given this house to Boone. True, it had been with the intention of bettering his daughter's future, but it sure was a cruel hand dealt to his sister.

'He was my partner on the ranch.' Words cramped his throat, felt like a blamed snake was coiled around it.

'On a ranch?' Her voice sounded steady and her back looked ramrod stiff, yet her fingers trembled. 'But you have parted ways?'

Knowing what he must say it felt as if his throat was bound in barbed wire. Each swallow stabbed him with rusty, twisted spikes.

'I'm sorry, Miss Malcomb, your brother has passed away.'

'What?' Her hand flew to her mouth, her posture sagged. He lowered her to the chair but he doubted she noticed. 'No!'

Feeling saggy himself, he sat in the chair across from her.

'I'm sorry.' Pitiful words, he knew.

He had grieved horribly in his life as well as comforted the inconsolable.

Experience did not make this any easier. Each death was new. The grief raw.

The lady's shoulders trembled, she covered her eyes with pale, slender fingers.

She seemed so small and vulnerable.

Instinct, an innate need to comfort the hurting, made him lean across to wrap her in a hug. He patted her back, made crooning comforting sounds like he had when he given the news to Marigold.

'He didn't suffer,' he promised, although Boone was not certain he had not.

Freezing, he'd heard, was not an awful way to pass to the Great Beyond, once a person got numb. He had no way of knowing if it was true or not. There was only one truth in that moment and he knew that to be that he must do what he could to help this lady in her pain.

Hesitantly, at first, she lowered her head to his shoulder, clutching his shirt and weeping. In the moment they were not strangers, but folks bound in common loss.

Hers was raw, his scabbed over, but cracked and bleeding again. And so, they held one another for a moment, bound in grief.

When her sobs quieted, he drew back but held her hands to keep the comfort passing between them.

After a moment or two she let go of his hands. She

covered her mouth with her fingers, shaking her head in what he knew would be denial.

'Shall I go fetch your kin?'

'They…no…they are not my kin. It seems I no longer have any family. Grant was all…' She wept once more, perhaps harder with the shock wearing off and acceptance beginning to set in. 'There is no one else.'

He reached for her hands again, cupping them in his and giving her quivering, fragile fingers a squeeze.

'Look at me, Miss Malcomb.' A shudder went through her. She did not look up but stared at her fingertips where they peeked out from his palms. He let go of her hands, lifted her chin with his thumb. She blinked at him through a wash of tears. 'You aren't as alone as you think.'

'Oh, but I am. I have no one Mr…' She swiped moisture from her cheeks with her knuckles. 'I'm sorry, I've wept all over your vest, sir, and I do not even know your proper name.'

'Boone Rawlins. And little Marigold…she's Grant's daughter.'

Ambrin sucked in her breath all of a sudden, pressed one curled fist to her heart. 'My brother…a father?'

'Yes, it's true. So, you see, you are not alone after all.'

'I have a niece,' she whispered as if confirming the fact to herself.

Boone reckoned it must feel like a miracle to her. One life lost and another one given. It's something of how he'd felt when Marigold was born…grief and joy all rolled up in one moment.

It was for the best, he decided, to wait and tell her about the house. There was only so much a person could take in a moment of time.

'Would you like to tell Marigold you are her auntie? Or shall I?'

'I think…if you do not mind…would you? I'm quite undone and would only weep all over her.'

Boone stood up, reached a hand down to help her up. He gave her fingers a squeeze of assurance.

'I reckon she's going to be as pleased to meet you as you are to meet her. It's only been the two of us since November when…' He shrugged, not needing to say the words. She would know he meant since her brother died.

He turned to walk in the direction the others had gone moments earlier but Ambrin touched his arm, stalling him.

'Mr Rawlins, I apologise for earlier. I believed you to be an intruder.'

'That's understandable. I was as surprised as you were.'

For a moment she appeared confused, looked as if she would say something but then the sound of Marigold's laughter came from the hallway and she glanced towards the doorway.

New tears glistened in her eyes, not tears of grief

he guessed. He well remembered how one could cry tears of joy right upon the heels of tragedy.

'I want to thank you for bringing my niece home… and for bringing me news of Grant.'

Damn it, he was not here for that reason. Until he entered the house he hadn't known Ambrin Malcomb existed.

Sure did know it now, though. Watching her wrestling with grief, finding joy in meeting Marigold in spite of it, he respected the lady every which way.

At some point he would need to tell her the truth, but it would not be tonight.

It was an hour before dawn when Ambrin decided to go for a walk in the garden. No surprise really that sleep had evaded her, refusing to give even a few moments of forgetfulness.

She had retired to her quarters last night shortly after preparing the guest chamber for Mr Rawlins and Marigold.

What she had hoped is that her niece would share her room for the night but the child clung to her Uncle Boone, refusing to be separated from him.

One of the many things that had kept her awake last night had been worry over how difficult it would be for Marigold when the cowboy returned to America and left the child in England.

She had many questions to ask Mr Rawlins about her brother's life and…and his death. All she knew of the last is that Boone Rawlins did not believe Grant suffered.

All well and good for Grant, happy in his new heavenly home. As usual, he'd left her behind to do the suffering.

The thought had not finished crossing her mind when she felt wretched about it. Her brother was thousands of miles away in his grave and she was thinking about how he had deserted her for the final time.

She sobbed again but without tears. They had run dry hours ago.

Grant had not intended to leave her this time. She must convince herself that, had he not died, he would have eventually come home to Greycliff House.

But it seemed…oh how it seemed…as if he had forgotten her.

What was she to do now? The funds that remained would not last much longer. Her brother's partner had not mentioned that he was leaving any money with Marigold so she could only assume their ranch had come to naught. Which meant that she would come to naught, along with Marigold, Millie and Frederick.

There was only one way for her to provide for them. But oh how she despaired of even imagining wedding for funds.

Very well, she would not imagine it. Not now. Perhaps in a day or two…next week would be plenty of time.

This morning she would walk in the garden and take

comfort in this exquisite hour before sunrise when the world was fresh and expectant.

What she must try and think of were the good times she had shared with her brother. The times they had laughed at silly jokes they told one another. The times they raced about the garden and begged treats from the kitchen staff. If it were possible, these were the things she would dwell on.

Common moments are the memories she must cherish.

In the end, each one of them made her choke on her sobs.

She had not gone far along the path when she heard a deep bark, spotted a huge four-legged beast lumbering at her.

Hurrying towards one of the benches scattered along the path she stood on it. Wild beasts terrified her and just because this one was named Petunia did not change the fact that she looked wild, or half-wild at least.

The dog had a wide mouth, which was open, and its tongue lolled out to one side.

How faint-hearted of her to be standing on a bench and waving her skirt at a dog. Her niece was quite comfortable wrapping her small arms all over the animal even though it was as tall as she was and weighed a great deal more.

'Sit!' came a voice from the darkness. The inky silhouette of the cowboy strode out of predawn shadows. His strides were long, purposeful. He brought to mind a cougar prowling her garden. A shiver pricked the fine hairs on her neck. She was used to gentleman who were more like graceful housecats.

He lifted his hand to help her down from the bench. She hesitated several seconds before placing her fingers in his.

In spite of the cool clear morning, his hand was warm, firm and as comforting as it had been last night. For some reason the strength of his grip made her want to weep all over again.

'I reckon you had a hard night,' he said, his voice as supportive as his hand.

'It was awfu—' then her voice caught and she could say no more about it. She prayed to never have another like it. 'Would you tell me what happened to my brother, Mr Rawlins?'

'Call me Boone, ma'am. I figure with Marigold between us, it's fitting.'

'That being the case…' And she was not certain it was. Marigold was her blood kin, not his. There was really no 'between them' involved. However, having been so closely comforted by him, perhaps it would be appropriate to call him by his given name. '…you must call me Ambrin.'

She would have bet her remaining ball gowns that she was incapable of responding to his smile. But it was a compelling smile. It reflected the aura of reassurance he had about him...but that was not what she reacted to.

Heaven help her, but her heart fluttered the way a woman's heart does when she is attracted to a man. Nothing could be more inappropriate in this moment.

'How did my brother die?' she asked, coming back to the matter most pressing upon her heart.

'It was in a snowstorm. May we sit here? I'll tell you about it.'

He sat down, patted the space beside him.

When she sat, Petunia placed her wide head on Ambrin's knee, gazed up at her with soulful looking eyes. Curiously, it was as if the dog was trying to comfort her.

She was half tempted to pet the animal, but only half.

In the east, the sky was beginning to brighten. Hopefully knowing what happened to Grant would help her face the coming day.

'I don't know if you heard anything about the blizzards of '86 and '87 in America, but they were worst anyone can remember. Grant and I weren't the only ranchers to suffer from them. But the first one, the one in November, that is the one that took Grant. It had already been snowing for three days with the wind wild and contrary. The temperature was well below zero. We were rightly worried about the cattle. If they would survive or not. If our business would. One afternoon your brother took it in mind to check on them. I told him it was a fool dangerous thing to do and no point to it. But I reckon you know more than anyone how strong headed he could be when he set his mind on a course.'

'Yes… I…' She shook her head, shrugged because there was no need to say more. Clearly this man knew her brother as well as she did…perhaps better.

'I'd have tied him up to keep him inside but he went out while Marigold and I were in the kitchen having lunch and I didn't notice him go out the door. I only wish…but I reckon it's useless wishing for the past to change. Well, that afternoon you couldn't see your hand in front of your face the snow was so thick. It's easy to get turned around and lost and that's what happened. I tied a rope on myself and the porch post, and went looking. I found Grant only a few steps from the house. There were others who met the same fate. But like I said, I do not think he suffered in passing.'

She swallowed hard over the image presenting in her mind.

'Did your cattle live?' she asked because she could not bear dwelling on how horrid it must have been for Boone when he found Grant that way…and so close to safety.

'Most of them did, then. But then there was another blizzard in early January, which was the worst of them all. I lost nearly all of the cattle in that one. And then the ranch your brother and I worked for.'

'I'm sorry to hear it, Boone. It must have been crushing to lose everything.'

She ached for Boone. She was too close to financial ruin not to understand the awfulness of losing the place one loved.

But worry over losing her home and what she must do to save it would wait until later.

'Was the ranch everything Grant dreamed of? Was he happy?' Was it worth leaving her and his place in society, is what she really wanted to know.

Boone gave her a half smile, one that indicated yes and no at the same time.

'We worked hard and the ranch prospered for a time.'

Prospered? And still Grant had not sent what she needed to get by.

'Early on your brother met a pretty Mexican girl and fell in love with her. I've never seen a fellow so besotted and happy. Guadalupe was her name. They wed within a week of meeting.'

Where was her sister-in-law now? Something was not right. Why would Boone bring Marigold home to London without her mother?

'I'm glad for Grant.' She was, truly. At least one of them had experienced being in love.

Abiding love was not something she could wait for any longer. Abiding security for her household, and now Marigold, was what she had to strive for.

'It was a joyful thing watching the two of them together.' Boone took a deep breath, his gaze seemed distant all of a sudden, as if he was looking at the ghosts in his mind. 'I hate to say…but Guadalupe died giving birth to Marigold only a year later. Your brother was a broken man for a long time. I don't believe he ever truly recovered.'

'I am grieved to hear it. I suppose I should quit my sniffling and be happy for him. He found his love in this life and is now reunited with her.'

'I reckon it's true. And there is Marigold. I see your brother and Guadalupe both in her.'

Just then the first rays of sunshine topped the trees casting fingers of light across the garden. It was an inspirational sight. It lightened her heart, gave her hope for the future. She would not have her brother, nor would she have her love match, but she would have her niece and that was perhaps enough to give her the fortitude to face this day.

'Boone, I cannot express how thankful I am that you came all this way to tell me about my brother and to bring Marigold home.'

Her heart swelled so full of gratitude that she leaned sideways and kissed Boone Rawlins on the cheek. Her lips lingered inappropriately in expressing thanks because the stubble of is beard felt delightfully ticklish. And because he smelled like fresh morning air and aged leather. Also because she had not done anything that felt so unrestrained and oddly luxurious a long time.

'Although I have known you for such a short time, Boone, I will miss you when you leave,' she murmured, quite amazed at how boldly she was speaking to a man who was a stranger.

But then, perhaps the length of a friendship did not matter. One could know a person for many years and they could still be strangers. Or, as she had just discovered, one could know a person for a day and develop a regard for them.

Boone's expression clouded. Perhaps she should not have spoken so openly. She certainly should not have kissed him. He stared at the tips of his boots while second by second darkness in the garden gave way to daylight.

'There is something you have to know, Ambrin. I reckon I ought to have said it right off.'

All at once she remembered something. A comment of his that had made no sense to her but that she'd dismissed when she'd heard Marigold's laughter coming from the hallway.

'You said you were surprised to see me, but why would you be?' She scooted further from him on the bench to better look at his face to see what she could decipher from his expression. 'If you were bringing Marigold home to me surely you knew I would be here.'

'Damn it, Ambrin. I was not bringing Marigold home to you.'

* * *

Curse him for a fool. He ought to have told Ambrin the reason he had come as soon as he entered the house. But there had been Grant's fate to be told. Of all the bad news he found himself having to deliver that one had seemed most pressing in the moment.

Nothing had turned out like he expected it to when he'd arrived here. What he'd imagined is that he would bed down his horse, give Marigold something to eat and then thoroughly explore his vast new house.

Not that it could be done in a couple of hours. When he finally did get to explore the place, it might take all day.

Now, here he sat, feeling like a heartless cuss having to break her heart again.

'Of course you were bringing her home. Here she is, after all.'

'The reason I was surprised to see you…' Words felt like acid in this throat. '…is that your brother never told me about you.'

Ambrin's eyes grew wide as she stiffed a small gasp. The first, fragile sign of healing he had seen in her a moment ago was now snuffed out.

It wasn't right to curse the dead but, damn it, Grant ought to have mentioned his sister.

'He never…' her voice caught, trembled. 'He never spoke of me?'

Except for having to deal with the death of a loved

one, this was the most heart-rending situation he'd ever landed in.

While he might have been able to comfort Ambrin over the death of her brother, what he must reveal next… Damn it! There was no condolence for that.

'I'm so sorry, darlin'.' As sorry as he'd ever been. 'He didn't.'

'But how could he…' She shook her head, clearly not believing him.

'Grant did not always make wise choices. You know that. He didn't speak of his past and curse me for not asking. All he said is that he never felt he belonged in London. The ranch was his new start. I ought to have pressed him about what he left behind. Forgive me, Ambrin.'

'Did I mean so little to him, then?'

'I cannot pretend to know what was in his mind. If I could go back in time and give him a comeuppance, I'd do it.'

Gradually her expression changed, sorrow becoming bewilderment.

'It makes no sense to me. If you knew nothing about me how did you know to bring my niece here?'

He did not like himself in the moment but he liked his partner even less. How did a man crush the heart of a woman who was already grieving?

Picking each word with care, he went about it as gently as he knew how.

'As I said, Grant and I were partners. Part of that

was watching out for one another. We were as close as kin. We shared a dream of having a ranch. That life, it's not like anything else. It gets in a man's blood until he can't live any other life. But ranching is dangerous, unpredictable work. Death can come all of a sudden. It did for his wife and mine. After Guadalupe went to her glory, Grant and I made promises to each other in case one of us died. We vowed them and made them legal.'

'What promises?'

'There were a few of them, mostly having to do with protecting Marigold.'

'Which you have done. You may return home confident that I will care for her.'

The truth could no longer be postponed.

'The thing of it is, I am home. Grant left this house to me in his will.'

Chapter Three

Everything turned red. Anger flashed through her in a way she had never felt before.

None of this was true!

'You, Mr Boone Rawlins if that is indeed your name, are a cad. How dare you, a complete stranger, come into my home and tell me outrageous lies!'

Ambrin stood up, paced back and forth in front of the villain. If she'd still had the poker, she would have run him through.

Oh, he had fooled her for a time. She'd let him comfort her in grief, even. But now she saw matters clearly. Did he believe she would simply pack her belongings and surrender her home to him, a thief and a squatter?

'You have no proof of any of what you say.'

The cowboy simply sat where he was, head half bowed while peeking up at her with regret shimmering in his eyes.

Yes, shimmering. She would be more confident in her accusation if he did not look so regretful.

'There is Marigold. I reckon she's proof enough.'

Yes, there was Marigold. The realisation that she was the image of Ambrin's mother, except for having brown eyes and black hair, made her go half dizzy.

Even if the part about Marigold was true, and she glad it was, it did not mean the cowboy was telling the truth about the house.

'I will accept that my brother is dead. Also that Marigold is my niece. I will not accept that you own this house.'

And that was the end of it.

Except… 'You will leave here by noon or I will summon a constable.'

She spun about and walked towards the house. Her house!

Morning light glistened off the wet cobbled path as it caught in the raindrops of last night's storm in a wash of sparkly prisms.

This was a bright new day. What the man claimed was not true. With a dismissive flick of her skirt she put the cowboy and his lies behind her.

Not Marigold, though. The child was an unexpected blessing in her life.

'I have the will…and the deed.'

A lie of course, but still, she felt like she had been smacked by a stone between her shoulder blades. For a moment she could not catch her breath. It was as if the ghost of her brother had dealt her one last blow.

'I will send for Greycliff's solicitor. He will set you

straight on whatever documentation you claim to have,' she announced, her chin lifted a notch.

Not that she could spare the funds to pay Mr Adams, but she would not lose her home. Grant had taken quite enough from her already.

Given her more, though. She did have to credit her brother for the gift of her niece. Not that he'd meant Marigold as a gift. Had he not died she might never have known the child existed.

Were Grant not already dead, she would strangle him.

Ambrin became aware of movement beside her, then of a large, damp tongue scraping her hand.

'The dog is sensitive to your suffering,' Boone said, coming up on the other side of her. 'I promise you, I never intended for any of this to happen.'

'You may prove it by going back to America, then. You and your beast.'

'Reckon I can't do that. There is no place for me and Marigold to go back to.'

'My niece is no longer your concern Mr Rawlins. She will remain with me no matter where you go after this.'

He looked as if he meant to say something, to argue perhaps, but then did not.

With a grave expression, he walked beside her as silent as the cobbles under her damp shoes.

When they came to the garden door, he opened it.

Without a glance, she brushed past him.

'I'll do my best to make this fair for you,' he said. 'I truly mean you no harm.'

Ambrin rushed into Grant's chamber then slammed the door behind her.

The visit with Greycliff's solicitor this afternoon could not have gone worse had it been a nightmare.

Boone Rawlins, it turned out, was not a liar. He was the owner of her home. He was also Marigold's legal guardian!

Her brother had made it clear in his will that Mr Boone Rawlins would be the one to adopt and raise her niece. In the eyes of the law, it made no difference that the child was her blood kin. Even if she tried to contest the injustice, Boone was a man and therefore viewed as more fit to raise a little girl than she was.

It was unbearable. All of it!

Oh, the cowboy had seemed regretful over the whole matter but he did not give her back the house. Nor did he offer her custody of her niece.

What was the point of regretting something if one did nothing to rectify it?

All she wanted to do was scream, which she could not do while claiming to be self-possessed enough to raise a child.

'I am sorry you were my brother, Grant!' Although she meant it, she groaned and wrapped her arms around her middle.

She had not thought that of him yesterday and might

not think it in a week, but now…oh how she needed to rail at him.

Just then she noticed the dime novels that he took so much pleasure in. The very books that had caused him to dream his foolish and fatal dream of a life in the American West. Crossing to the table where they were neatly stacked, she swiped her arm. The books hit the floor with a satisfying thump. Still, the gesture was not enough to express her bitter resentment so she kicked them, then she slipped to her knees, ripped one down the spine. It was a fragile volume and tore easily, just like her brother's absurd dream.

'*The Baron's Golden Land*,' she read a title then ripped that one too. '*The Baron's Fool Mistake* more like it.'

The chamber door creaked open. Boots crossed the floor. Having known Boone Rawlins for little more than a day, she already recognised his long, bold stride.

The space next to her grew suddenly warmer when the cowboy knelt down. Oddly, his presence soothed her.

Crushed her too.

How puzzling.

He smelled wild…like leather and what she guessed pastureland would smell like. In that moment she detested anything or anyone to do with farms or ranches.

'So this is where Grant came by some of his fool-headed notions,' he murmured.

'These books ruined my life.'

She was tempted to blame the turn her life had taken on the man kneeling next to her. He would make a logical target to vent her anger on. Not a fair one though. He had been as stunned by this mess as she was. The blame lay on one person only and he was quite beyond her reach.

His dearly loved novels were not and so she continued to shred them.

'May I help?' Boone picked one up, his brow arched in askance.

Although she understood he was not to blame for what Grant did, she still felt prickly towards him. He was the one taking her house, was he not?

'You are not offended that I am insulting your former, and glorious, way of life?'

Was that truly her sounding so snappish? Indeed, yes it was! She was rather entitled to a bit of a snit, she thought.

He laughed, or snorted. The sound was some of both. Under no circumstances would she be charmed by Boone Rawlins.

Thumbing open the book, he began to read.

'"The noble cowherd swung his lasso in the air in a valiant effort to—". Blamed fool thing to try and lasso a cougar,' he mumbled. 'Must be where your brother got the idea.'

'He did that?' she asked, curiosity getting the better of indignation.

Boone smiled and, of all things, she smiled back

at him. Out of one corner of her mouth only, but the fact remained that she had done so. This was no time for smiling. This was her time to be angry at her late brother.

She was quite done with weeping and so she would express her feelings by ripping up this nonsense that Grant held dear.

'Only once.' The simple answer was softly spoken and Boone's gaze grew distant, as if he was not seeing the dime novel in his hand.

He set it beside him then picked up another book and ripped the pages from that one.

'Your life is not ruined, darlin'.'

Darlin'? A shiver slid through her at the endearment. A delightful quiver, which she could not in all honesty claim to dislike. It did, however, cause her anger to skip a beat.

As lovely as 'darlin'' sounded, she was in no state to be soothed by a word.

She regathered her bitterness. 'Is it not? I have two elderly servants to support and no home to do it in.'

'I will not ask them, or you, to leave,' he said.

'It is not as if I can stay.' It was not as if she could leave either. Where would she go? 'Gossip will spread. You might find yourself forced to wed me.'

'I would not take advantage of a lady under my roof. No need to fret about that.'

'Perhaps not. But it hardly matters. Society will label me a fallen woman no matter what the truth is.'

'I will speak for your innocence. The matter will be put to rest.'

'Perhaps where you come from that would be the case. But this is London and appearances are all that matter.'

'Damn unreasonable thing, if you ask me.'

My word, but a frown was not supposed to look like that. It was far too well formed and handsome for anyone's good.

'You will be considered a rake.'

'I reckon I don't care what narrow minds accuse me of. You and I know the truth.'

'If you intend to live here, you must care.'

Wrinkles, also disturbingly well formed, creased his forehead when he frowned. He shook his head. A hank of brown hair, frosted with blond, dipped over one brow.

A handsome face was neither here nor there, in importance. It was imperative for Boone Rawlins to understand the necessity of avoiding gossip.

Being financially ruined, Ambrin had no wish to be socially ruined, as well. Also, Marigold's place in society needed to not be jeopardised.

Weary of ripping books, she shoved them away from her. The gesture hadn't helped overmuch anyway.

'I do not know how to go on from this,' she admitted and wondered why she had. Just because he had called her darlin' it did not mean they were chums. She had known him but a day. An intense day to be certain but still only a day. 'How does a person get over feeling embittered?'

Boone picked up the book he had set aside, thumbed the pages but did not speak.

Either he had no more idea how than she did, or he did not wish to speak of it.

But then he said, 'I told you that your brother lassoed a wildcat. What I didn't say is that he did it to save my life. The cougar made a leap for me but Grant caught it around the neck with his rope. The cat went after him instead.' Boone gave her an odd, half smile. 'I fired my rifle in the air and the cat ran off. Your brother was right proud of the scar on his shoulder from that fight.'

'I am happy that the cat did not get you, Boone.' What would have become of Marigold if it had? There would have been no one to protect her.

'There was a reason I told you the story.'

'To point out that my brother had redeeming qualities, I suppose. I know he did, Boone. It's only…'

That she was having a hard time remembering what they were in the moment.

'What I mean to say is that we can't get past this misery we are in without forgiving him,' he said.

'I am not certain I can do that. But why do you say "we"?' She was the one grieving and angry.

'Grant was like a brother to me and I loved him. But you know he had his ways. After he died I was bitter at him for going out in the blizzard like he did. For leaving his child an orphan and killing our dream along with himself. It was a foolish thing to do and it took me a while to come to peace with it.'

'But you did come to peace?'

It would be easier for him to do, she supposed, given that Grant had saved him from the cougar. Her brother had not saved her from anything. Not a wicked storm when she was small nor the financial straits she was now in.

'I needed to. I had to move on with life, if only for Marigold's sake.' He took one of her hands, squeezed it then let go. The gesture felt like 'darlin''. 'She'll need for you to do the same.'

'Am I to be a part of her life, then? It seems my brother and the lawyers say otherwise.'

'You are her aunt. Her only blood kin. You must be a part of her life, only, not a bitter part.'

'How do you propose I forgive him for not even mentioning me? Clearly I meant nothing to him.'

'It sure won't be easy. You've got to try, though. Resentment is too heavy a load.'

'If you have an idea how to, I would like to hear it.'

'First thing is to understand it's hard to do all at one time. Little by little is the way. May I share something my mother taught me?'

She nodded, but could not imagine anything would help make her feel kindly towards Grant.

'What you do, is speak out loud. Say what makes you angry about the person. Then right after, say something good about them.'

'I am not certain I can do it.'

'I'll begin so you get the feel of it.'

With a wink and a smile, he brushed the hair back from his brow. She caught her breath. How was it that this man could make her feel flutters in the most unlikely moments?

'Grant put me in a position to break your heart and I resent the hell out of him for it, darlin'. Now, I need to forgive him for it or it will fester away at me and I won't be any good to anyone. So, here it goes.' He huffed out a breath, paused a moment before speaking. 'Grant was enthusiastic. There was no one like him for getting excited about a plan.'

Boone nodded, indicating it was her turn.

This was a silly thing to do and she was certain it would not work but his gaze at her was expectant, encouraging. So… 'I am so angry that my brother abandoned his place in society and went away.'

She shrugged. There was much more to it but this was a start. 'When I was seven years old I broke a vase and Grant took the blame and the punishment.' Very well, he had saved her from something, after all. She had nearly forgotten.

'You see how it works? We don't say that what he did wrong is excused. Only that we are willing to move past it. To remember the good. It takes some practice.'

While she was not convinced that it would help, that she would come out of the exercise feeling any better, she listened while Boone continued.

'I need to forgive Grant for not mentioning you.' The frown creasing his brow indicated he was having trouble with this bit of forgiveness. Well then, so was she! 'My partner loved to dance in the parlour with his bride. His laughter made the whole household happy.'

That much was true. Grant did have a joyous laugh.

'I need to forgive my brother for leaving me lost in a storm. Once I awoke with a nightmare and Grant rushed into my room. He spent the night on the floor next to my bed so that anything coming for me would step on him first.'

Boone nodded, looking thoughtful. 'He always did like being a hero. I reckon it's why he thought he could save the cattle that day.'

'All of a sudden I miss my brother…' She could scarcely believe it to be possible given how resentful she felt towards him. 'Nearly as much as I want to rail at him.'

Boone nodded. That twirl of hair dipped between his brows again, making him look quite playful. It nearly made her smile, which would have been most ill-timed.

'Reckon that's the way it goes at first. But we've made a start. What do you say we practice at this every day at mealtime? One day we might find we forgive him.'

One day? Since this was no longer her home, there would be no opportunity for practicing. She must find a man of means and marry him at the first chance.

There really was no other way for a woman in her situation.

'Your mother's solution might work but it would take time, which I do not have. As I said, I cannot continue to live here. I will be utterly ruined.'

'Not by me.'

'Be that as it may, I cannot live in a man's home and not be married to him.'

Boone stood up, reached down a hand to help her up. His gaze was so intent that she could not look anywhere but into his blue eyes. Once again, frown lines cut his brow.

That silly twirl of hair was quite distracting. She would brush it away for him if… No, she would never do that!

'Surely you would be allowed to entertain guests?' he asked.

'Yes, naturally.'

'Then we won't tell anyone that this is no longer your house. I will be the man from America who brought Grant's daughter home and I am staying here as your guest for a time.'

For a moment all she could do is blink and fight a new bout of tears. Grateful ones this time.

'You would truly agree to it?'

'As long as it will keep your friends from getting wrong ideas about you, I'm agreeable. I wonder though, what kind of friends you have. Not loyal ones, I reckon.'

'You are a decent man, Boone Rawlins.' She did not particularly like saying so since she had not fully forgiven anyone for the situation she found herself in.

And yet the truth was the truth. He was a decent man.

One other thing…he was loyal. He stood by Grant, no matter that her brother was dead. And in turn, he stood by her because she was Grant's sister.

It might be a stretch to believe Boone Rawlins to be a friend…and yet, given the past days, he seemed as close as one.

'I'm just a cowboy, darlin'…you going to kiss me again?' he presented his cheek.

Kiss him! Why, she was still stunned that she had done it the first time.

Oh, that is something that would never happen again. Her lips so near his mouth…it would be risky. Last time she kissed his cheek, she had experienced a great deal more than gratitude.

'That was certainly not a kiss. It was simply a peck. A simple act of gratitude.'

For all that her world had turned over, this man, who had no reason to, was helping to set it right. She found that she liked him more than was prudent.

He was a handsome fellow of course. And charming. Who would not like him? What an odd sensation, liking and resenting a person at the same time.

A small voice in her mind asked what exactly he had done for her to resent him.

Never mind that, the small voice also reminded her that it was urgent to begin searching for a husband. A fine man who would offer both financial security and insure her place in society.

Boone Rawlins could not remain her 'guest' forever.

The time had come to put away her fantasy of a love match in which some handsome man would cherish her above all women.

When all was said and done, it was better to be an unloved bride than a starving spinster.

While walking down the hallway, Boone heard Frederick Haver's voice coming from the kitchen.

'Our Mr Rawlins is the talk of Mayfair.'

He paused at the door to listen, figuring it wasn't eavesdropping when folks were talking about you.

'Invitations will start arriving at the door quite soon I imagine,' answered Millie.

'Folks are curious and you can't blame them. Never seen a fellow like him around here before. He could have come right out of one of those Wild West shows, he could.'

Boone stifled a snort. Those shows had as much to do with real life as lizards had to do with the stones they sunned themselves on.

If he got an invitation to some fancy event he would turn it down. Ranching was his life and the sooner he got back to it, the better. All he wanted was to sell this giant house, take the money and then purchase cattle for his farm.

He and Marigold would remain in London no longer than they must. This vast city was no place to bring up a child, not with its foul air, congested streets, and so much noise.

'I don't know what's to become of us, Frederick. We are too old to seek other employment. It is only out of Ambrin's good heart that we remain here.'

'Aye. I suppose Mr Rawlins will want his own staff.'

'We won't be able to go with Miss Ambrin when she weds. Her new husband will already be staffed.'

Ambrin was to wed? It was a relief to discover there was a man who would take care of her once he sold the house. What he could not figure is why the news didn't sit well in his gut.

Boone stepped into the kitchen. The elderly brother and sister appeared as distressed as they sounded. Whether it was because they feared he had overheard them speaking about him or that they feared being put out on the street, he did not know.

'I'm sorry to bother you,' he said. 'I was looking for a bite to eat and I thought I heard you say Miss Malcomb is engaged to be married?'

He wouldn't have guessed it to be true, since she had not spoken of it, but he'd known her only a week.

A glance passed between the elderly pair. Probably wondering if it was their place to speak of Ambrin's business.

'Well, sir, she is not…not yet. But given how things are, she will need to seek a husband soon.'

Hunt up some fellow she did not love? Now that would be a crime. Ambrin Malcomb was too fine a woman not to be loved. Made him a bit queasy in the gut, hearing of it.

To his way of thinking, this society she lived in seemed cold at heart. Marriage was meant for love and family.

'I wonder, would I be able to persuade you both to come and work for me…starting from a few days ago?'

It was only right that he take over the expense of running the house that now belonged to him.

More, it was his place to watch out for the people who had been Grant's. It is what partners did for each other. Death did not cancel the commitment.

'I'd take it as a favour if you both accept.'

'As long as Miss Ambrin approves, we will be happy to,' Frederick said.

'And be grateful to you, sir,' added his sister.

'Thank you, ma'am.' He tipped his Stetson at her and started to walk out of the kitchen.

'Mr Rawlins, you came for a bite to eat,' Millie called, then wrapped half a loaf of bread in a cloth and handed it to him.

Going out he heard Millie whisper to her brother, 'He'll have to fight the debutantes off with a switch, mark my words.'

As if that would happen. He wouldn't have cause to

be anywhere near a debutante. He was going back to ranching as soon as he could manage. Continuing on his way, he went up the stairs, down a long hallway. He opened the door to Grant's chamber.

It was his chamber now, but it didn't feel like it. Everywhere he looked he saw the fancy things his partner had left behind.

No wonder Grant had been happier in the wide-open spaces of Montana.

The room did smell fresh, though, like someone had just polished the wood. Drapes covered all of one wall making the room feel heavy and too dark.

He pulled the drapes aside. There was a window but the view was of the street, of carriages bouncing over uneven cobbles. There were people in refined clothes strolling past. People in humble clothes, too, pushing carts and calling out what they were selling.

'Herring!'

'Mince pies!'

'Apples and carrots!'

'Get out o' my way you ugly, careless lout!' called one carriage driver to another.

Too much motion and too much noise. He drew the drapes closed again.

Boone was glad he'd found such a good horse to buy when he'd arrived in England. He couldn't imagine how it would feel travelling in a confined coach like the ones down below, having to trust someone else to do the driving.

From what he had seen of London, it could stifle a man. He didn't blame Grant for needing to get away from here. But his sister? How could he have not wanted anything to do with her? His own kin?

'You made a mistake partner and I'm having to deal with the mess you left,' he whispered. He fell silent for a moment, listening to the din beyond the window, and then continued. 'I remember the time you carried an orphaned calf on your shoulders for a mile to bring it back to the barn.'

What his mother taught him had worked in the past. He sure hoped it would this time. He was finding it was a mite easier to forgive a wrong done to himself than done to someone else.

He sure was struggling with what Grant had done to his sister.

Chapter Four

Ambrin lifted her black mourning gown from a box in her wardrobe then briskly flicked the dust off the shoulder with her fingertips. She had not worn the gown in the ten years since her parents died of influenza. Back then she had hoped to never put it on again.

Perhaps she would not.

Nearly six months had passed since Grant died. With the mourning period ending she might be excused from the formal observation. Some might judge her to be insensitive. Others would not. Grant had been absent for so long that society had given up on him doing his duty as baron.

Indeed, she had heard the whispers.

What she needed to do is wed in a hurry. Spending six months in mourning would only postpone it.

'The lavender gown it is, then.'

She folded the black gown, placed it back in the box. She would wear lavender, the colour acceptable for easing out of formal grief. She would wear it for a week and be done with it.

'It is not as if he would have worn black for me. He would not have known I had died… Drat… Grant taught me to climb a fence even though he knew father would forbid it.'

Changing quickly into her lavender gown she judged the effect in the mirror. Not deeply somber, not cheerful as sunshine either. The one week of wearing it should be appropriate. In her own mind at any rate. What was in other people's minds was not for her to dwell on.

What she needed in that moment was a nice brisk walk in the park. A good stretch of her limbs was what she needed to clear her brain and set her course for what lay ahead.

A course she did not wish to run. Not that it mattered what she wished. When had it ever? Her brother had been the one with choices and he'd made poor ones. Fatal ones that meant the end of the peerage, for there was no male kin to inherit it.

Nothing for it now but to move ahead and find whatever future she could for herself and for Marigold.

Perhaps she would spot a gentleman in the park who would suit her needs. Someone she might already be acquainted with but would now regard in a new light. No longer could she look for a fellow who made her heart flutter. Rather, she required a man of influence whose position would help Marigold when the time came for her to be presented to society. It was many years off, and she was glad of that, but the time to prepare was now. More than that, she needed a husband who could support her niece if Boone's farm failed. It had happened to him once before and could certainly happen again.

One thing Grant had taught her was that security came from one's position in society, not from smelly bulls and cows.

Coming across the garden from the small stable in the back of the property, Boone spotted Ambrin waving her hand at him from the terrace.

Well now, wasn't she a sight to see? She brought to mind a purple blossom shimmering in a ray of sunshine.

'Right pretty isn't she, Petunia?' The dog whined. 'Stay beside me, girl. The lady is afraid of you.'

Coming down the steps she lifted the hem of her skirt in one hand while pressing her bonnet to her head with the other.

He thought of the flower he had plucked from beside Susanna's grave. His wife had been one for signs. From the first he'd figured the flower a message from her, suggesting that he ought to move on.

Was the color Ambrin was wearing a sign that she was the one he ought to do it with? It was a leap to think so. Just his imagination playing tricks.

'Damn it, Susanna,' he muttered in case it was true.

'I'm here to build a business, not get married. Besides, I've learned how marriage can end as quick as a blink. Don't reckon I want to learn it again.'

Chances are that the reason the thought of marriage crossed his mind was because Millie and Frederick had spoken of Ambrin needing to wed. The purple flower and the gown being the same shade had no meaning whatsoever.

Wildflowers were common this time of year. They bloomed in all colours in Montana. He wondered if it would be different at his new farm.

Many things would be different, he thought while watching Ambrin hurrying towards him on the path.

More than an ocean separated England from Montana.

Everything here was unfamiliar. From food to houses and the sounds of the town. Even the feel of the air was different. Being close to the sea, it was often damp and foggy.

In London a man could not see a thousand acres of grass while sitting on his saddle. There were not majestic mountain ranges topped with snow. Maybe, though, he didn't need to see for miles on end. In the moment, he was happy enough watching Ambrin Malcomb rushing towards him with her purple skirt billowing about her.

'Boone,' she gasped, reaching him winded. 'I would so love to go for a walk in the park. Millie and Frederick are busy playing with Marigold and I have no one to accompany me. Would you mind?'

He'd seen the park from a distance and had been meaning to visit. Besides, Petunia could do with a run in an open space.

'A walk sounds mighty fine. I'll meet you by the door after I check on Marigold.'

'Oh, please let me do it. I can't bear to be away from her for long.'

Her smile when she turned to hurry towards the back door of the kitchen was the happiest he'd seen from her. Being with Marigold could do that to a person, light them up inside.

He probably ought to tell her that he'd purchased a farm and that he meant to sell the house. She needed to know that Marigold would be living with him there. Millie and Frederick too.

But he feared that when he told her, the news might plunge her into misery once again.

Standing near the front door, Boone put on his hat. He strapped his weapon on his hip then put on his buckskin coat. They were not likely to encounter bears or wolves but he'd noticed predators of another kind while riding his horse on London's crowded streets.

Thugs and thieves lurked, even in daylight. Snake-like, they slithered among decent folks.

Just because he no longer lived in the wilds of Montana didn't mean that there was a reason to be unprepared for danger.

Ambrin rushed into the hallway, saw him and came up short.

'There is no hunting in the park, Boone.'

He opened the door, whistled for Petunia who was never far away. The dog dashed across the floor. She was still getting used to tiled floors so she skidded trying to stop.

'Sure there is, darlin'. I aim to keep us from being the prey.'

Out on the porch, Ambrin placed her small hand in the crook of his elbow. A sudden sense of protectiveness had him glancing around even as they went down the front steps.

Just as when he was back in Montana, he was glad for the presence of his sidearm and his dog. Life, as precious as it was, could be taken in an instant. He aimed to protect this woman in any way he could, whether she thought it necessary or not.

'Have you no lead for the animal?' Ambrin asked as they walked down the street to the park.

The afternoon was warm, gentle. The park was green, lush with grass hedges and trees. If ever there was a setting to lull a man and make him unwary, this was the one.

'She won't wander.'

'But she looks ferocious. People will be frightened.' Ambrin frowned up at him with those amber shaded eyes. The colour was so rich and warm that in his mind, he tasted honey, savoured it, and wondered if her lips would taste the same.

Well, that was not something he wanted to dwell on. Lavender gown notwithstanding, he was not ready to wed. He had a farm to build.

'That's the point,' he said.

'Is it also the point for you to look as ferocious as your dog?'

'Yes ma'am, it is.' Her eyes went so wide he couldn't help but grin. 'If you did not wish for my protection, why did you ask me to accompany you?'

'Not for safety's sake. I would be quite secure on my own. However an unmarried lady must never walk in public alone. It would be a scandal. There's probably one brewing right now. I ought to be taking the air with Millie, not with a gentleman.'

'Darlin', that's the most senseless thing I've heard in a while. How would you expect an elderly lady to protect you from harm?'

'It is not harm I am concerned about, Boone. It's gossip.'

'It isn't gossip that's going to steal the necklace off your throat. It's that man over there who is thinking about it.'

'What man? Where?' She pressed the jewels to her throat.

'The one who's been keeping pace with the couple we just passed by.'

'Truly, Boone, he looks like a perfect gentleman to me.'

'That's what makes him dangerous. Why do you think Petunia is keeping so close to you?'

'To get dog hair on my skirt.'

'Petunia has a sense about people. Also a nose that can smell bad intentions.'

Ambrin stared at the man when he walked briskly past them. The fellow tipped his hat, smiled slyly.

'How do you know what the dog knows?'

'I raised her from a pup.'

'If that man is a villain, why does she not attack him?'

'I haven't given her leave to.'

'You, Boone Rawlins, are making all of this up to justify carrying a weapon in a perfectly safe park. I am certain that gentleman is respectable.'

'He's a thief. A pickpocket.'

All of a sudden, the woman behind them cried out in dismay and began franticly searching the path near her skirt.

'Wait here, darlin',' he ordered then gave Petunia the gesture that meant stand and guard.

Boone dashed after the man. Catching up, he blocked the thief's escape.

'I'll take the lady's property.'

'I ain't got her—'

Boone slid his coat aside, rested one hand on the hilt of his sidearm.

'Turn out your pockets. All of them.'

Luckily, the fool criminal complied.

A necklace of green stones hit the dirt. The culprit turned tail and dashed towards a fountain, shoving his way through a crowd of people. The man who had been walking with the victim gave chase.

Boone plucked the necklace out of the dirt then returned it to the distraught owner.

People nearby began to clap. He hadn't meant to make a spectacle of it, but crimes did attract attention.

Returning to Ambrin, he picked up her hand, tucked it into his elbow and walked on as if nothing dramatic had occurred.

'Very well, Boone. That particular man was a ruffian. But they are not lurking behind every shrub.'

Even with what just occurred, Boone feared Ambrin did not appreciate the danger an ordinary day presented.

'When you look for a husband, darlin', don't settle for one who is an ornament on your arm. You'll need a fellow who can protect you.'

'Oh? Perhaps I should have you pick him for me?'

'Yes, and maybe we should find one soon. '

She sighed, nodded her head. 'It must be. I cannot keep you as my house guest for ever, after all.'

'I reckon not. I can't live in London for ever, either. This place isn't healthy for Marigold to grow up in. And there is the dream your brother and I had. I mean to carry on with it.'

'Men and their dreams.' It sounded as if she spat those words out of some bitter place in her heart.

Boone wondered if Ambrin realised she had her fingers curled in the fur on Petunia's neck. Her hand had been anchored to that very spot since he had ordered the dog to remain beside her.

'Where is it you intend to live if not in your own home?' she asked.

The question was casually presented but Ambrin's eyes gave away her apprehension. Rightly so, he reckoned. She had to be wondering what connection she would have with her niece if he did not live in the London house.

'I've bought a farm in Oxfordshire.'

'And you mean to take my niece with you?'

All at once Ambrin must have noticed her grip on Petunia. She gasped and snatched her hand away.

'But, Boone, I have only begun to get acquainted with her. Surely there is no rush.'

'I don't fit in here, darlin'. I don't aim to stay in London longer than I have to.'

'Have you seen this farm? Is it prepared for a little girl to live there properly? No, Marigold must stay with me until everything is ready.'

There were two problems with her idea. The first being that he was not willing to be separated from the child he was sworn to love and protect as if she had been born of his blood. He'd been as devoted to

Marigold as her own father had been, ever since she took her first breath.

The other problem was that he was selling the town house in order to purchase cattle. He couldn't very well leave a child in London with no place to live.

He couldn't very well leave Ambrin that way either.

How fast could a lady find a husband in high society, anyway? And not just any old fool of a man. The fellow to marry her must be fine and upstanding.

'I won't be ready to leave London for a while yet. Between now and then I'll help you select a man, since you asked.'

'I said that in jest, as you surely must know. I am quite capable of picking an appropriate husband.'

Saying that, she hurried on ahead of him, purple skirts swaying like a flower in a prairie breeze.

'I thought you weren't supposed to walk alone,' he called after her.

But she wasn't alone, she had him.

And damn if he knew what to do about that.

'Miss Ambrin, I've brought the correspondence.' Ambrin looked up from where she knelt, scrubbing vigorous circles on the parlour floor with a soapy brush.

'That is kind of you, Frederick. Please just set it there on the table.'

'We haven't seen so many invitations since before the baron went to America. Lord rest his soul.' He placed the invitations where directed. 'Let me help you with that, my dear.'

He tried to kneel but seemed to become stuck someplace between up and down.

'Do not trouble yourself. I am all but finished.' At least in another hour she would be. 'But if you would cut some roses for the vase on the dining table I would appreciate it.'

'It would be my delight,' he answered but made no move to do so. 'Our young man has certainly gathered attention since his heroics in the park.'

Oh, indeed. Three days had gone by and it seemed everyone was wanting the honour of having the hero cowboy attend their entertainments.

Wiping her hands on her apron, Ambrin stood then took the invitations off the table.

'The floor will not need to be spotless, my dear girl,' Frederick pointed out before he went out of the room.

Ambrin sat down on the armchair. Oh, but it did feel good to get up off the floor. And Frederick was wrong about the floor not needing to be spotless. If she entertained a caller she did not wish it to appear that the estate did not have enough help and was failing. No one wished to wed a woman who was openly destitute.

'My word,' she muttered, shuffling through the invitations. 'Three of them for tea, one to join Lady Hasberry in her box at the opera, two musicals, oh, and Lady Dewhurst's ball.

Each and every invitation was addressed to her and to Boone Rawlins.

Even she would be worn out attending them all. For all that Boone was big and bold, he would never survive the ordeal.

Still, for the sake of Marigold's future, Boone must make himself known to society. Which meant she must present him in as elegant a manner as possible.

Heaven help her, it did seem she had a challenge ahead of her.

The ball would suit best, she decided, since the highest-ranking members would attend.

But perhaps Boone would not hate society as much she suspected he would. If he somehow learned to enjoy entertainments, he might decide to forsake his dream of a farm.

Perhaps her dream, for once, would come true and she would live near her niece. The child had come into her life rather like a miracle on the heels of heartache and she could not imagine being without her.

If she was very lucky, and Boone remained here, she would be allowed to visit this home she cherished so often that she would not feel the loss so sharply.

While a wedding was not her dream, perhaps it would lead her to what now was her dream. Residing near her niece.

Although it limited her prospects, she must wed a man who was a neighbour.

The sound of familiar boot steps came down the hallway and Boone entered the parlour.

'I just spoke with Frederick,' he announced.

My word Boone Rawlins had a handsome manner about him. The way his hair dipped over his brow... well, what lady would not lose her wits just looking at him. And that was before he had squatted on the floor and picked up the scrub brush. She, for one, would not lose her wits. Not for long at least.

'Seems like some younger knees are needed here.'

'I will not ask you to do my work, Boone.'

Setting the invitation to the ball aside, she rose from the chair, knelt beside him and picked up the drying rag.

'Reckon it's not your work anymore. My house, my work.'

Yes...his house. As much as she hated it, there was nothing to do but accept reality. There was so much reality she had been required to accept of late, but losing her home hurt dreadfully.

'I suppose you will hire more staff soon?'

It only made sense that he would. Someone would need to care for the place even after Boone moved to his farm and she moved to the home of her, yet to be known, husband.

The thought of strangers filling the house made her want to weep. Hired caretakers would not put their love into dusting the furniture or scrubbing the floors the way that she did.

However, she would not weep. What she would do instead is move on with her life and see that her niece found her place in society when the time came.

And to that end she told Boone that he'd been invited to Lady Dewhurst's ball.

Ambrin might have announced that he had been invited to spend an evening sitting on an ant hill, the news was that unwelcome.

He'd never attended anything fancier than a barn dance.

It only seemed right to attend the get-together, though. Without intending to, he'd turned Ambrin's life upside down and he'd done it again when he confessed to selling the house.

At first, he'd thought the sooner he sold it, the better. He'd been anxious to get Marigold settled in Oxfordshire and have cattle grazing on the land. But he'd decided since, that it would be wiser to wait until Ambrin had found a good man to marry.

Boone spread soapy bubbles in circles on the wooden floor.

His thoughts were not on attacking dirt, but on how he would guide Ambrin towards someone worthy. A dandy, well-appointed fellow who would appreciate the fine woman she was.

'Well?' she asked, probably wondering why he'd been silent for so long. 'Will you attend…with me?'

He nodded and stopped scrubbing in order to judge

her expression, although he couldn't see it because she was staring out the window at the mass of black clouds diming the afternoon.

Since she wasn't paying attention to drying the floor, her fingers slid across his.

She went still. He went still.

The only sounds Boone could hear in the room were the sounds of the soap bubbles popping where their hands touched. And their breathing. And quite possibly his heart slamming into his ribs.

A sense of awakening shimmered along his nerves, pumped in his blood. He'd felt nothing like it since… Since Susanna.

Eyes of deep amber blinked at him, not sea green ones.

He felt shaken from his fingertips to his heart. Not since Susanna had he indulged in this sort of sensation and he oughtn't be indulging in it now, either.

That wasn't what a man ought to be feeling when he was meant to judge a lady's candidates for a husband and that candidate was not him.

Marriage is not what he'd set his cap for. No, ranching was. The fellow Ambrin needed was not a cowboy but a gentleman.

He waited for her to move her hand…and kept waiting. All the while she continued to look at him, maybe as stunned as he was that neither of them had made a move away from the other.

'I'd be proud to go with you to that shindig, darlin',' he said, coming back to what she had said a moment ago.

He squeezed her fingers, felt them sliding between his, all slick and sudsy.

'Oh,' she gasped. She blushed and looked even prettier than she had seconds previously.

She wiped her hand on her apron. He wondered whether she was brushing off the suds or his touch.

'Very well, I shall let the hostess know.'

Dwelling on how fine it had felt when their fingers touched was not what he ought to be doing and that was the plain truth.

He wrangled his thoughts, reminding himself that Ambrin would be husband hunting, and he would be helping her.

He stood up. 'Reckon I ought to hire a couple of maids to clean the house.'

For a short time only. Just so the burden would not fall on Ambrin for the time that remained. Here and now was the time to tell her of his intention to sell the place, but the words wouldn't come.

Better to let her find a husband first. Once she was in love and engaged, the blow wouldn't be as hurtful.

'When is this hoedown?'

'Next week.'

'Well now, darlin', I can't promise I'll show up looking like a shiny penny.'

'I'll help with that. It is important for you to make connections. For the sake of Marigold's future.'

Just as he'd kept quiet about selling the house, he thought that this was not the time to press the matter of his child's future. Although, he did know it would be spent in fresh air and wide-open spaces. Marigold would enjoy the freedom of life in the countryside and would not be bound by the constrictions of society the way Ambrin was.

'It's your connections I'm giving thought to, darlin'.'

'Rest assured, I've had a lifetime of them, which should help Marigold greatly.'

Links to society would not do the child a lick of good, not on the farm where she would be raised.

'I was speaking of your connections in the light of lassoing a husband.' It would be an interesting pursuit. He meant to take a deep look at each man she took a notion to. 'I aim to help you.'

'Don't be ridiculous, Boone. I've been trained in the pursuit since I was Marigold's age.'

That was a notion that sat sour in his gut. A person did not get trained to fall in love and get married.

'Well, darlin', you asked for my help and now you have it.'

'I was making a joke… I told you so already.'

Her dander was rising, and she looked right pretty.

It wasn't smart of him to wonder, but it wasn't as if he could help it. What would it be like to kiss a woman when she was all bristled?

His wife had been as even tempered as a dove, so he'd never had a prickly kiss.

He wouldn't have one now, either, but it didn't hurt to think about what it would be like.

It was interesting. He'd never kissed anyone but Susanna, yet now he found himself wondering about Ambrin's lips.

'You may dismiss the idea altogether, Boone Rawlins. I will not need your advice.'

What he needed to dismiss was the vision of kissing her. It had taken hold of his mind and was hanging on like a dog chewing a bone.

Ambrin Malcomb was meant for a fancy gentleman with polite manners.

The sooner she found him, the sooner Boone could get on with the life he'd envisioned for himself and Marigold. The life where, if he listened with his heart, he could hear the mellow lowing of cattle.

Chapter Five

If the idea of attending a ball gave Boone the sensation of sitting on an anthill, shopping for fancy clothes to wear to the event made him feel as if the ants were crawling under his collar. And they were fire ants at that.

The only thing that made the experience of being measured and poked for a suit bearable was that Ambrin and Marigold were waiting on the other side of the curtain for him.

Through a gap in the drape he could see Marigold sitting on Ambrin's lap. The both of them giggling at his grunts of discomfort. The sight warmed his heart but it also troubled him.

Hang it. For this morning he would set anxiety aside.

He would fret over how Marigold was to have close family ties with her auntie when they would live such a distance from one another later. Once Ambrin was wed, she would go and live with her husband. Boone's task was to direct her towards a fellow who lived closer to Oxfordshire, rather than further away.

With the ordeal of fitting finished, and the suit having been ordered, the three of them left the shop. Petunia rose from her spot on the top step of the porch, her long hairy tail wagging.

Ambrin had urged him to leave the dog at home, along with his side firearm, but he'd declined.

If a walk in a park was a risk, being here in the expensive shopping district was even more so. All those people out on their strolls would have money in their pockets, which would attract thieves.

'Uncle Boone.' Marigold let go of Ambrin's hand to grab his. She had been clinging to her auntie so tight that it seemed her small fingers had taken root. 'Auntie Ambrin told me if I was well behaved in the suit shop, we could go to the sweet shop.'

'The sweet shop is just up the street.' Ambrin gave him a hopeful smile.

As if he needed convincing. It had been a good long time since Marigold had been someplace that sold sweets and just as long for him.

It would be worth the walk just to see his two ladies grinning in anticipation.

Ah well, one of them was his lady. The other was meant for someone else. He needed to keep that in mind or risk feeling the way he had when they had touched hands.

That was something he could not risk. Those sorts

of feelings led to love and to the risk of losing it in a tragic way.

Funny though, how just walking down the street with Ambrin made him all sunny inside. Made him forget that tragedy could come in an instant.

Feeling the presence of the dog, and the weight of the gun strapped to his thigh, he knew he was as prepared as he could be. He might as well relax and enjoy the company of his companions.

'Why are people looking funny at us?' Marigold asked.

It might have been wiser to leave his dog and his weapon at home, just like Ambrin suggested. He did have a rougher appearance than what these fancy folks were used to seeing.

'People aren't used to seeing a dog so big and fine as Petunia, little darlin'. Reckon they are wishing they had a pup like her.'

'I am certain that is the case,' Ambrin confirmed. It gave his heart a squeeze hearing her take his side when he knew she didn't agree about the dog or the weapon. 'But look, here we are at the front door. Just look at all the sweets in the window! I will never decide what to bring home and what to eat now.'

'I want to eat all of it now!' Marigold hopped up and down. Boone could not recall ever seeing the child's eyes so round in anticipation.

'The sweet shop back in Montana is only a counter in the mercantile.' He figured his eyes must be as round in wonder as Marigold's were.

Going inside, he was overwhelmed with colourful displays of gumdrops, toffee, peppermint sticks and lemon drops. Going past the first long glass case, he came to a display containing every kind of chocolate he'd ever thought of.

He supposed big cities in America would have places like this, but he'd never been in one.

Well then, London did have something he liked. Besides, Ambrin, he meant. His admiration for her was growing as fast as a dust storm sweeping across the plains.

He needed a good tight lasso around his feelings so they wouldn't wander where they should not.

Problem with a lasso though, is that it is made of rope. Watching Ambrin lead Marigold from treat to treat, admiring and exclaiming over each one, he felt his heart melting right out of any restraint.

Concern for how it would be for his little girl when she was separated from her auntie pressed upon him once again. She had already lost her father and not so long ago. It was harder to corral worry to the back of his mind than it had been even moments ago.

A problem was emerging, and he didn't know a way around it.

He could hardly prevent Ambrin and Marigold from forming attachments. They were the only blood kin each other had.

'I hope there is candy in Heaven,' Marigold declared. 'My papa would love to eat a peppermint stick.'

Boone noticed Ambrin's breath hitch. To her credit, her smile did not falter. It would be a while before she would be able to think easy thoughts of Grant.

'I reckon Heaven's got candy so delicious we haven't thought of it yet, little darlin'. What do you say we go home and try some of what is in that bag you filled up?'

Having had a bit too much sugar, Marigold fell asleep quickly. Ambrin smoothed the hair away from her niece's sticky mouth then Boone carried her upstairs for her nap.

My word, how was it possible to fall in love with someone as quickly as she had with Marigold?

In part it might be due to the fact that the child was the only family she had left. More than that though, the little girl was utterly enchanting—a brown-eyed, dark-haired reflection of her grandmother.

With the day being lovely and sunny, Ambrin decided not to stay inside. The things she'd had to get accomplished would wait for a few moments while she sat in the garden enjoying a peppermint stick and listening to a dove cooing in the branches overhead.

In all, the morning had gone well. Boone had not waylaid lurking thieves while shopping. He'd acted polite and well mannered, smiling and tipping his disturbing Stetson to the people they passed by.

The dog had not attacked any passing shoppers but merely wagged her broom-like tail at them.

Boone's delight while visiting the sweet shop had been endearing. Ambrin had found herself seeing the place that she had frequented all her life with fresh eyes.

Sharing the experience with Marigold, though, that made her feel young again. In those moments of choosing the sweets, Ambrin had been carefree and her problems had been miles away.

The only trouble with the outing was that it was tempting to imagine the three of them being family. Naturally, such a thing could not be.

Boone Rawlins was a cowboy, rough and…well, not at all the sort of genteel fellow she would wed.

Oh bother. Hearts, it seemed, did not care about what could or could not be. They simply felt things.

It was a bit wicked of her to be setting her cap for some unknown gentleman while at the same time be wondering what it would be like to kiss her cowboy.

But he was not her cowboy. Indeed, she did not want him to be! Boone and her brother had caused her no end of misery. She must do better at remembering that.

Truly, she did not want a man who wore a dead snake on his hat. She wanted a refined gentleman. In fact, she needed one.

Sighing, twice, she closed her eyes and became lost in an inappropriate thought. Indulged in it, to be truthful, when she ought to be scouring it from her mind.

She had never known herself to be fickle. But what if she were eating a peppermint stick when along came Boone Rawlins, all handsome in his Stetson and his rugged boots. And what if he were sucking on a lemon drop?

And then, what if they kissed? The flavours would meld and…

The bench sagged with the weight of a big, solid body sitting down.

She opened her eyes, slid her gaze sideways and up.

Oh, indeed, Boone was handsome. The reality of him was even more enticing than the daydream.

With his Stetson dipped over his brow, she had a close view of the snakeskin band. Had he purchased it that way, or had he shot the creature? Marigold did say that he shot snakes.

Unlike in her fantasy, he was not sucking on a lemon drop. Oddly enough though, she could still taste peppermint and lemon on her tongue.

'Nice spot to enjoy your sweets,' he commented.

Indeed. If he only knew how much she had been enjoying it.

Giving herself a mental slap, she doused the fantasy. Peppermint and lemon kisses were not in her future. They were not in her present either.

She had a future to seek and must not dream there was another path open to her. Especially not with a man who was her…not adversary quite, but something akin to it.

An adversary through no fault of his own, a tricky voice in her mind pointed out. In return, she pointed out that he owned her home and that was not right or fair.

'Sunshine can be rare at times, here in London,' she answered, carrying on the conversation as if she were not in an argument with her heart. 'I take advantage of pleasant weather when I can. But I imagine it is different where you come from.'

And that is what she must bear in mind when her imagination went on a flight of fancy. Where he came from is not where she was going.

'Everything is different.'

'I wonder how you will adjust to the change, Boone.' He must feel like the proverbial fish out of water.

'I've had to travel new trails more than once in my life. Marigold and I will find ourselves at home in time.'

At home on his farm is what he surely meant. But perhaps if she wed very well and Boone saw the grand sort of life her niece would have in London, he might change his mind. She must do her best to make him see it her way. The daughter of a baron did not belong on a farm, no matter what that said baron would believe otherwise if he were alive and able to state his opinion on it.

Boone adjusted his hat, shielding his eyes from a ray of sunlight stabbing through the branches.

A question persisted in her mind. Did he kill that snake?

'What sort of snake is that?' She had to know. 'Did you kill it?'

'A Prairie rattlesnake. I killed that one and all of its kind I could hunt up within a half mile of the ranch house.'

'Grant used to go on and on about them. He learned in his novels how they rattle their tails and how the venom can kill a man.'

Boone nodded, his gaze suddenly somber.

'Or a woman. My wife, my Susanna, got bit. That's how she died.'

Oh, no! How Ambrin wished she had not spoken of snakes.

'I am so very sorry, Boone. What a horrid thing…'

She was at a loss at how to carry on with the conversation but she could hardly let what he'd confided fall into a conversational abyss as if he had just mentioned a bout of bad weather.

'If you wish to speak of her, I would like to know about your wife. Did my brother know her?'

'He didn't. She was gone before I met Grant. It was a lonely year between the time I lost Susanna and the time I met Grant. Only part of the reason we partnered up was financial. He had money to buy cattle but no land, while I had land but no cattle. But your brother came along when I needed a friend and he was a good one. Then later, when he lost Guadalupe, I did what I could to carry him the way he carried me.'

Boone grew silent, seeming far off in thought. Perhaps he was finished speaking of his loss.

Oh, please let her not have opened his wounds. While she did wish to know about the woman he had… or still loved, she would not pry.

'I don't mind speaking of Susanna. She and I grew up together on neighbouring ranches. We never loved anyone but each other. Reckon it might sound odd, but even after so many years, it seems like the love we had for each other never went away.'

'I've heard of people who never love anyone but their first love, even after they are torn apart like you and Susanna were.'

'That's not quite what I mean. It's more like she's a glow in my heart. Can't explain how I know it but she is urging me to go on and make a new life, even if that means finding love again. If that makes any sense?'

She wanted it to, but having never been in love she could not fully understand.

'Boone, am I wicked that I do not feel that glow for my brother?'

He touched her cheek, wiped away a tear. My word, when had she shed it?

'Not now, but you will. It takes getting over the grief before you recognise the love has survived.'

'I'm so sorry, Boone. We were speaking of your grief and I have turned the attention on my own.'

'Don't be sorry, darlin'.' His voice was soft, assuring. 'My mourning has turned to dancing. Yours is still raw. Give it time.'

'Having Marigold helps.'

As unlikely as it seemed, being near Boone helped, too. There was something about him. A quality that she could not put a name to. Only, she felt less troubled when she was with him.

For all that she resented the fact that her brother had chosen a stranger, along with a new and foreign way of life over her, and had indeed completely dismissed her from his life, she knew that did not mean Boone and Grant were cut from the same cloth.

She thought just perhaps, Boone was not the foe she had cast him as.

Unlike her brother, Boone Rawlins appeared to be a man she could trust.

'Sorry, darlin', that's no hat. It's a stovepipe.'

He swiped the stiff black thing off his head and tossed it on to the parlour couch.

The suit was as bad as the hat. The tailor must have done a poor job of measuring because he felt as confined as a sausage in a casing.

Ambrin was doing her valiant best to spiff him up but the ball was in four days. He couldn't rightly see how she was going to turn this tumbleweed into a trimmed hedge.

'Try on the shoes, then.' Ambrin pointed to a pair

of black boots so shiny he figured he could see the reflection of his frown if he looked.

To make the lady happy, he put them on. He tried to smile even though the rigid leather pinched his toes and rubbed his heels.

'Perfect!' Ambrin smiled, walking around him in a circle. 'You look every bit a gentleman.'

'I'm not, but for your sake I'll act the part.'

'Not for my sake. For Marigold's. The day will come when she needs to take her place in society. You will want to reflect well on her and that begins at Lady Dewhurst's ball.'

'Marigold will take her place wherever she chooses.'

'Nice words, Boone. But it is not how it works here. You will see. Society has certain expectations of its members.'

'Marigold is not one of them. She is a little girl.'

'One day she will grow up. You will want her to be invited to all society events.'

'You reckon having her pa look like a strutting peacock will do that?'

She gave him a look over, hairline to boot toe. Her gaze lingered on his mouth for longer than the rest of him, which made his heart slam an unexpected thump against his ribs. Not just any sort of thump either. It was the sort that made a man yearn for a woman.

'A peacock? No, an eagle perhaps. And as for strutting…that is something I do not expect to see.'

An eagle was it? That was a flattering notion but

that was not why he had stuffed himself into this suit of torture.

He did not want to shame Ambrin in front of her suitors. There was no other reason than that.

'Teach me what I need to know.'

'Well, it is the ladies you must impress more than the gentlemen. Many women will wish to make your acquaintance, of course. You know that you are the talk of Mayfair?'

Ambrin tapped her lips with two fingers, looking him over again. This time the inspection made him squirm. He wasn't used to having his appearance scrutinised. He was a practical dresser not a fancy one.

'Darlin', I'll give a fine howdy. No need to worry.'

'Yes, I believe you will, but there is so much more to it.' She picked the stovepipe of a hat off the couch then placed it on his head, then with a delicate frown, she removed it. 'What dances do you know? There is a great deal of dancing at a ball. Gentlemen are expected to participate.'

'I've stomped about the floor at barn dances and such. I only bruised Susanna's toe twice…that she let on about.'

'Stomping about isn't…' She bit her lip. He got the impression she was trying not to grimace. 'Do you waltz?'

'Too fancy for me.'

'Polka?'

'Fun, but risky for my partner's toes.'

'Well, never fear. I happen to be an excellent dance teacher. I think the waltz will be the one to learn.'

'Fancy moves to go with my fancy clothes,' he murmured sullenly but she only laughed at his aversion.

Grinning, Ambrin wound up a music box, which was conveniently placed on a shelf in the parlour.

'When we were younger Grant and I used to practice the latest dance fads,' she explained while winding the ornately carved box.

A tinkling tune filled the room. While a great deal fancier, the box didn't sound so different than the one he'd had at the ranch.

'It goes like this,' she said.

Then she demonstrated by moving in a tricky looking pattern of stepping and twirling. One, two, three, pause…one, two, three.

He'd seen it done once or twice but had never been struck by how graceful it was. Ambrin made it look as if she was floating about the parlour with her feet barely on the floor.

'Now you try.' She smiled and nodded as if she believed he could.

For her sake he attempted what she had done but he felt like a donkey next to a prize pony.

'I suppose it would go better if we tried it as partners. Place your hand here.'

On her? He was to place his hand on her back? He didn't rightly know how he was supposed to concentrate on the dance steps when he was touching her.

But then, it did feel nice having her so close. No one would catch him complaining about that.

Next, she placed one hand on his shoulder. She wriggled the fingers of her other hand indicating that he should hold it. Not like they were holding hands for a romantic stroll, but in some way that looked formal.

Formal isn't how he felt, though. The slide of her palm on his was downright intimate.

If she felt the same it didn't show in her expression.

With a nod, she slowly manoeuvred him in the one, two, three, pause, and twirl configuration she had demonstrated.

It was going better than he'd expected in that he had not trampled on her skirt or foot and hadn't smashed her toe, either.

With the heat of her skin on his, the scent of her breath so close, he almost yanked her in for a kiss, but managed to restrain himself. It was all that was on his mind though.

The afternoon had grown cloudy during the past hour. A timely peal of thunder bounced across the roof.

All at once Ambrin went stiff, glancing about as if seeking a place to hide.

'Nothing to be afraid of, darlin'.'

'But of course there isn't. I was only startled for an instant.'

Startled and trembling.

'What's got you so riled?'

'I dislike storms.' She stepped out of his arms,

clutched the fabric of her skirt so tight that her fingers blanched.

'It's just a little one. I reckon it will pass before you can hide under that table you are staring at.' Catching her hand again, more because he missed the feel of it than to lead her, he drew her towards the couch then eased her down to sit beside him. 'Tell me why it's got you so riled.'

'You might think it's silly, but I got lost in a storm once when I was Marigold's age. I was convinced I would die.'

'It's not silly. They can be fearsome and that's a fact. How did you end up lost?'

'When I was quite little my family went to the country to visit friends for a week. Grant wanted to go out exploring but he didn't want to do it alone. He convinced me to go off without telling anyone. We wandered a long distance. We walked through a meadow with cattle grazing in it. They made me nervous but my brother called me a baby so I went along with him to prove I was not. We also went into some woods,' she paused slightly before taking a breath and continuing.

'A big storm came up. Later, people said it was the worst they had seen. It was so terrifying I could not move from where I stood. Grant could though. He ran back the way we had come and left me behind. I was four years old and had no idea of how far we had gone. Less idea of how to get back. I was too frightened to do anything but stand where I was getting wet and cold.

Then a bolt of lightning hit a tree not far from me. A frizzle went up my legs and my hair stood straight up from my head. I cried and cried. I found a bush to hide under. That is when I was convinced I would die. I was not quite certain what dying was but I feared it so much I couldn't move. Then the ground rumbled even without thunder. When I peeked out from the bush I saw a great, horrid bull who must have been as spooked by the lightning as I was. It was running straight at the bush I was in.'

'Ah, darlin', were you injured?'

He hadn't let go of her hand so he gave it a squeeze.

'No…not on the outside. But, if you can believe it, lightning hit again. This time between me and the bull. The animal dashed off in another direction.'

Ambrin was quiet for a time. Looking back was clearly stressful for her.

'Cattle will spook on occasion. What happened after that?'

'I heard my father calling me so I crawled out from under the bush. He carried me home. After what happened, we never went visiting the country again.' Glancing down, she must have just noticed he was holding her hand because she slid her hand away.

Ambrin Malcomb had womanly fingers. Slender but far from weak. He reckoned when she wed, her husband would never tire of holding her hand.

'It's silly, I know, to continue to be frightened after all this time. I am striving to get over it.'

He could talk until he was blue about how lightning was a part of life and storms were followed by pretty blue skies, but the lady felt what she felt and who could blame her? The fact was thunderstorms were dangerous—even deadly on the rare occasion.

Life, one's beating heart and one's lungs expanding in breath, was not something one could take for granted.

'No, darlin', it's not silly. It's wise.'

What would not be wise was leaning in for a kiss that belonged to the man she would wed, one day soon.

But damn it, the gent probably was not worthy of her. And hadn't she leaned forward an inch? Hadn't he?

As if summoned, Marigold skipped into the room rubbing sleep from her eyes.

'You up already, little darlin'?' He asked, dropping his hand in the act of reaching to touch Ambrin's cheek to draw her into a kiss.

'Thunder waked me up. I dreamed fairies were bouncing balls on the roof.'

Marigold had been through worse thunderstorms. They did not frighten her.

'Your auntie was just teaching me a fancy dance.' It was not a lie, she had been before he drew her down on the couch. 'How would you like to help me teach her something not fancy?'

'I would! Dancing is soooo much fun, Auntie Ambrin.'

'Do you think she would like El Jarabe Tapatio?'

'Yes!' Marigold clapped her hands then hopped happily about waving her skirt in anticipation.

'It's been her favourite since she could walk. It's also called the Mexican Hat Dance,' he explained. 'It's the national dance of Mexico. Our cook back at the ranch was Mexican. She taught it to us.'

'It's about falling in love,' Marigold said, giggling.

'And about having fun,' he clarified because he'd stepped a little too close to that flame a moment ago.

'Please do teach it to me, then.'

Boone took off his hat and placed it on the floor.

'So, Auntie, you wear a big, big, skirt and hop from one foot to the other. Then Uncle Boone hops too.'

'We won't have the music, which is half the fun, but Marigold likes to sing it.'

With that, Marigold began to swish her skirt and bounce about on her toes.

'La…la…lalalala, lala…lala…lalalala…' she sang.

Within a moment or two, the three of them were dancing around the hat, laughing and singing.

It was a good sound, Ambrin's giggles mingled with Marigold's la-la-las.

He wondered how long it had been since Ambrin had allowed a moment of light-heartedness to lift her out of her cares. Even before the recent upheaval in her life, she had borne the responsibility of keeping her household together.

Likely it had been a very long time.

Watching her open her heart to frolic and fun, with the storm apparently forgotten, he just wanted to grin.

More than that, he wanted to please her by putting his best foot forward at the ball. To that end he would practice the waltz in private until he had the tricky steps right.

While he cared little for what society thought about the cowherd from Montana, he cared very much for what Grant's sister thought of him. Although she would move on with her life, find herself a rich husband and have a family, he wanted her to think of him with a smile.

A noise in the night brought Ambrin upright in her bed.

She listened for it to come again.

There…it was faint and not issuing from within her chamber but rather from below in the garden.

Relieved, she slid from her bed and padded across the cool floor to the window.

She bit her lip to stifle a gasp. The very last thing she wished to do is make a sound that would disturb the goings on below.

The sound that woke her had been the chime of the music box. It had been placed on a bench close to the greenhouse.

Within a circle of lantern light, she spotted Boone. Greeting a bush, was it?

He made a gentlemanly bow in front of a tall camellia.

Lifting a branch, he appeared to be introducing himself to it, then he lifted it to his lips and kissed a leaf.

If shrubbery could swoon, no doubt the camellia would have.

From her spot at the window, she grew curiously heated.

Within the circle of lantern light, Ambrin watched him pretend to be escorting the branch to what must be a ballroom dance floor.

Then he placed one arm around the back of the shrub and took what he must believe to be the correct stance to begin a waltz.

He backed away from the bush and began to dance, quite off time with the tinkle of the music.

One step, glide, two, three and then a curse to go with a misstep. He tried it over again, failing each time.

She clapped her hand over her mouth. She could not decide whether it was to stifle a laugh or to keep her heart from floating out of her body and down to the garden.

If she were able to seek a husband where her heart led, she would consider Boone Rawlins to be at the top of her list. Such a thing was not possible, naturally. He had neither fortune nor social position, both things that a baron's daughter and sister must consider. It was especially true now that she had Marigold's future to consider.

Oh, but the cowboy in the garden…her heart twirled along with him.

For all that he had been part and parcel of her trouble, the blame lay more on her brother. Had she met Boone Rawlins in different circumstances, she might believe him to be a man she could count upon.

However, what she had learned over the past several years is that there was only one person she could count upon and that was herself. But not herself as much as her ability to find a gentleman who would watch out for her and those who depended upon her. It was the way society worked.

Apparently though, her feminine heart worked in a different way. Watching Boone now, she grew tingly inside.

The cowboy was graceful in his own way, which was robust rather than sophisticated. And yet, it did not seem likely that he would learn to waltz in time to perform it at the ball. Bless him for trying though. She was touched beyond words at his effort.

She turned away from the window and went back to bed. If she watched much longer, she might dash down to the garden to take the place of his imaginary partner, the bush. With her blankets pulled up to her chin, Ambrin listened to the music box. She did not know how long Boone practiced because she fell asleep with it tinkling away into night.

Chapter Six

The day had come. The hour had come.

It was time to depart Greycliff House for Lady Dewhurst's elegant extravaganza.

The event at which Ambrin would let it be known that she was encouraging suitors.

A carriage was waiting and so was she.

Standing at the foot of the stairway and gazing up, she waited for her escort to descend.

She fluffed her skirt then tugged the bows adorning her sleeves.

What if he changed his mind? What if he was not going to attend?

She would not blame him if that were the case. His way of seeing life was an ocean away from how the London elite saw it.

The snobbish among her circle were bound to greet him with disdain. Luckily, she knew there were more people eager to meet the hero in the park than there were swell-headed ones.

'Oh, but please do come down,' she whispered under her breath. She could hardly go unescorted. 'And please let him be dressed like a gentleman.'

Boone had shown nothing but dislike for his new suit since the moment he took it out of the box. But he simply must make a good show for the sake of Marigold's future.

As far as dancing went, she would not expect that of him, in spite of his clandestine practice in the garden. Most gentlemen learned the intricacies of the dance as children. Boone could hardly be faulted for not being accomplished in it.

Truth be told, the hat dance she had learned from him and Marigold was far more fun and he was brilliant at that. Brilliant and so very masculine.

Hearing the pad of soft leather on the stairs, she looked up…and caught her breath.

Boone was not wearing his elegant, polished boots, but rather his worn every-day ones.

Nor was he wearing his fine top hat. No indeed, he wore the Stetson with the snakeskin band. At least, though, he had left his holster and gun in his chamber.

To her relief he did have on the black suit and the white shirt…even the tie, which at one point he had sworn was choking him.

With each step he descended, her chest grew tighter, her breathing quicker. The sigh rising in her heart made her go utterly soft inside.

She stifled the sigh, scarcely able to take him in.

The man was a vision of virility balanced between two worlds. Half of him was gleaming gentleman, but the other half…oh my word. Half of him was as rugged as a stable stone.

The sight of him left her scrambling after her wits and half hoping she did not find them.

The two images Boone presented made him by far the most dashing man she had ever seen.

Coming to the bottom of the stairway, he dipped his Stetson in greeting. Then he extended his elbow in a most gentlemanly manner.

'My lady.'

That sounded terribly wrong coming from him. She much preferred darlin'. It implied a connection. Oh, but she must not read too much into it. He probably called many women darlin'.

There was no doubt whatsoever that society would be charmed by Boone. Ladies would be smitten and melt in their corsets. Gentlemen would envy him.

Boone, she imagined, would be far more likely to return home with prospects for courting than she would.

If people were staring at Boone, he was also staring at them.

In appearance, he was dressed somewhat like they were. He was a cowboy though and not a gentleman and the difference showed. Reckoned he was breaking some sort of code by wearing his Stetson, didn't mean he aimed to take it off to please them, though.

Glancing about he decided the money spent on this shindig would probably be enough to purchase a dozen farms in Oxfordshire.

The awe he'd felt while visiting the sweet shop was dwarfed by this display of prosperity.

'What do you think, Boone?' Ambrin clutched her fingers tight in the crook of his arm while they stood at the top of a short staircase leading down to the party.

Some fellow, who looked dressed for his own wedding, announced his and Ambrin's arrival with great flair.

What he thought is not what he would tell her.

He had never seen the like of this place. A wall of mirrors reflected the flames of countless candelabras. The floor was polished to such a gleam it looked like another mirror that caught the glow of the chandeliers hanging over it.

As pretty as the ballroom looked, the stench of perfume rose up powerful enough to make his nose itch.

'The music is as fine as I've ever heard,' he said. 'Half the flowers in London must have been picked to make the room look so pretty.'

'From what I hear, Lady Dewhurst feels quite grateful to have engaged the orchestra. They perform all over the world and are in great demand whenever they visit London.'

Boone figured he might as well enjoy himself since he would never attend anything like this again. This night would be something to tell people about for the rest of his life, and that was a fact.

Going down the steps he had an eagle's eye view of folks mingling. He paid special attention to the men. Which ones would Ambrin encourage as suitors?

All along she had insisted it was not his concern. Which did nothing to deter him from making it his concern.

His partner was the one who had put her in a position of need. It fell to Boone to make sure she came to no harm because of it.

'So, darlin', who you are going to flash your dainty little fan at?'

That's how it was done, she'd explained to him earlier. A lady gave subtle messages with her fan that would tell the men she was interested…or not interested.

Curious. But was this secret language understood by men? Could be that he would have to give the fellows she was interested in a shove in her direction… as long as he approved of them.

Over the course of an hour, he'd met several fine people and some pompous ones. As far as folks went, they didn't seem so different at heart than where he came from. Miles apart in manners though.

One woman who was stuffed in lace and bedecked in jewels had taken offense when he'd tipped his hat and greeted her as 'ma'am'. She'd stared at his Stetson in revulsion then declared with a lifted chin that she was Duchess Grendolf and would be addressed with the respect due her.

Other ladies, though, seemed charmed to be called ma'am. Fluttered their fans at him, even.

He sure was in a foreign land. It would be a relief to get to his new farm. The sooner he settled in, the sooner he would make an easy, comfortable home for himself and for Marigold.

While he was busy meeting folks, he got separated from Ambrin for a time. When they reconnected, she had a card hanging from her wrist by a satin ribbon.

'What's that for?'

'Why, it's my dance card.'

He must have looked pretty confused because she added, 'When a gentleman asks me for a dance, I write his name on the card. That way everyone knows who they will partner with for each dance.'

'You got a spot or two for me on that card?'

'You may have one. You cannot dance with me twice or people will speak of it.'

'What will they say?' he asked, feeling bewildered. For all the elegance of this party, he preferred the simplicity of a barn dance.

'That we are fond of one another.'

'I am fond of you, darlin'.'

Pink bloomed in her cheeks. The sight made his insides melt like beeswax. He hadn't thought she could get any prettier, but here she was looking sweeter than a purple flower petal.

'As I am fond of you, Boone. But to dance twice with a man indicates another sort of fondness. A romantic one.'

'Too many complicated rules, if you ask me.' How did folks learn them all? And why did they put so many restrictions on their behaviour?

One thing for certain, Marigold would not be bound by them. He was sorry enough that Ambrin was tangled in rules.

'Let me have a look at that little card.'

Giving him a pretty smile she lifted her hand, which was encased in a silly transparent glove. He looked the card over meaning to ask her later what purpose the gloves served.

'Here is an empty spot,' he said. 'Write my name on it.'

'It's a waltz.' She frowned while taking a pencil out of the little jewelled bag she carried. 'Are you certain?'

He could understand her reluctance. She didn't know he'd been practicing in the garden.

Seeing the hesitation in her expression, he plucked the pencil from her fingers and wrote his name on the appointment card.

'How much longer before we dance?' He couldn't deny being uneasy. While his partner of the other night, Lady Camellia, had not complained about his skills, the folks whose gazes trailed him since he came down the stairs would be a sight more critical.

'I've got Lord Gilmore and then Mr Dawson. And then it will be your dance.'

Before she finished speaking a tall, skinny gent strode towards them.

Lord Gilmore, he suspected. What sort of lord was he? A baron like Grant, or someone higher up?

After a polite greeting, Lord Gilmore led Ambrin away. Boone had no reason whatsoever to dislike the man, but the fellow made his nerves itch.

Boone wandered across the room towards the champagne bowl, stopping a few times to greet young ladies and their hovering mamas.

A servant handed him a glass of champagne. He took it to a secluded spot near a potted plant to sip and to watch Gilmore—to judge what sort of fellow he was.

His impression was that the man was a fortune hunter. The fellow wore scuffed shoes and, Boone noticed, he had a missing button on his coat. Every other man here was as polished as the floor.

Gilmore would not know that Ambrin had no fortune to go with her. He probably expected that with the baron gone Greycliff House would be easy pickings. The man bore watching.

When the dance ended, another man took Lord Gilmore's place. Must be Mr Dawson.

Dawson seemed young, on the portly side and too shy to carry a conversation. There didn't seem to be anything wrong with him, except that a middle-aged woman stood near the dancers watching him as if he were her fledgling fallen from the nest.

Seemed to Boone like Dawson was a calf too long with its mother. Not enough of a man for Ambrin and that was a plain fact.

The orchestra quit playing. Ambrin turned her gaze towards him as if she had been keeping an eye on his whereabouts within the throng of elegant folks. It would be flattering if he didn't know her attention had to do with him being her next dance partner and probably being worried about how he would perform. Not that he could blame her. He was worried too. He wanted to put on a good show, but he'd probably look like a bull trampling on a meadow of wildflowers.

Ambrin sent him a smile and a nod.

With a nod back, he strode towards her but then she turned and walked in the other direction.

She spoke a few words with the orchestra conductor who nodded at her with raised brows and a wide grin. Next Ambrin hurried to Lady Dewhurst who was not far from the orchestra.

Whatever Ambrin had to say must have met with their hostess' approval. Lady Dewhurst laughed although he could not hear her from so far away. Then she nodded at the conductor.

It must not be usual for a guest to speak to the conductor because when Ambrin crossed the room to claim her waltz, folks watched her.

As elegantly as he knew how to, he extended his arm

to lead her to the ballroom dance floor. To his probable place of shame. But maybe not every fellow here had the gift of dance and could be he would blend in with them. Or, just as likely, a herd of cattle would thunder across the floor.

With the eyes of all the fine people upon him, knowing they were wondering how the cowboy from Montana would perform, he lassoed a steadying breath.

Best to get it over and done with.

She'd done it now.

For good or ill, Ambrin was about to act more boldly than she ever had.

Glancing about, she recognised that people knew something different was about to happen. They could not guess how different.

Stepping up to Boone, she lifted the hat from his head, dropped it on the dance floor between them.

She heard someone gasp, then three more. It sounded as if the rattlesnake had come to life.

'Darlin'?' Boone cocked his head at her, his gaze questioning. A hank of dark blond hair slid across his brow.

Ambrin imagined she heard feminine hearts sighing all over the room.

Gripping her skirt in both hands, she waggled it, stomped one foot on the floor.

Suddenly understanding, Boone nodded, grinned.

'How unorthodox,' a male voice declared. Ambrin heard feet shuffling away from them.

'El Jarabe Tapatio!' the conductor announced with a wave of his baton.

Then the music started. The tune was vastly different from Marigolds lalala's. It might be the happiest and most lively music she had ever heard.

Boone placed his hands behind his back, near his waist. Nodded at her then grinned.

He tapped his feet on the floor, his worn boots making muted clicks. She tapped her feet on the floor, her dancing shoes making sharp reports while she waved and twirled her skirt the way Marigold had taught her to do.

Boone circled the hat; she followed on the opposite side.

The music box at home had not done justice to the liveliness of the orchestra. The sound was thrilling. Magic. She let it run through her. Overtake her.

Her steps might not be quite what they were supposed to be but when it came to the way it made her feel, she knew had the joy of it.

More than that, Boone's attention rested fully upon her. It was all a part of this courtship dance, she knew, but his eyes looked so deep into her that she sensed his soul calling hers.

All she had meant to do is save him from the embarrassment of the waltz, which he was not accomplished at.

Oh, but circling around that snake banded hat, it was as if no one existed but the pair of them and, over the progression of the music, they were being drawn ever closer to one another.

Although he was not touching her, no waltz had ever been as seductive.

Then too soon, the music ended. Lady Dewhurst clapped and cheered. Many others joined her.

A few turned their backs, huffing their indignation but she scarcely cared. Flushed with delight and exertion as she was, the whole assembly could call 'boo', and it would not distress her in the least.

Grinning, his intent gaze never leaving hers, Boone stooped and snatched up his Stetson.

Rising, he placed it on her head.

She touched the brim, inhaled his scent which seemed alive within the hat.

The queen herself could not wear a finer crown.

During the short carriage ride home Boone wondered if he was falling in love, or half falling if there was such a thing.

The lady sitting across from him was one of the most spirited people he had ever met. Far bolder than her brother had been and with a great deal more sense.

Even with the weight of all Ambrin had dealt with recently, grief and financial setbacks, tonight he watched her rise above it all and give herself over to joy.

Although her only training in the Mexican Hat Dance had been from him and Marigold, she had become one with the music…and with him. In that moment he'd gotten the same fullness of heart that he did watching prairie grass blowing under a full moon. That was all it had taken for her to capture a part of his heart forever. Someday, when she was wed to some fortunate man, he would remember this night and long to live it again.

Although he had no intention of marriage, a thought nagged. Years from now would he regret not being the sort of man she needed?

He could not recall when someone had risked humiliating themselves to save him from shame. The risk she had taken was real, he knew. The stuffy folks of society seemed to hold power over who was, and who was not, deemed respectable.

Ambrin had behaved unconventionally for his sake. This is something he would never forget.

Hopefully she had not discouraged quality suitors by what she had done. But then, if they rejected her for it, they were not quality. Only the best sort of man would do for her, and damn it, he had yet to encounter one he fully approved of.

While he stewed over the matter, she closed her eyes and began to hum the tune they had danced to.

Maybe he should ask for her hand.

But no. He was not the sort of fellow she had in mind. She had her cap set on a man with plenty of money. That would not be him until he sold Greycliff. Ambrin admired gentlemen who wore tall black hats and shoes so shiny they reflected the wearer's aristocratic grin.

Mostly, she needed a man who wanted to marry. Even given the lavender crocus and what he believed his late wife wished for him, he was not ready. So much loss over the last years left him skittish.

The old prophet Jerimiah said a leopard could not change his spots. Same held true for a rancher. Boone could never be the gentleman Ambrin needed. The best he could do is sort through the men who would come courting. Sift out the weeds from the wheat.

Pretty hard thing to do when a fellow might be halfway in love.

Chapter Seven

In Ambrin's opinion, Lord Gilmore looked decidedly uncomfortable having a cowboy as chaperone for his visit. And no wonder. Boone sat in a chair near the window, arms crossed over his chest, peering out from under a frown. If Boone's intention was to discourage Lord Gilmore, she thought he was succeeding.

Later she would have a word with him about his attitude, explain that entertaining callers was something she must do. His scowl was not helping.

'It is a lovely day, wouldn't you say, Miss Malcomb?' Lord Gilmore asked.

'Oh, indeed, quite lovely.'

An awkward silence fell during which her visitor glanced at an expensive vase on the mantle and then a crystal decanter on a side table.

'Judging by those clouds there's a storm coming,' Boone declared.

Clearly Boone needed a lesson in the duties of acting chaperone. He was supposed to blend quietly into the background, be present but not involved.

With Lord Gilmore's attention focused on the painting of a fruit bowl, Ambrin shot Boone a frown.

Clearly it was not stern enough for he answered with a grin.

She countered with a huff because there was no way this man could possibly blend into the background.

'I beg your pardon.' Her caller swung his gaze back to her. 'I fear my attention was caught by that exquisite painting for an instant. It must be a costly piece of art.'

'Is it the apple or the pear that intrigues you, Lord Gilmore?' Boone asked.

In a clear snub, Lord Gilmore acted as if he had not spoken.

'I would have admired the orange,' Boone went on, seemly undaunted. 'My parents own an orange orchard in California.'

Next time, she would make certain her visits were chaperoned by Millie.

'What do you think of what was reported in the Daily Whisper last week, Miss Malcomb?' Lord Gilmore asked. 'It was quite irregular was it not?'

'I believe Hestor Givens was quite right to investigate rumours of misconduct at the city orphanage.'

'But surely that is nothing for you to worry about, my dear lady. No, what I was speaking of is Lady Fenton's hat. It made quite the stir at Mrs Brewster's charity tea. Those ostentatious orange feathers were large enough to have come from an ostrich and it was rumoured that they smelled rather…foul.' Lord Gilmore chuckled at his joke.

Apparently Boone did not see the humour in it any more than she did. He shook his head, brows and smile flat.

'But surely, Lord Gilmore, you are not suggesting that the welfare of orphans is not everyone's concern?' she asked, not at all pleased with the man's attitude. Not towards helpless children or his condescending demeanour towards her.

'The problems at the orphanage will be sorted through without you having to trouble yourself, my dear. I am certain you have enough to do directing the staff of this grand home, which your brother has left you. He has hasn't he? There was no one else, I assume?'

A fortune hunter, then. He would be disappointed to learn his prey was penniless. But she could hardly fault him for his motives since hers were no different.

She stood indicating the visit was at an end.

'As it happens there was someone else Lord Gilmore.' Better to get the news said and spread. It was pointless to have men courting her who hoped to gain Greycliff House.

'But who?' Her former potential suitor gasped, his expression reflecting the blow he'd been dealt.

How to answer that? She could not say it was Boone. The only respectable way for them to be living under the same roof is if he, along with her niece, was her guest.

'That...' Boone declared while rising from his chair, '...is surely nothing for you to worry about, Lord Gilmore. Better for you to direct your attention towards Lady Fenton's hat and to saving society from overly smelly feathers.'

'Good day, my lord.' She nodded crisply in dismissal.

'Allow me to escort you to the door.' Boone inclined his head towards the hallway.

When her caller began to grumble about the sudden end to his visit, Boone pronounced, 'Better hurry or you'll get wet in the storm.'

Watching Lord Gilmore go, Ambrin was relieved rather than disappointed. Not because of discovering him to be a fortune hunter, she was indifferent in that. But to suggest she should put objectionable feathers above the well-being of orphans?

The man was an overbearing, pompous—

'Snake,' Boone declared striding back into the parlour with Petunia trotting at his side. 'Dog didn't think much of him either. The next fellow to come calling better give you the respect you deserve, darlin'. Otherwise he'll be out the door faster than frog can snatch a fly.'

That would be Mr Dawson. He was scheduled to pay a call tomorrow.

The man would need to be quite derelict not to meet with her approval.

It is not as if she was a fresh and dewy debutante with dozens of suitors begging for her hand.

Truly, young Dawson was a pleasant sort. He was also her last hope.

'And you know, Miss Mead is in a tizzy over my boy, but so is her sister. You can understand how a marriage in that case would create quite the muddle,' Mrs Dawson said while Boone and the lady walked in step behind Ambrin and young Dawson.

By daybreak the storm had scooted off leaving the air this noon uncommonly fresh. A walk in the garden suited well.

Except that the matron beside him had not ceased to praise her son's brilliance since the second she set foot in Greycliff House.

As far as Boone could figure, it was Dawson's mother who was doing the courting and not her son.

'I have advised him to not pursue either of those ladies. It is not as if he is desperate, you know. For all that he is not in the direct line of a title he does carry the same blood. Since his dear papa's passing he has come into quite a fortune, which makes him wealthier than many a viscount. So naturally my boy is sought after and can have his pick of this season's well-bred ladies.'

It didn't take long for Boone to quit listening to the woman chanting her offspring's praises. He nodded every now and then to make her think he was listening, but his attention was on the young paragon's attitude towards Ambrin.

It was damn hard to judge since Dawson didn't have more than a pair of words to string together.

Hard to determine the nature of a man when all he said was 'yes' or 'no' with nods added in.

'He was top of his class at...'

Any fool knew that it was the heart of a fellow that made him a decent man or not.

'He was nearly engaged once but then the girl...'

Boone nodded, even glanced sideways and smiled but what he wondered was whether—

Well curse him for thinking what he shouldn't, but he couldn't un-think something when it was already in his mind. But the plain truth was, he didn't think Dawson was enough of a man to kiss Ambrin the way she ought to be kissed. To leave her thoroughly satisfied and feeling—

'A man's first duty is towards the woman who bore and raised him after all, and that girl wanted all of his attention. I did not allow that engagement to come to pass, as you can surely appreciate.'

'I can't say that I do appreciate it, ma'am.'

'What was that?' Her gasp caused Ambrin and young Dawson to glance back.

Boone waited a moment for the couple to move

ahead before he answered. 'Seems to me when a man and a woman get hitched, they set up a new family. Between the two of them.'

Which is something he could not see happening between Ambrin and Dawson.

He'd keep quiet about the intimate spark he knew to be cornerstone in marriage. For Ambrin, it was financial stability which must be cornerstone.

Blamed shame though, a woman like Ambrin should experience the spark.

'I would not expect a man of your sort to understand.' Mrs Dawson gave him an arch look, one that lingered on his hatband in clear scorn.

After that she had little to say.

An hour later Dawson and his mother rode away in their expensive carriage. Boone hadn't seen anything wrong with the suitor, except that he didn't find anything worthy in him either. Reckoned it was because he hadn't been out from under his mama's wing long enough to grow his flight feathers.

Could be he'd grow to be a decent fellow. What chafed at Boone, was thinking of Ambrin waiting for him to do it.

Ambrin sat at the kitchen table listening to the clock chime midnight. Her fork pinged on the plate when she stabbed it at an apple tart that would never make it to her mouth.

How could she possibly eat when faced with marrying Mr Dawson? As far as she could determine, he was only considering taking a bride because his mother had deemed it time.

Oh, she could predict the outcome of a union with him all too well. After the wedding, her groom would share the manor house with his mother while dear Mama would manage a way to hide away Ambrin in a cottage on the outskirts of the property.

Wedding vows notwithstanding, the woman had no intention of sharing her son.

And yet she must wed and soon. Too bad her options were so limited. There was no time for her to search for the ideal man. So, it appeared that her choice came down to two men. One of them did not appreciate that a woman could contemplate matters more important than fashion. The other would be more influenced by his mother than his wife.

Dawson then. Between her two prospects, he was the one Boone had not escorted off the premises.

'Drat it, Grant,' she grumbled then felt bad for it.

Yet it remained that, had her brother not given her house away, she might have lived a satisfactory life as a spinster. With her marriage prospects dim, she would happily live out her days here in the home she loved. Indeed, she would have been grateful for it.

No use dwelling on it though. She did not have the option of living life as a spinster.

Boone walked into the kitchen. 'Can't sleep?'

He settled on the chair across the narrow table from her.

My word but the man looked like he stepped out of every woman's fantasy.

With his feet bare, his hair rumpled and dipping over one eye, with his shirt buttoned but aligned wrong, he was simply… She really had no word for it, but her imagined satisfaction at spinsterhood laughed at her. Loud and hard.

But then, at least as a spinster she could dream of a man like him. As a married woman she could not. Should not at any rate.

'Not a wink.'

'I reckon the decision you are facing would keep anyone from sleeping.'

'Not the decision. I must wed, after all. More it's the outcome keeping me restless.'

'You'd have to pick the Dawson boy, I reckon.'

Boone did not say why but they both knew. Not only did Gilmore have no respect for her, but he had nothing to offer. All he wanted is what he thought she had.

She nodded, not even able to utter the words that Dawson was the one she would share her future with.

'What's his given name? I never heard it.'

'Willard.'

'Darlin', seems to me that Willard Dawson is a nice enough fellow. He'd treat you decently.'

The expression on Boone's face did not look as hopeful as his words sounded.

'His mother won't,' she answered. 'She's not likely to want her boy's affections to wander.'

'She wouldn't be able to prevent it if you were...'

'If I what, Boone?'

'Darlin', I've been married, and I know some things that you maybe don't.'

'What things?' she asked even though she had a basic understanding of what he was referring to.

'Important things. Without them there can be no proper marriage.'

'If I am to make an informed decision about encouraging Willard, I will need a bit more of an explanation.'

'It's hard to put into words, darlin'.' He shook his head, his expression going soft, thoughtful. 'It's like—'

Boone reached across the table, lifted a hank of her unbound hair from her shoulder. He stroked the strands between his thumb and fingers. He lifted it to his nose, drew it across his lips, seeming to be breathing in the scent. Then he ran one finger over the curve of her cheek, under her chin, all the while looking at her as if she was a midnight treat.

Then he drew his hand back, making a fist on the table.

'Did you feel anything when I did that?'

Anything? Or everything?

'Warm,' she admitted in a whisper.

Heat swirled through her in the oddest way. It rolled

over her nerves and thrummed in her blood. She could give no name to the sensation except…longing.

'That's the sort of feeling you need in order to make a marriage hold together. It's the glue that binds a man and woman when the problems of life try and rip them apart…it's what I've learned.'

And what he'd just taught her. Words could never have conveyed the message delivered in one heated touch.

'I have much to consider,' she whispered, still pulsing with a glow that was spreading from her cheek to her heart.

If only…but no, she did not dare consider Boone as a potential husband.

His future was a risky one. Farms did not always thrive. His and Grant's failed dream was proof of that, and he had even less experience in the English climate. If the dream failed again, someone must be in a financial situation to provide for Marigold.

Financial security was what marriage was all about. There came a time when the poetic notions that dewy-eyed girls entertained must be put away.

Dreams were often dashed, but society remained constant. Reliable.

Drat that lock of hair brushing his brow. She wanted to touch it…brush it aside and then—

Drat, drat, drat! Cowboys were an utter distraction when it came to seeking a dependable monetary future.

'Goodnight, Boone.'

Rising, she could not let go of wondering what it would be it would be like to kiss him. Would it bind them in the way he had just spoken of?

But perhaps that was a bond he would not feel again. It was quite clear how much he had loved his wife. Maybe he would never feel that way for another woman.

An hour after speaking with Ambrin in the kitchen, Boone needed a good strong dose of fresh air. Being inside when he was troubled always made it seem like walls held and magnified emotions.

Back on the ranch being under a starry sky, where a soul could reach for the ends of the universe, helped him get right in his mind. Could be a walk in the park would help set him right.

Boone reached for the high shelf where he kept his gun and holster inside a pot. He strapped the holster around his hips and whistled softly for Petunia.

The dog must have been close by because she was beside him within seconds.

Going outside, he discovered thick fog pressing the ground instead of a sky full of stars. It made eerie, vaporous halos around the gas lamps lining the cobbled walkway leading the short distance to the park.

He reckoned there were thugs about, but he wasn't worried, not with Petunia trotting at his side.

What did gnaw at him, was the demonstration he had presented to Ambrin of what was needed in a committed, happy marriage. Turned out, he was the one to have learned a lesson. While Ambrin had admitted to feeling warm, he'd gone past warm to boil the instant he lifted her hair from her shoulder.

What he'd felt when he touched her cheek had been outright longing. Until that moment he'd never felt desire for any woman but his late wife.

Not that he felt wrong or guilty. Susanna would want this for him. What he felt was overwhelming and something akin to fear.

One thing was certain, he should not be living under the same roof as Ambrin. Given the sensations simmering his nerves, he might be tempted to dwell on matters that were not appropriate, given he was not wed to her.

Pacing through thick swirls of fog, he wondered what to do about it.

All of a sudden he wasn't so inclined to help her find a husband. Which did not change the fact that she needed one.

It was not as if she could go on living in the home she had grown up in since he was going to sell the place. Even if he felt a villain for doing it, he had no choice. If a man were to have a farm he needed cattle on it. In order to get the cattle, he would be forced to sell Greycliff house.

There was Marigold's welfare to consider, as well. She needed someplace safe to live. A place to grow strong and to breathe fresh air. A place to run free and be happy.

It is what he had promised her father. The agreement had been that if anything ever happened to Grant, Boone would raise Marigold the way he and Guadalupe had intended to.

Boone might not be a fancy gentleman, but he was a man who took his responsibilities to heart. His partner had never mentioned a sister as being one of them, since he'd never spoken of her. But Ambrin was under his watch, nonetheless.

Besides, a man didn't just take a woman's home and leave her to her own ends.

Last week he'd meant to watch out for Ambrin by pointing her to a decent husband.

A decent husband, he reckoned, was not to be had. Even if there were such a fellow, Boone had misgivings about handing her over to him. Especially now that he was beginning to admire her in a particular way.

A rustling noise came from up the path. The fur on the dog's back stood up. She growled. It wasn't a bear or a snake that had her riled. No such beasts in England.

Before he had a chance to worry a sleek little fox slipped out of the brush and crossed his path.

Going along, past the park fountain, he heard more rustling. This came from a critter bigger than a fox. One that was meaner too.

Petunia growled again. Whoever had been lying in

wait must have changed his mind when he spotted the dog because he never came out of hiding, curse his sorry soul. If there was any doubt as to what he needed to do next, this reminder of a villain's intent upon pouncing on the unwary, made up his mind.

Grant might have thought it to be appropriate to leave his sister alone in London, but he hadn't always made the wisest choices.

Boone would not make that misjudgement. Too much was at stake.

Ambrin was at stake.

He could no more leave her to the Dawson boy than he could the lurker in the bushes.

He exhaled long and slow. His mind was made up. And his heart? Could be it was less certain, but it was made up too.

'Well, girl—' Petunia looked up at him, her tail wagging '—looks like I'm getting married again.'

It had been a week since Ambrin first wondered if it would be preferable to remain a spinster than to wed. Wondered and concluded that it would be. She loved this home. If she remained here she could enjoy a lifetime of afternoons like this one.

Truly, what could be nicer than playing hide and seek in the garden with her niece?

A giggle came from around the corner of the house. In order to prolong the game, Ambrin pretended to search bushes and hedges.

'My word, but you have hidden so well you might miss naptime,' she called.

Marigold's laughter might be the sweetest sound she had ever heard. Her heart quite melted over it.

While she shook a bush, she thought again about an idea that had occurred to her. It was bold and in some respects preposterous. Still, it might very well solve her problem.

Why, she wondered, could she not seek a position as Greycliff's housekeeper?

Boone would have to be willing to keep the matter secret. It would be ruinous if people knew she worked for a wage. The reality was that nothing would change from what she was doing now. She had performed this duty since her mother died and was accomplished at it.

And perhaps she could convince Boone to allow Marigold to come for extended visits. It would only be right of him to allow it since she must get used to life in society.

Evidently with her thoughts wandering, so had her attention to the game. All of a sudden Marigold was hugging her skirt.

'You couldn't find me, Auntie! Your turn to hide.'

What a sweet and endearing smile her niece had. When Ambrin bent to kiss her cheek, she imagined that she was looking at a sun-brushed vision of her own mother.

'Close your eyes and count to a hundred,' Ambrin said, her throat growing tight with emotion.

Marigold shut her eyes tight. 'I can only count to twenty.'

'Do it five times then,' Ambrin called while she dashed around a tall hedge then knelt behind the fountain where she could not easily be seen. Small drops of water splashed on her but no matter. This was the most fun she had experienced in a very long time.

Oh but it had not been all that long, she realised, only since the ball when she and Boone performed the Mexican Hat Dance.

Truth be told, life was far more fun since Marigold and Boone burst into her home.

With every passing second, she felt more hopeful that all would be well.

Surely Boone would see the wisdom of allowing her to work for him. It is not as if he approved of either of her suitors, not any more than she did.

It was taking a rather long time for Marigold to find her. The top of Ambrin's hair was getting damp from fountain mist, so were her shoulders.

'Found you!'

'Boone? Where did you come from? Where is Marigold?'

'I sent her in for her nap. Millie's orders.'

'Already? Time got away from me.' She stood up wiping a spray of mist off of her cheeks and nose. 'I'd forgotten how much fun Grant and I used to have playing hide and seek.' And then she laughed. 'And how much mischief we got into doing it.'

It was beginning to feel good recalling moments spent with her brother and funny little things about him without so much heartache.

'If you have time there is something I wish to speak with you about,' she said.

The sooner she sorted out her future, the easier she would feel.

'There is something I'd like to speak with you about too, darlin'.'

It was not common for Boone to look nervous, but there was something about the set of his mouth and jaw that made him seem so.

But then he reached for the stray hair curling to her temple. Smiling, he lightly brushed away small droplets of fountain spray.

She must have been mistaken then that something was amiss.

With the sun shining down and water tapping cheerfully in the fountain, she felt more hopeful than she had in some time.

Ambrin waved her hand towards a bench, indicating they should sit across from the fountain. Boone followed her then sat down even though he felt like he was perched on a prickly cactus.

'What did you wish to speak with me about, Boone?'

Her smile looked cheerful. Sunshine dappling a flowered meadow is what it reminded him of.

That might change in a hurry since what he had to ask her would not be what she was expecting.

'Well, darlin',' he began, searching for perfect words as he went along. 'It has to do with your marriage prospects. We both know that Lord Gilmore is wrong, not a worthy fellow however you look at him. And Willard Dawson. He's of an age to marry but not nearly ready to.'

'This is exactly the conclusion I have come to, as well. It has to do with what I wish to speak with you about. I do have an idea which will make it possible for me not to wed at all.'

Not the best words to hear when a man meant to propose.

'You are frowning, Boone, and I have yet to present my idea.'

Frowning? A man ought to be smiling when he proposed. Just went to show how on edge he was.

'Tell me your idea, darlin',' he said, rooting for a smile.

'It's this. You will be going to your farm soon,' she wrung her fingers together, giving away how much what she was presenting meant to her. 'You will need someone to run your house for you while you are away. I imagine you will be hiring servants. The house is huge after all. Greycliff used to engage a full staff until Grant went away and left me to…oh drat…rather, my brother and I used to have mischief at the servants' expense and he always took the blame.'

She shook her head, smiled. 'I am making progress at forgiving him. But what I meant to ask is...will you let me act as housekeeper of your home?'

Hire her to run a home he would be selling? It grieved him to have to tell her how impossible this was, but it seemed he could no longer postpone the news.

'Do you like me, darlin'?'

'Yes, Boone, I think you know I do.' She smiled, and she blushed. 'You will not be sorry if you leave me in charge of running Greycliff. You know it is home to me and I will treat it with the greatest...'

At a loss for words, he touched her lips to keep her from going on about the home she was about to lose.

'It won't work,' he murmured.

'Oh... I thought...' She glanced away but not before he saw disappointment darken her eyes. 'But, of course, I cannot accept employment from you.'

He prayed that what he had to say next would put the bloom back in her cheeks...from pleasure, not displeasure.

Now that he'd made up his mind, his future was at stake as well as hers.

'But I have an idea, darlin'. A damned fine one.'

She did not answer, but cocked her head at him. Her lips pressed and the corners of her eyes creased in seeming confusion.

'If you agree, you will not be separated from Marigold.'

'Oh… I am to be her nanny then?' She gave a great sigh, slowly shaking her head. 'It is not as if I do not wish to, but we could not make it known. Again, a baron's daughter must not work for a wage. I will do everything a nanny would but as her aunt.'

What kind of sense did that make? Where he came from, if a woman on needed money, she was not looked down on for earning it.

Curse it, this was not going as he intended it to. He'd better get to the point before matters grew more muddled.

'Ambrin, darlin', I admire you more than anyone I know. Even when life goes against you, you hold strong. You weep like anyone would but then you shake it off. You collect yourself and do what you need to for the sake of the folks depending on you and…you smile.'

Although she was smiling now, it was only halfway. Those clear blue eyes of hers revealed a good dose of hesitancy.

'You are a mighty fine woman and I admire you.'

Although he was not offering his heart the way he had with Susanna, he was offering all of himself.

He meant to be a husband the second time as fully as he had been the first time. The marriage would be very different but he meant to be a devoted spouse.

Compared to the fortune hunter and the boy, he would be a good pick.

In the moment, Ambrin probably believed she had

a choice to wed or not. He'd like for her to accept him before she knew she did not.

Once she found out he'd been keeping the news of selling the home she'd likely be as mad as a hornet. She must feel that her life changed according to everyone's will but her own. And damn if he wasn't always at the heart of that change.

The last thing he wanted was for her to revile him. There was more to this proposal than she would suspect. It was not as cold as it might appear. How was he to make her understand that, although he admired her, it was not some distant regard he felt?

There was one way.

He hesitated for an instant before tracing the curve of her cheek with his thumb. Odd how his hand was steady when his insides were quaking.

'You are so beautiful, Ambrin. Sometimes I find myself unable to quit looking at you. I've got a powerful urge to kiss you...will you let me?'

'You do?' Her mouth formed a pink pretty circle of surprise. 'I do not understand.'

But he thought she might. Her deep honey eyes grew soft and dreamy, or maybe it was only curious. Either way, he figured she was willing.

'Reckon you have an idea.' He traced his thumb under the curve of her bottom lip, slowly to better savour the smooth skin of this woman he meant to make his bride. 'I admire you in more ways than I told you, darlin'.'

'I suppose I admire you, too.' She blushed, turned her cheek into the curve of his palm, closed her eyes and sighed.

Deep down need for her hit quick as a match strike, igniting and engulfing him. When he dipped his lips to hers it was not the sweet, patient wooing he'd intended. He felt the instant when she gave herself over to the flare and gave herself over to it…to him.

When the kiss ended, he had trouble catching his breath, so did she.

'I've never been kissed before, Boone. It was…' She took her time saying what it was.

Clumsy? Suave? Too demanding or not demanding enough? If anything, he prayed that she felt it for what it was—open-hearted.

'Very lovely and…' She blinked and shrugged her shoulders. 'I liked it.'

He'd damned liked it and then some!

'Ambrin, there is so much more to lovely than just this. I want to show you all that lovely can be.'

She bit her bottom lip, gave what might pass for a hesitant nod.

This was the time. He went down on his knee and withdrew the ring he had purchased three days ago.

'Will you marry me?'

It occurred to him that this was the first time he had proposed to a woman. With Susanna, they had grown up knowing they would wed one day. There had never been a moment of decision.

Now though, he was nervous. Would she turn him down? He had no other way of fulfilling his duty towards her if she refused him.

And now there was the kiss. It was like a seedling reaching for the light. He was right certain that something wonderful would grow in time.

If only she wasn't staring at him, silent as the moon. His stomach got tied in a hard, achy knot.

'What do you say, darlin'? Will you marry me?'

'Boone I…well, I only wonder… You do not approve of my suitors. Are you riding to my rescue? Taking care of me in my brother's place?'

She was not wrong. Caring for her was his intention. The last few moments had proven that it was not her brother's place he wanted to take.

But maybe he was mistaken about the kiss and she hadn't felt expectation for the future as deeply as he had.

While disappointing, it did not change his intention to wed her.

'Surely you can see the benefit of marrying me?'

'I am not a babe in the woods awaiting rescue. Nor am I an obligation to be fulfilled for my brother's sake. So no, I will not marry you.'

She stood up. Moisture pooled in her eyes. When blinking rapidly didn't make it go away she swiped the tears with the back of her hand.

'You must marry me, though—'

'Truly, Boone? I do not think I must. You take your perceived duty to my late brother too much to heart. I am not a problem for you to resolve. Were you in my place, would you wed a woman who considered you an obligation to be fulfilled?'

He understood her point. Not that it changed the position she was in. In fact, she was seconds from discovering that she had no place else to turn but to him…as his wife.

'I applaud you for your noble intentions, Boone Rawlins. I am certain Grant would appreciate you correcting his failures.'

If she applauded him, it didn't show.

What did show was that he'd hurt her pride. Anger at him and at her brother must be blinding her to common sense. Not that he could blame her for feeling that way.

Clamping her hands at her waist, she bent towards him where he was still on one knee. 'One day I will wed and it will be because I love the man who proposes to me. You may put that pretty little ring away for I shall not wear it.'

With a head of steam rising, her eyes flashed in a show of indignation.

'I will take care of your home and my niece as well as receive my due wage…in secret. What I will not do is pay for a place to live by committing my life to a man who does not want me. I will not marry you under any circumstances.'

'Damn it, Ambrin, there is one circumstance.'

'I am certain there is not, but please do enlighten me.'

'I told you hiring you would not work.' He stood up. What he had to tell her must be spoken eye to eye. 'And it won't.'

He had an urge to soften the news with a comforting hand. He reckoned, though, the last thing she would want is the touch of a Judas. Instead, he stood as rigid as one of the logs he'd built his ranch house from.

'I'm selling Greycliff House.'

Chapter Eight

'Sell Greycliff! You cannot!' The idea was so outrageous, so completely preposterous, that she wondered if she had misheard. 'Such things are not done.'

'Of course they are.' He looked up, seeming to give all of his attention to a cloud passing over the garden. 'That solicitor fellow you have, Adams, he knows a man or two who might be interested.'

'You, Boone Rawlins are a wretch with no heart at all if you intend to sell a home that has been in my family for generations. How could you not have told me?'

'You had suffered so much already. It was a hard thing to tell you.' He glanced away from the cloud that now covered the sky leaving no blue at all. 'And I do have a heart, Ambrin. It's hard to even find the words to tell you how bad it hurt when I sold the place I built out of my own sweat and dreams. I left three graves on a hill overlooking that house. I promise you, my heart was cleaved down the middle when I rode away.'

'I suppose we may thank my brother for giving you

a place to come and make a fresh start.' Her temper was bitter and she was not using the kindest of words but… 'And for turning me out on my ear as if I did not exist.'

'You are mistaken, Ambrin.' His gaze sharpened on her as if he meant to force her to see it his way, which was not going to happen any more than she was going to marry him. 'First thing, when Grant made his will he never expected to die. But there were already two graves on the hill by then so we both knew what could happen. When he left Greycliff to me it was understood that he was providing for his child's future.'

Well then…yes, as much as she did not wish to, she could understand. Naturally Marigold came first.

Already stunned at Boone's proposal, his news about selling her home, left her beyond undone.

What was to become of her? Of Millie and Frederick?

Feeling rather weak in the knees, she sat back on the bench with a thump.

'I would appreciate a moment to myself,' she said.

For all that she wished for Boone to leave her alone, he did not, but sat beside her close enough for her to feel the brush of his jacket on her sleeve.

'I do not know why your brother never told me about you. It wasn't right. But I promise you, darlin', when he left me this house, he knew I would watch out for you right along with Marigold.'

How could the man promise anything of the sort?

Who knew what had gone on in Grant's mind? Clearly he did not spare her a thought.

What she did know, is what was on Boone's mind. It made her feel like a piece of baggage. A worn satchel to be dragged about by one man or another.

No matter that she longed to have a choice for her future, it seemed she did not, nor perhaps would she ever.

Why would the man not leave her alone so she could indulge in a good weep?

'And so, you will sacrifice yourself on the altar of honour?' she asked. 'You will give up any hope of loving a woman of your choice and take me instead? And all in the name of loyalty to Grant?'

Once she said it she understood that, in his mind, he had no more choice than she did.

'Surely there must be another way,' she muttered.

'If you can think of one I will take back my ring.'

'You will not need to take it back because it is not on my finger.'

Indeed, the gold band was curled tight in his fist. She imagined it imprisoned, the same as she would feel if she'd wed him.

Not that he would intend to imprison her, only that is how she would feel having no choice in her future. If she were to marry Willard Dawson, that would, at least, be her own decision. Except that she had already made up her mind not to.

Not only could she see no future with the boy, just now she could see no future at all.

She was an unmoored vessel with no safe place to dock.

Boone stood up. She felt cold where his warmth had been.

'I reckon you could use the night to think things over.'

Thinking things over would not change her situation. She saw herself as adrift with rough seas keeping her from her safe harbour.

'Come inside, darlin', it's getting chilly out here.'

And cloudy. A storm was coming, she thought.

He reached a hand down to her. Looking at it, how broad and capable it was, she wondered if she ought to take it.

Like a boat adrift, she was being dragged by a current that would, in time, land someplace.

When she placed her hand in his she wondered if Boone was the place she would land.

Was he her safe harbour?

Boone's proposal had been shocking, he knew, and had clearly left Ambrin unsettled.

What he had not expected is to be unsettled as well. It wasn't like him to decide on a path and then be unsure of his footing.

Time outdoors under the stars was what he needed, but he would probably find the sky foggy or too bright with city lights to see stars. Hopefully once he took up living at the farm he would see Heaven's bright show more often.

When he reached for the doorknob Petunia rose to follow but he indicated that she should remain beside Marigold's bed.

Once outside he was grateful to see a full moon illuminating the garden paths.

An owl hooted. The sound of beating feathers ruffled the night air. A small cat scrambled up a tree, probably used to having the place to itself at this hour.

Just as Boone was used to snoring in his bed at this hour.

But there was that one thing Ambrin said that was leaving him sleepless.

It did not make him regret asking for her hand, it was what he needed to do. And he sure had not offered for her hand dragging boots and cussing in protest.

The thing she'd said, though, did give him pause.

It had to do with giving up hope of loving a woman the way the way he had Susanna. Of abandoning that hope for the sake of duty.

Glancing up at the windows, he saw that Ambrin's lamp was out.

Either she was tossing and fretting on her bed in the dark or she had come to terms with the matter and fallen asleep.

'The truth of it is, darlin',' he murmured at her shut curtains. 'I'll never love anyone like I loved Susanna.

It's impossible since there is no one else just like her. If I do love again, it will be all new. Unique between me and her.'

The question teasing his mind was, who was the 'her'?

The way matters stood, if he did not fall in love with his wife, it damned well would not be with anyone. Wedding Ambrin was a risk that, only a short time ago, he'd believed himself unwilling to take. Life could end in an instant. The pain of loss a harsh thing to endure.

Although he had great affection for Ambrin, he was not in love with her. Although, as he'd just discovered, he desired her greatly. Which was just as well if they were to wed.

All of life was a risk, he reminded himself. A man should not be fearful to take part in it.

It could be that not being heart and soul in love with Ambrin was for the best.

Nothing in this life was certain except duty, and he knew where his lay.

Looking up at Ambrin's window, imagining her looking all tussled and pretty in her sheets...he'd be damned if he didn't think there could be a real marriage between them in time.

That kiss they'd gotten lost in gave him hope they could get there.

Even if he were wrong about that kiss and the fire had been all on his side of it, they had friendship to build on.

Or they used to. He didn't know for certain how she felt about him now that she saw him as her betrayer.

It could be she'd have a hard time abiding his presence and he couldn't blame her for it. Everything involving him had meant loss for her…one hurtful surprise after another.

Except for Marigold. The child had been a delightful surprise for her. He knew Ambrin loved the little girl.

He cast the moon a glance to judge how long until dawn.

Not enough time to get a decent sleep but plenty of time to fret and worry.

Yes, Ambrin was angry over having no choice in what happened in her life but when it came to it, who really did?

Boone didn't have a choice that his wife got bitten by a snake any more than he did when the storm took his partner and all they had built together.

What a person did have was a choice about how he moved on from tragedy. How to take up life and live it.

There was a dried-out purple flower in his bureau drawer urging him to do just that.

Life might not have turned out to his choosing. But that did not mean it would not end up a mighty fine one in the end.

Too bad he did not know the words to bring Ambrin around to his way of thinking.

Then he remembered there was a way. Problem was,

if he tried to kiss her any time soon, it would be like dropping cold water in sizzling fat.

He wanted to get married, not burned.

Ambrin didn't mind washing dishes. Water warming her hands and soap gliding between her fingers was something of a balm while she came to terms with the turn her life was going to take.

She was to wed. Without fanfare, without an elaborate gown from Paris, without society making a fuss… and without being in love.

She shook her head, wished she could curse without feeling wicked.

'Drat,' she managed.

It was not as if she had not intended to wed. Doing what she must to get by was nothing new. It was what she had been doing since Grant went away.

However, she had intended to make her own decision on who her groom would be. She was beyond weary of being dragged every which way by the choices men made.

Rain pummelled the window while in the distance lightning scattered over the city.

For some reason the storm did not bother her as much as it normally did. It could only be because she was preoccupied with thoughts of the high handed, overbearing, knight in shining armour she must wed.

Of how he had not seen fit to inform her that he was selling her home. How, she wondered for the hundredth time since last night, had the man assumed it was in her best interests to keep the secret that he was selling her life!

She was so sick of secrets springing out at her that she could spit. Let Boone Rawlins go on about how he kept them to spare her grief. She was still in no frame of mind to forgive and forget.

For pity's sake, she was hardly a shrinking violet, too timid to hear bad news.

Not that her being either bold or timid changed her current situation.

She had no reasonable prospects for a society marriage, nor did she have the funds to become a respectable, if pitied, spinster. And curse the day, she would soon have no home to live in.

There was simply no way forward but to accept the single option available to her.

Her future was decided. Albeit, not by her.

All that remained was for her to wear his ring on her finger. There had been a time when she would have seen a pretty gold band as a symbol of love. Now it was a reminder that she was not loved but taken out of obligation.

Oh, it did have to be said that her future groom was handsome. Which by no means made him the type of husband she had envisioned as a starry-eyed young miss. What daydream ever involved a beloved who would rather herd cattle than attend a ball?

What an odd couple they were going to be.

She a proper lady of London. He an American cowboy with a rattlesnake skin on his hat and who wore his weapon even on the safe, affluent streets of the city.

The rancher was far too rough for her sensibilities.

Not for her senses, though. She would be a liar if she denied how attractive he was.

She shook her head and sighed. She must not spend another moment daydreaming of how she'd felt when he kissed her. It was far too confusing.

Never in her life had she spent nights tossing in her sheets alternating between being vexed and delighted.

Ambrin reached for the next cup to be washed. The glass glided under her soapy fingers with an almost sensual feel. Oh, indeed, it could not be understated what a fine kisser Boone Rawlins was.

A lovely kisser. And he had boldly hinted that there was much more to lovely than he had given her in that kiss. What, precisely had he meant? She had a vague idea, naturally, but what were the particulars he'd been speaking of?

All of a sudden the glass slipped from her fingers. She tried to catch it but it broke in her hand and sliced her palm.

'Oh drat!' Blood dripped from her palm. She grabbed a dishtowel, wrapped the wound and waited for the pain to come. She had no idea how deep the cut was, nor did she want to look and see so she stood still, pressing the towel to her hand.

That just went to show what came of drifting away

on a fantasy. The bubble always burst and dropped one on the hard ground of reality, bruised and bleeding. Wounded by secrets.

A lesson served, she decided. While she might be forced to wed, she would not be forced to give her heart. No one could make her do that. Her affections were her own. She would choose to keep them or to give them away.

'And I will very well keep them,' she muttered while watching a red stain seep through the towel.

'Keep what? Here let me have a look at that.'

There was no 'letting', not with Boone. He simply took her hand and drew the towel away from the cut.

'Keep whatever I wish to,' she gritted.

One thing about Boone, he did seem to be at her side when she needed him. Loyal to a flaw is what he was.

If it were not the case, what would become of her?

Oh, mercy, it was a difficult thing to be resentful and grateful at the same time.

Boone put pressure on the cut and it did not feel so bad.

'I have decided not to keep my hand,' she told him.

'This little bitty cut isn't enough to sever it, darlin'.'

'I mean in marriage. I have decided to give it to you.'

Not that there was a decision involved but she was glad to say the words which sounded as if she had made one.

'Ambrin, darlin', I'll be a good husband to you. I

promise I won't give you cause to regret marrying me.' He said so while dabbing the towel on the cut.

'There is one thing, Boone. I will have this promise. I cannot wed without it.'

'Anything, darlin'.'

'No more secrets. I will not be protected from bad news.'

'No more secrets, I promise.'

With her hand wrapped in the cloth and cradled in his large fingers, he gave her a grin and a wink. She got the oddest sensation in her stomach. Far from unpleasant but distressing nonetheless, given that she meant to keep her heart to herself.

'There is something rare between us, Ambrin.' His eyes had a certain look, the same as they had when he'd kissed her. 'If we nurture it, we can build a good marriage.'

'I am giving you my hand. The rest I shall keep to myself.' Best to have that understood between them for good and all.

'If you wish,' he murmured, but his eyes glittered. His grin quirked higher on one side.

With a jerk, she drew her hand out of his because… why the nerve of the man speaking words that smacked of a challenge.

Very well, her future husband would soon learn how set her mind could be.

And it was set on keeping her heart independent and to herself.

* * *

This was Boone's wedding night.

He stood in the hallway staring at his bride's closed bedroom door wondering how to proceed.

This morning, he entered a marriage of obligation and for the life of him he'd not been able to sense a romantic moment in the ceremony.

Couldn't say it was a surprise since he and Ambrin were not in love. But he wasn't mistaken that they were better than friends.

What, he wondered while staring at the polished doorknob, were the bedroom rules for a marriage of this sort?

The last thing he wished was to widen the distance that had grown between them in the two weeks since she had agreed to wed him. Did she want marital intimacy? It was not something they had discussed. To him, being close that way was a natural part of being married. Until he stood in front of this door, he had not given proper thought to the fact that she might feel otherwise.

Curse him for being insensitive. He'd been married and she had not. The only reason she was married now is because she had no other choice.

Thing was, after that kiss they'd shared, she must have been thinking about tonight. It hadn't been off his mind for more than a couple of hours at a time.

Whatever her feelings on the matter, there was no way of knowing until he knocked on the door.

She might be waiting for him, as eager to be with him as he was to be with her, or she might turn him away.

He knocked, waited. Knocked softly again. He could not recall a time when he had been edgier.

It almost felt as if he were the one who was a virgin. Of course, when he gave it a few seconds more thought, he was a virgin when it came to her.

In the dragged-out moments it took to hear footsteps on the other side of the door, he wondered if he would remain one.

The door creaked open inch by slow inch.

'Boone?' Ambrin blinked up at him with a little frown between her brows. 'Did you want something?'

Seeing her in a soft flannel nightgown with a blue satin ribbon tied at her throat, he damn sure did.

He wanted his bride. From the look on her face, he didn't get the sense that she wanted her groom.

'Figured we ought to talk.'

'I have a busy day tomorrow, getting ready to leave for the farm.' She indicated the garments spread over chairs, tables and most of her bed.

'It's important, darlin'.'

She sighed and then stood aside for him to enter.

'I suppose you've come to tell me you sold the house to the gentleman who called this afternoon.'

It had been the solicitor of a fellow called Lord Brunswick who had an interest in purchasing Greycliff.

'It was just someone asking about it. I won't sell without telling you first. You have my word on it.'

'Thank you for that.' She turned away then walked to the window and looked at the night. He didn't know what she could see out there with fog suffocating everything.

'I'm not selling Greycliff out of meanness, Ambrin. It's got to be done so we can make our farm prosperous.'

'Your farm. But I imagine the sale of the house is not what you came to discuss.'

'No, it isn't.' He joined her at the window, careful not to stand too close until he understood her thoughts on what their wedding night would consist of.

'You were a beautiful bride,' he said, feeling his way. 'You plain took my breath away.'

Snatched his heart out of his chest, was what she'd done.

Ambrin looked as pretty as a dream in a white gown that flowed about her like a dozen doves fluttering their wings. He wasn't surprised to see the sleeves and hem decorated with lavender flowers.

In the moment he'd taken it as a good omen. Since then, he wasn't so sure.

She glanced away from the window, her gaze at him softer than he'd thought it would be.

'You've come to claim your husbandly rights?'

'I've come to ask what you want of our wedding

night. I'm not here to claim anything you don't wish to give.'

'I do not know that I have anything to give you, Boone. Not with everything I had taken from me.'

'I understand that is true and I damn regret it. But, darlin'.' He tipped her chin up hoping she would look deep in his eyes and see his heart. 'Everything I have is yours. Your future and mine are all bound up now. You, me and Marigold are family.'

'Marigold…yes. She is the good to come out of all that happened. I will be like a mother to her now. I will be for ever grateful to you for that.'

'Well now, there are some things a man appreciates his wife being grateful for…and he's grateful for them too.' Hopefully she understood he was speaking of the marriage bed. 'But there are other things she has a right to. I promise you will never have to worry about having a good solid roof over your head, a warm fire in the hearth and food on the table.'

'Because the farm will be successful? I believe you mean those words, but your ranch failed once before. It can fail again. We would be far better off to live in this house, which is already established. Life is safer in London.'

'I disagree with you about safety. That aside, though, I don't have the income to support a place like this. Not without selling it.'

She didn't answer but he could tell by the resigned tug on her lips that she recognised the truth.

What he also could tell by the set of her mouth was that she wasn't thinking about kissing him or doing anything else common to newlyweds.

Remaining in her chamber any longer would only cause them both to feel uneasy.

'I reckon I should turn in. You are right about tomorrow being a busy day.'

He kissed her cheek, looked into her eyes one more time, disappointed to see there was no invitation for him to stay.

'Some things take time,' he said, but it was more to himself than to her.

Chapter Nine

Ambrin stepped onto the rustic conveyance that Boone had purchased for their new life and to take them the long drive to the farm in Oxfordshire.

Sitting on a slat bench, that had been altered to fit a cushion, she adjusted her bonnet strings making an effort not to look back at her home.

If she did she would weep.

So far she had managed not to, even though she had lovingly touched the banister then clung to the door-frame for several seconds on the way out.

Very likely the next time she saw Greycliff it would belong to someone else. However, Boone had promised not to entertain an offer without telling her first. If her new husband was anything, he was reliable.

Perhaps in time matters would change and the house would not be sold.

And perhaps the moon really was made of green cheese and maybe one could catch a falling star.

An early rising neighbour from across the street

drew her curtain aside, her curious expression evident even from here.

Word of Ambrin's hasty marriage had probably spread by now. She would have been spotted going into the church in her wedding gown.

Her peers would believe she had been forced to wed and they would be correct. Only not forced for the scandalous reason they would be whispering about. No matter, she was off to a new life now and what they believed was of no consequence.

Boone lifted Marigold and placed her on the bench beside Ambrin. The child bounced on the cushion, grinning and giggling.

'Uncle Boone bought us a fancy wagon, Auntie Ambrin. It's like I'm a princess.'

Clearly the child thought so for she fluffed her skirt and then pretended to adjust an invisible tiara on her head.

'It's quite the prettiest wagon I have ever seen,' she declared, trying to latch onto the spirit of her niece's joy. 'And your crown is dazzling. Your uncle will have to fight off all the handsome princes trying to take you off to their castles.'

The wagon shifted when Petunia jumped on it and settled into a space between boxes. What furniture they needed for the farmhouse would be brought in a few days along with Millie and Frederick. The boxes behind her contained a few precious items she did not trust with the movers.

Most of Greycliff's furnishings would, by necessity, be left behind and sold with the property.

Breathing deeply and blinking hard she tried to close her mind on the loss.

What she would do is rejoice over the miracle of having this sweet child to raise.

'Petunia will bite those princes,' Marigold declared. 'She is a very good dog.'

Boone tied his horse—the finest quarter horse alive he called it—to the back of the wagon.

After securing the animal, he took his place on the wooden bench then snatched up the reins of the team he had purchased along with the wagon.

'Get along,' he called. Wood creaked as the wagon lurched forward.

Do not look back, do not look back, she repeated in her mind. If she did it would crush her spirit to see her home vanish from her sight as they turned the corner.

Losing this house felt like another death to be mourned.

Marigold leaned against her, hugged little arms about Ambrin's middle and looked up through long dark lashes.

'Don't cry, Auntie. Me and Uncle Boone love you.'

'And I love you too, sweetheart.'

That was the truth, she did love her niece. The fact that she was now able to live with her for all time is the only thing that made this long ride from the place she loved to a place that was unfamiliar, bearable.

A weight settled on her shoulder. Damp, warm breath huffed near her ear.

'Petunia is sad for you, Auntie. She will lick away your tears if you wish.'

'It is quite sweet of her but I shall dry them on my own.' Weeping would gain her nothing. It was time to look forward, not back.

Glancing about she noticed a few early morning risers strolling on the sidewalk. The stares being cast their way were understandable, if uncomfortable.

What a sight they must make. She, wearing her best travel gown and bonnet while riding down an affluent street in a farm wagon accompanied by an armed man, a grinning child and a drooling dog.

But, she realised, it would do no good to dwell on what her neighbours might think of her fall from society.

Straightening her spine and gathering her resolve, she set her eyes on the glistening hindquarters of the horses pulling the wagon. She would simply ignore anything else.

'Howdy,' she heard Boone call.

Unable to resist, she glanced over to see who he was tipping his Stetson to.

Oh dear…

'Good day, Mrs Dawson… Willard,' she called, nodding at the astounded looking woman and her peach-faced son.

She offered a smile that was not completely false

because in the moment she realised things could have been much worse for her.

Having kissed Boone how could she ever have thought to share the feelings he had awakened in her with a boy like Willard?

Not that she meant to share those feelings with her husband, either. But at least the thought of intimacy with Boone was not repulsive, as it was with Willard.

Glancing over at Boone, seeing his smile in profile and how his face reflected the joy he felt this morning, she thought to herself that, indeed, things really were not as awful as they might have been.

She had wed a loyal, bold and handsome man. Which made resisting him in certain ways rather difficult.

Perhaps she was foolish to do so. Most brides would leap happily into the marital bed with a man such as him.

But then, most women would have chosen their groom. And although they may have chosen them for reasons other than love, still, those ladies would have decided upon their life path.

Had matters been different. Had her brother not given away her home, had Boone not been set on selling the place she loved...well, she had to wonder what might have taken root between them.

They had been companionable from the start. Well, once she'd understood he was not a thief, they had. Since then, their friendship had deepened.

Now that she thought about it, it occurred to her that she had never become close to another person so easily.

If only things had been different then perhaps… But there was no perhaps. Only what was.

Since they were travelling by wagon and not by train, this was going to be a very long day. She had hours to think and dwell on what could and could not be in her marriage, in her life.

The whole thing left her emotions in a knot. What she must do is step out of her herself, of her tangled thoughts.

Look at life as Boone saw it in the moment, as Marigold did too.

They both seemed as happy as could be, facing the adventure of moving to a new home.

For the past quarter of an hour Marigold's conversation had been all about chickens. How many could she have, would she be allowed to collect the eggs and play with the chicks?

'Ambrin, darlin', how many chickens do you think we should have?' Boone asked, clearly trying to engage her in conversation.

For all her effort not to be, she been quiet and moody, which was unlike her. She did not admire the quality in others and so should not act it towards others.

'Why, I really have no idea.' How could she? In her experience chickens came neatly packaged by the butcher and eggs were collected from the back porch. 'What would make you happy Marigold?'

'One hundred hens and one rooster,' Marigold announced.

In her excitement the child stood up, wobbled precariously. Ambrin grasped her arm, drew her down to the seat.

'Whoa there, little darlin'. That's a lot of hens.' Boone shot Ambrin a grin. 'Let's let your auntie decide.'

No hens and no roosters is what came to mind. Life on the farm was going to be too much for her city-raised self, she feared.

'I would think ten hens should suffice,' she bravely answered. She really had no idea what the correct number would be.

'But there must be a rooster, Auntie, otherwise we will have no chicks.'

Ambrin arched a brow at Boone, sent him a disapproving glance. Even though the child had spent her life on a ranch, five years old was rather young to know how baby chicks came to be.

Mischief sparked in Boone's expression.

'Looks like your auntie doesn't know how that works. Seems like she'll need to understand now that we will have a farm.'

'May I tell her how it works, Uncle Boone?'

Oh, what a grin her new husband had. She would need to learn not to get lost in it.

'Can't have her wondering how chicks just pop out of some eggs and not others,' he said.

'Well, you see, Auntie, roosters like to dance, even more than they like to eat. So, when they do their happy jig with the hens, eggs become chicks…like magic, my papa told me. When the eggs are for eating it is because the rooster got tired of dancing…but I don't think they do that very much.'

Dancing?

Inappropriately, a vision of Boone knocking on her chamber door on their wedding night sneaked her mind.

Even she, a maiden, knew he had come asking for a dance. The temptation to accept had been much stronger than she had let on.

She was saved from further thought on the matter when Marigold asked, 'When will we get cows? I love cows.'

When indeed? Ambrin did not love cows, she feared them. And not only because of nearly being run down by a bull. The creatures were huge. Probably smelly too and plagued with flies.

She was, however, fond of cheese and milk, and steak.

Lord have mercy on her, farm life was going to be quite a different thing than she had even imagined.

The question of when they would get cows and chickens was answered sooner than Boone expected.

As it happened, he stopped to water the horses at a

clear, cold stream. While they all rested under a shady tree a farmer came down the road.

He and Boone struck up a conversation. As luck would have it, the man was from a neighbouring farm and had been planning to take a pair of milk cows, a few crates of chickens, a donkey and a collection of sheep and goats to market the next day.

Boone made the deal to purchase the cows, ten chickens, including one brooding a clutch of eggs and one rooster—or cockerel as the man called it—and arranged for them to be brought to his new farm later that day.

This was a bit of good luck since it might be a while before he was able to purchase his herd of beef cattle. While there had been some interested buyers for the London property, no offers had been presented yet.

A farm needed animals and the ones he just bought were a start.

Lying back on the grass, Boone closed his eyes, let his mind wander and imagined what his property would look like.

He knew some things having seen the map and read the description.

The farm was not a terribly far distance from the nearest town, which would be convenient. Back in Montana, it had taken several hours to ride to the nearest town on horseback, longer when they took the wagon. Most trips took two days.

He'd noticed two or three streams drawn on the map. It looked like they flowed through a valley, or glen it was called here. He'd been told there were rolling hills, too, that were always green because of frequent rain.

It set easy on his mind knowing he wouldn't live in fear of withering drought. Or snakes whose colouring blended in with the earth and had the venom to strike a person down.

This, he thought, was a gentle land compared to where he had come from.

No bears, no cougars. As far as he knew there were no predators to ravage his herd.

Like anywhere else, there could be rustlers he reckoned. Or floods.

The swishing sound Ambrin's skirt made when she walked drew his attention.

'Have something to eat, Boone,' she said, settling down next to him on the blanket he had put down. 'You will need something before we get to your farm.'

He sat up, rolled his shoulders. Her words, although quite common to wives gave him a sense of contentment. It was good to have someone care that he was eating.

'Our farm,' he reminded her. 'What's mine is yours.'

'Is that how it is where you come from?' She handed him a piece of bread and some cheese. 'Here, when a woman weds all she has becomes her husband's.'

'Depends on the folks, I reckon. It will not be so in our marriage.'

Ambrin nibbled on a piece of bread while giving him a pointed, raised brow glance.

'Let me understand, husband. You own the farm and so it is mine as well as yours.'

'Yes, wife. What I have is yours.'

'So then, the London house is yours but now that we are wed, it is also mine?'

He nodded sensing that he was being corralled into a corner and no way out.

'Then I do not wish to sell my half of the house.'

'Do you know of another way of providing for our farm, darlin'? If you do I'll be glad to hear it.'

Apparently she did not, for her answer was, 'I dislike cows.'

That said she rose from the blanket then walked towards the stream where Marigold was knelt looking for frogs.

Watching his bride kneel down beside her niece, hearing them laugh, made his insides go soft.

What he hoped is that one day Ambrin would understand why he must sell the house.

What he prayed is that on that day, his wife would laugh with him the way she was doing with Marigold.

Ambrin was as tired as she could ever recall being. It was well after dark when Boone drew the wagon to a halt in front of the farmhouse.

A full moon was sitting fat in the sky, which gave her a decent view of her new home.

The place was long and had only one level. A chimney poked up from the centre of the roof. There were many windows. She liked windows. Only, in the moment, these windows resembled dark eyes staring—blank and creepy.

But there was also a heavenly smelling flower growing nearby, only she could not tell where.

Water must be close at hand for she heard it gurgling.

Boone helped her down from the wagon and it was a good thing he did. She felt stiff in all her joints from the day-long journey.

Next he lifted Marigold, who had fallen asleep hours ago. He placed her sweetly limp body in Ambrin's arms.

'I'll take the horses to the barn. I think it's around back, not too far away. Maybe you can find a spot to lay her down inside.'

'It looks like a good, solid home, Boone,' she told him wanting to make amends for her snippy attitude earlier.

Since this afternoon she had given a great deal of thought to his question about how to provide for the farm, but so far no answer had presented itself.

If he was to fulfil his dream, and her brother's, the London house must go. And she must deal with it as best she could. This was her home now, like it or not.

Once there were lamps burning cheerily inside, it was sure to look less foreboding.

Carrying her niece up the porch steps she reminded herself there were things to be grateful for. The lovely weight of the child in her arms being first and foremost of them.

She noted that the front steps were solid, not warped or splintered. What a relief since, from what Boone had told her, the house had not been lived in for more than a year.

It gave her hope for the rest of the house.

She opened the front door but didn't go in. With no lamp to guide her through the darkened interior, it seemed prudent to remain outside until Boone had finished settling the animals.

Luckily, there was a chair on the porch. She sat on it gingerly, hoping it would hold the weight of both her and Marigold.

It creaked but held their weight easily. She relaxed and arranged her niece's small form comfortably across her lap.

What a delightful sensation to no longer be jostling and bouncing in the wagon.

One thing she immediately liked about this place was the way the air was so crisp and clean.

One thing she immediately disliked was the silence. Or more, the rustling noises in the night that filled the silence.

In the distance she heard the cattle Boone had purchased lowing. Surprisingly, she found the sound soothing.

But there was another noise coming from a bush growing near the porch steps that was not soothing.

Some sort of creature must be lurking in it.

A fox? Hedgehog? Or…rat?

While she devised a plan to protect Marigold from whatever the beast might be, two small bunnies hopped from the bush and into the moonlight.

'Why, aren't you the sweetest things,' she murmured softly so she would not frighten them.

They really were adorable, nibbling grass and hopping in circles about one another.

In that instant, Marigold woke up. Ambrin motioned for her to be still and pointed to the frolicking babies.

If this docile scene was any indication, life on the farm was going to be more pleasant than she thought.

All at once a shadow swooped out of the tree. It made no sound whatsoever.

Only when it snatched a bunny did she recognise the silent hunter as an owl.

Ambrin screeched.

Seconds later she heard thumping boots running through brush. Boone burst out of the shadows and into the clearing, glanced about with his hand curled about a rifle.

'What happened?'

'Why it was horrible… I cannot believe what I just saw!' Such things did not happen in London. Or if they did, she did not witness them.

'It was only an owl, Auntie.' Marigold patted her hand.

'It snatched that poor baby bunny and flew off with it!' Why was she the only one shaking over the incident?

'But, Auntie, it probably had babies to feed. We feel sad for the bunny, but if the baby owls didn't eat we would feel sad for them too.'

'Our girl is right,' Boone said. 'It is the way of nature.'

Ambrin was not at all certain she would ever become comfortable with nature's way.

'Let's go inside and see our new home.' There was no mistaking the emphasis Boone put on the word 'our'.

He carried an unlit lantern in his hand, which she had not noticed when he charged into the yard.

Whatever the conditions inside, they had to be better than out here where a peaceful moment could turn tragic in a heartbeat.

Unless you were a hungry baby owl. In that case you would be quite content to have your mother fly in with dinner.

In London one did not fret over such things. She must challenge herself to be as practical in her thinking as Marigold was.

* * *

Boone entered the house first and lit the lantern. Ambrin came in leading Marigold by the hand.

The home he had built with his own hands was far different than this one, the one he'd purchased.

Although these walls were not made of good thick logs, they still looked sturdy.

He walked about the front room with the lantern raised high to shed better light.

No water stains. The flower-patterned paper on the walls was not peeling.

The fireplace was huge, like the one he had before, but it was in the centre of the room and open on both sides.

Seemed a good, practical idea to heat both halves of the house at the same time.

'It is soooo pretty!' Marigold twirled about on the wood floor, which still had a sheen even though no one had lived here in a while. 'I will never let a prince carry me away even if he is handsome.'

'Good girl.' He and Ambrin spoke in unison, which made all three of them laugh.

It was good to hear his bride laugh. She had not done so in days.

The last thing he'd intended by marrying her was to make her miserable. She might just as well have wed Dawson and been miserable in London.

Life was going to be so different here than there.

Damn it though, he meant to do his utmost to make

her happy here. Truth was, he meant to do all he could so that she would rather live here than there.

He carried the lantern through to the room on the other side of the fireplace.

'Dining room, do you think?' he asked Ambrin and Marigold who kept close, walking in the circle of lantern light.

'It could be used for a parlour, but since it seems that the kitchen might be through that door, dining room makes sense,' Ambrin answered.

Going on, the next room did indeed turn out to be the kitchen.

'What do you think, darlin'? Will it be comfortable for you to work in?'

'Adequate enough.' She walked the room in a circle. He followed with the lamp.

It was smaller than she was used to. The stove wasn't bright and shiny like the one in London.

There was a good-sized window, though. Spreading the curtain aside he peered into the dark. Moonlight cast a glow on his new barn. It looked like a pearl sitting on the rise of the hill beyond a paddock.

It was a good spot for a barn. Set on high ground, it would fare well in a flood.

Even though he'd been here for such a short time, the place was already settling into his heart.

He reckoned that Ambrin didn't have the same warm spirit for the farm that he had.

The owl hadn't helped with a good first impression.

Marigold was still twirling about so he figured he would not need to convince her to love her new home.

Moving on from the kitchen they came to a hallway, which seemed to circle back to the first room they entered. Off the hallway were four, no five, doors that must lead to bedrooms.

He opened them one by one, holding the lantern high so they could all have a look.

Each of them had a small fireplace.

First chore of the morning would be to set aside a big store of firewood. His understanding was that England did not have the severe winters that the Great Plains had, but a man could not be too careful when it came to the care of his family.

Opening the third door he noticed a bit of trouble. The room had stains on the ceiling and the plaster was peeling in at least four places that he could see.

'Leaky roof,' he commented.

Until he'd opened the last bedroom door, he'd been wondering where the three of them would sleep tonight since the beds were still in London.

But there in the centre of the room with a beam of moonlight illuminating it, was a good-sized bed. He couldn't say what condition the mattress might be in but it was at least off the floor.

'I'll go back to the wagon and fetch the blankets,' Boone said, catching Ambrin's eye and grinning in that way he had.

He dashed out before she had a chance to question how all three of them were to occupy that one rather small bed.

Not that she would do such a thing even in a large bed.

Marigold hopped onto the mattress, bounced and sneezed.

But of course, there would be dust after the house being shut up this long.

She hated to imagine what it all would look like in the light of day. What a fortunate thing that she had not been a refined lady in a good long while. The layer of dust that was probably coating every surface would not cause her to faint.

Apparently this house was going to require a great deal of labour to make it a decent place to live.

Both Boone and Marigold already believed it to be a decent place. Neither of them had quit smiling or pointing out wonderful things about the house since they came in the front door.

Had she been the only one to worry that a rat or a mouse might dash across their shoes?

Oh, yes, there had been some sort of rustling noise when they entered the kitchen. Which was not to say there had never been a mouse at Greycliff but they were city mice. No doubt the ones here had longer tails and beadier eyes.

It was a lucky thing Boone had left the lantern for them otherwise Ambrin would have had to return to the porch where she would probably watch all manner of nature happening.

No doubt in London right now fog was rolling in, blanketing the city in a peaceful haze.

When Boone returned a short time later carrying an armload of blankets, Petunia trotted in with him.

The great, shedding dog settled at once before the front door, the same as she did at Greycliff. Laying her head on her wide paws she wagged her tail.

Lucky dog, knowing where she would sleep. Ambrin had no idea where she would.

Not in the bed with Boone. While it was true that they were married, in her heart she was still Miss Ambrin Malcomb.

Oh, yes indeed she was. And Miss she would remain!

Joining Boone in his bed would change everything. It would make her truly wed.

While she struggled with the problem, Boone strode to the bed, picked up the mattress and carried it outside.

Hearing a thwack, thwack, sound, she followed him to the porch.

Boone was beating dust from the mattress with a thick stick.

She watched, or admired to be perfectly honest, his strength. His muscularity had not been so evident in London where gentlemen did not labour, except at sports.

While she could not see his muscles under his shirt she well imagined how they would look while he heroically made the mattress usable.

She would have watched longer but a creature slithered out of a hedgerow not far away. A fox on the hunt no doubt.

Spinning about she went back into the house before she witnessed the other bunny become dinner.

Better to focus her attention on the issue at hand. Which was, who was going to occupy the bed other than Marigold?

Boone came back inside, carrying the mattress across his shoulders.

She did not wish for her heart to flutter over the sight of his well-knit frame, but really what was a woman to do but silently sigh?

Sigh and find the fortitude not to share the bed of a handsome man who was her husband.

It was sensible to hold onto something of her former self. Just because she had been forced to give her future to Boone Rawlins did not mean she must give away her… Well, she was not certain of the name for it, but it is the part of her that kept her from being a puppet at the mercy of whatever man pulled her strings.

'It will do until the furniture comes,' Boone announced seeming satisfied with the situation.

'Do for whom?' she asked because she rather needed to know what he had in mind.

'Us.' With a nod, he indicated her and Marigold. 'It will be tight but we should all fit.'

Sweat glowed on his neck from the exertion of beating the mattress. The puppeteer jerked the string attached to her stomach and made it spin dizzily.

Stepping close to Boone so that Marigold would not overhear she whispered. 'I cannot sleep with you.'

He dipped is lips to her and whispered back, 'We are married. There is no shame in it.'

'I don't feel married.' His breath was too warm brushing past her ear. His voice too beguiling. Bait on a hook was what it was.

'I reckon that will come with time,' he murmured. She tried to read the expression in his eyes but by lamplight it was hard to decipher. 'You take the bed with Marigold.'

He lifted one blanket from the stack he had carried in then he went out of the bedroom.

Taking the lantern, she set it in the doorway way so both rooms had light.

Boone spread the blanket on the floor and Petunia lay down on it, with Boone lying down next to her. There was no reason whatsoever for her to feel wrong about putting him out of the bed.

'I am sorry but…' But what? Being sorry did not mean she was going to change her mind.

'No need to fret over it, darlin'. I've spent the night in front of the door with the dog more than a few times.'

But why? 'You must have had a bed in Montana.'

'A good one. What I also had were bears and cougars prowling the house every now and again. That's why Petunia took to sleeping by the front door.'

'From all I have heard there are no large predators in England.'

'Reckon the dog will figure it out in time. Sleep well, darlin'.' With that he rolled over on his side.

Ambrin took her slight sense of guilt and lay down on the bed with her niece.

But she could see Boone through the open doorway. His wide shoulders rose and fell with his breathing.

Although she was bone weary, it took her a very long time to fall asleep.

Her mind would not relax because it looped over and over what Boone said about feeling like a wife in time.

An argument went on inside her. One side of it insisted that she would never feel like a wife to a man she was not in love with, one she had not even chosen. Oh, but the other side was too quarrelsome to give her rest. That contentious voice kept wondering what it would be like if she was.

Chapter Ten

A ray of sunlight stabbed Ambrin's eyes, waking her with a start.

Marigold was not in bed with her.

Rising, Ambrin left the dusty little bedchamber. She tried to smooth wrinkles from her skirt, but having slept in her gown, it was impossible.

Boone was no longer asleep near the door. The dog was not in the house.

Apparently, no one was inside.

Walking through rooms that she had seen only dimly last night, she felt overwhelmingly alone.

Where had they all gone, deserting her to ramble about in a strange home?

Then a bird chirruped outside an open window sounding much the same as a bird would in London. The happy twitter gave her spirits a boost.

'Marigold!' she called but got no answer. She must be with Boone, then.

Her call did not go unheard, though. A pair of big

paws hit the windowsill from outside. Peering out and down, Ambrin saw Petunia looking up, her tail wagging madly.

'Hello, dog.' She slid the window open and then reached down to stroke Petunia between her ears. Any creature who slept near the front door thinking to protect her family from attack did deserve a grateful nuzzle.

'You are not as scary as I first thought you were. Where is everyone?'

As if Petunia understood proper English, she dropped to all fours then trotted in the direction of the stable…which Boone referred to as the barn.

Hurrying outside, she followed the dog through a meadow and then across a stone bridge. The area looked much cheerier by daylight. A family of quacking ducks passed under a bridge at the same time she went over it.

That now made two things she liked about the farm. Fresh air and ducks swimming under quaint stone bridges.

In the moment, she vowed to keep her mind open about this place where she would be living.

It was undeniably lovely with its green fields and low hills that spread far and away. She could only imagine how thrilled Boone must be to imagine cattle grazing across these acres.

She followed the sound of voices coming from the barn. Through the open doors she saw that the cows

Boone purchased yesterday were settled in their stalls and chewing hay quite happily.

She walked inside and spotted Boone sitting with his back towards her milking one of them. Marigold sat beside him on a shorter stool, her hair neatly plaited in one braid that shifted with her movements.

'Why won't the milk squirt into the pail, Uncle Boone?'

'It's your first time trying. And your hands are small.'

Ambrin watched the pair of them, listened to Boone's instructions on how to milk a cow.

A ray of sunlight filtering through a slatted window shimmered gold streaks in Boone's hair. She had the oddest impression that it was touching him in benediction.

Silly thought, she decided. The man was simply performing a necessary chore.

Hopefully it is not one she would be expected to learn. The last thing she wished is to be that close to a cow.

Funny, but simply standing apart and watching, not even involved in what was happening, made her feel less lonely than she'd been in the kitchen.

And yet she could not deny also feeling a certain alienation from Boone and Marigold.

While the pair of them seemed at ease sitting on milking stools, she would never feel that way. In a very real sense, she was an outsider.

If this is how Boone had felt in London, he did a far better job of hiding his distress.

She did not belong here. What was she supposed to contribute to this new life?

Useless, that's what she was.

Once Millie and Frederick arrived along with the household goods, she would keep busy putting the house together and making it shine. But after that?

What she had been trained to do is act graciously and entertain callers. She could pour tea, waltz and polka quite skilfully.

She rather doubted a neighbour passing by on the road would appreciate how well she could wield a fan.

Her place was in London.

'Good morning, Boone. Good morning Marigold,' she said deciding it was time to make her presence known.

Marigold spun about on her stool, giving Ambrin a sunny smile.

Boone turned, shot her a grin. The ray of sunshine shifted to his cheek. He hadn't shaved the way a proper gentlemen would before starting his morning in society.

But then, this was not proper society and he had no need to impress the animals he had risen so early to care for.

Nor to impress her apparently, for she rather liked the golden stubbles on his jaw putting the rugged cowboy within him on full display.

Show her the woman who would not be delighted by the brawny image he presented.

The contented image, too. Boone seemed quite pleased to be in a barn milking a cow.

She envied him that. Not milking a cow, but having a dream and being able to live it.

'Good morning, darlin'. I hope you rested well on your first night.'

'I did, once I got used to the sounds and managed to fall asleep.'

'Sure did sound like a lullaby once a body got used to it.'

That is not how it had seemed to her, but never mind, this was not London. Things were going to sound different.

'Auntie! The hens have arrived! I am hoping there will be eggs soon. I have been waiting for you to help me look for them.'

Although she had never collected an egg from a nest, it did not seem a terribly difficult task.

'Let's go and look for them, then.' She extended her hand to her niece. Marigold hopped up from the stool, dashed across the floor stones then grasped it. 'They might not have had time to lay any. But if we find some I shall cook them for our breakfast.'

Cooking was something she excelled at. Hopefully the stove was in good enough condition to be used. Afterward, it would need a thorough cleaning, she was certain.

'You must be careful, Auntie, and listen to what I tell you so that you don't get pecked.'

Marigold drew her along to the last stall against the barn wall where the chicken cages were.

'I will do exactly as you say. It sounds as if the hens do not like it when you take the eggs.' She would rather not be pecked by an angry chicken if she could help it.

'Oh noooo, they want chicks and so do I. But Uncle Boone says we must eat.'

'And so, we must. Shall we make a bargain? You will teach me to gather eggs and I will show you how to cook them.'

'Uncle says I am still too young to get close to cooking flames.'

'And so, you are. You will prepare the eggs and I will cook them.'

'I'm glad you married Uncle Boone, Auntie. It's like I have a mama now.'

'And like I have a little girl.' Ambrin picked her up and spun her about while listening to chickens cackling in their cages.

Well then, she did have purpose here. Or anywhere she might find herself. It fell to Ambrin to raise Marigold to be a fine and happy young lady.

Not that Boone had not done an exemplary job until now, but there were just some things a girl needed to learn from her mother, or aunt acting as one.

So many things about living on the farm were

going to be difficult, but loving her niece was not one of them.

As for loving her husband? She would like him. Even deeply. But she would have to do it without offering her heart.

Truly, she had no intention of giving herself away.

Ambrin awoke in the wee hours of night. She stretched, then feeling Marigold's small sleeping body, drew her closer. She listened for a moment thinking that Boone had been right about the sounds of the wee hours being a lullaby. After spending three nights here, she was beginning to hear the melody.

Not that bugs and night creatures rustling about would ever take the place of the comforting sounds of home, of London, but she held some small hope that in time she would appreciate hooting owls and lowing cattle in the night.

All at once her peaceful moment was interrupted by a grunt.

The house was dark since Boone had put out the lamp hours ago when he'd gone to sleep on the floor in the front room. Still, through the open doorway she saw him sit up, roll his shoulders and then lay back down.

A moment later he sighed and rolled to his other side. Petunia gave a soft woof of protest.

This was not the first time she had woken in the wee hours feeling guilty for keeping Boone out of the bed.

There really was enough room for all three of them.

Her husband worked harder than any man she'd ever known. He seldom rested. From the time he rose in the morning to the time he lay back down on the floor at night he worked at some chore or another.

By rights, he should have the bed and she should have the floor. Especially tonight, since tomorrow the items they shipped from London would arrive and he would have double the work to do.

Thought about in the right way, if she invited him to sleep in the bed it was not as if he would be spending the night since there not much of the night left. Only a few hours until morning. And, if she did not fall asleep, then they would not have slept together.

It was twisted logic, she knew, but it was not fair for him to be uncomfortable on the floor. She needed some sort of justification to tell herself that sharing a bed was the proper thing to do.

'Boone,' she called softly so that she did not awaken Marigold. 'Come to bed.'

Oh dear, the way she said that sounded wifely. Even seductive. She ought to have used other words.

She should also have considered that she was sleeping in her shift and not her gown as she had done the first night.

'Bless you, darlin'.'

Rising from the floor, he looked stiff in his joints.

Scooting to the edge of the mattress, she made room for him on the other side of Marigold.

'Feels like I'm floating on a cloud,' he murmured, and then as quick as that he fell asleep.

So much for feeling modest about being so close to him while wearing her shift. It was unlikely that he had even noticed.

He was lying on his side with his face towards her and so close that, even in the dark, she was able to indulge in gazing at his face.

What a handsome face it was, too. She was too tempted to reach over and trace the line of his jaw. He still had not shaved. What would it be like to touch his chin? To feel the beard scrape her fingertips? What would it feel like to trace the shape of his eyebrow or the straight line of his nose?

He would not know it if she did. They were wed so there would be no scandal in it.

What there would be was a great deal of risk. If she intended to keep her heart to herself, she would need to keep her hands to herself.

In order to do that she must close her eyes because the temptation to brush the hair away from his brow was even greater than the temptation to touch his beard was.

She squeezed her lids shut, which did little to help because she could still hear his deep, slow breathing.

There truly was nothing to be done about closing her nose against his masculine scent so she did not try.

The rest of the night would be lost as far as sleeping went.

It was only fair for her to sacrifice a few hours of sleep for her new husband who worked so hard for his dream. His dream for them all.

If only she shared that dream then life would be so sweet.

She must have slept after all because a noise woke her. There was no need to open her eyes, she was acquainted with the sounds that announced the coming of dawn.

The first was Petunia, coming to her feet and shaking out her fur.

Normally the next sound would be Boone groaning from having got all stiff and achy from sleeping on the floor.

In that moment light would change from inky dark to dim.

She sighed with her eyes closed. This moment was as peaceful as could be.

However, the coming hours were bound to present challenges aplenty. Boone mentioned something about her getting more comfortable with the milk cows.

Perhaps he was teasing but she was quite serious in her determination that it would not happen. Having once been close to being trampled by a fearsome bull, she would be happy to never be within snorting distance of a bovine creature again.

Just then she felt fingers at her temple, in her hair.

Opening her eyes she saw Marigold's small fingers wound up in the strands and Boone's large fingers gently working at untangling them.

At least that is what she thought was happening. It did rather seem that her husband was stroking her hair, perhaps using the excuse of freeing her from Marigold's grip.

'Good morning Mrs Rawlins,' he murmured.

How she wished he hadn't called her that. Although it was her legal name the way he spoke it, the whispery early morning tone of his voice, sounded far too intimate.

'It will be a busy one,' she answered replacing the intimate, predawn whisper with practical concerns.

Sitting up at the edge of the bed, he reached his arms over his head and stretched. The shirt he slept in was thin and worn. It was easy to see the outline of his muscles flexing and relaxing.

'Best get to it then,' he said.

The man had no shame. He did not remove himself to another room to dress, he simply yanked on his trousers in front of her. Then looking over his shoulder he shot her a grin, took off the sleep shirt and shrugged into his work shirt.

'Sure do appreciate you letting me sleep in the bed last night.'

'You are welcome. Marigold and I will be along soon to collect the eggs.' She answered casually, as if watching him dress left her unaffected.

The fact is it had not. The sooner she had her own bed in her own chamber, the better.

'I'll teach you how to milk Clarabelle.' He winked, quite clearly tossing her a challenge.

'I will teach you how to cook an egg.' She gave the challenge right back.

If there was one thing she'd learned about Boone Rawlins, it was that he did not excel at preparing food.

Her position as cook would go unchallenged, which made her feel a bit better about her place on the farm.

She did belong somewhere, after all.

Chopping firewood when the sun was at its highest was a sweaty job. Even here in Oxfordshire, where the weather was milder than what Boone was used to.

The task needed doing though, so he bent his back to it while keeping his ear open for the sound of wagon wheels on the road leading to the farm.

If nothing delayed the delivery, the goods from London would be here before the end of the day, along with Millie and Frederick.

He reckoned it would be a comfort for Ambrin when they arrived. Having their familiar company was bound to make her happier.

Could be he would even see her pretty smile again.

Ever since he revealed that he was selling the house her smile had been as scarce as rain in a drought.

Except for when it came to Marigold. The child lit up his wife's smile like nothing else and he was glad for it.

No man wanted to make a woman unhappy in marriage. His intention had been to protect her so that she could flourish, not shrivel.

It only took a few minutes of labour to work up a good sweat. Since he didn't want to make extra laundry, he took off his shirt then hung it on the branch of a nearby apple tree.

Grant used to claim Boone had a fixation with chopping wood. Maybe, but he had more of a fixation on making sure that the people depending on him did not suffer during a harsh winter.

In Montana, every winter was harsh.

He'd been told that was not the case in Oxfordshire. That the temperature rarely got below freezing.

Could be true but one thing life had taught him was to be prepared for the unexpected. No matter where he lived, his wood stacks would be high.

He stopped for a moment to wipe his brow and gaze at the road.

A movement at the kitchen window caught his attention.

Ah, his bride peeking out at him.

He'd like to think she was looking at him and admiring him in a way a woman admired her husband, but he had no reason to think so.

Any spark that had initially ignited between them had been extinguished before the wedding.

He lifted his arm and waved to her but she dropped the curtain as if embarrassed to have been caught looking.

He considered himself a patient man. Certain things were worth the wait.

The affection of his wife was one of them.

There was work to be done. He picked up his axe.

But then he saw her pretty, shadowy form moving about behind the sheer curtain. It gave him a glow in his middle wondering what wifely thing she was doing.

Reckoned she might not get the same glow, though. Ambrin was a society lady who had mostly had things done for her, not the other way around.

At least she had until he and her brother upended her life.

'Damnit,' he mumbled and lifted the axe. He needed to find a way to make her happy in her new home.

Halfway into his first swing he heard the wagon wheels on the road.

Ambrin rushed out to the front porch watching the wagon approach the house with her hand shading her eyes. Marigold rushed past her, skipped down the steps then dashed across the yard to peer over the fence.

'Millie, Millie, Millie!' Marigold called waving her hand while bouncing on her toes.

The wagon creaked and groaned when it pulled to a stop in front of the gate.

He'd been expecting two wagons, but did not see another lagging behind on the road.

If every item Ambrin had directed to be brought from London was loaded on this one, it would be dangerously overloaded. It was a wonder it had survived the journey. More a wonder that the team of horses had managed to pull the weight.

The driver, who looked far too young for the job, hopped down from the wagon seat. To Boone's way of thinking, any boy with peach fuzz on his chin ought to be in the schoolroom.

The boy helped Millie and Frederick down while Boone strode over to welcome them all to the farm.

While the ladies hugged each other, he had a few moments to speak to the driver.

Turns out the boy, Tom Gibson, was the son of the wagon owner. When his pa overbooked deliveries, the boy signed on to help bring the wagon out to the farm, bringing Millie and Frederick along with him.

Seemed too big a responsibility for a lad, is what Boone thought, but they were all safely arrived and that is what mattered.

The boy looked as strapping as a bull calf, though. When Boone asked if he would want to earn extra money by helping unload the goods and carry them into the house, he readily accepted.

Tom began at once, taking boxes off the wagon before Boone even got the team unhitched.

With the horses untethered, Boone took a step to lead them away but stopped cold when he heard a noise.

Groaning metal…splintering wood.

'Jump!' he shouted while yanking the horses away from the hitch.

A wicked snap broke the still afternoon. Birds flushed out of trees, flapping and screeching.

Petunia ran in circles around the wagon barking. Boone would have barked too if it would have helped, but the axle had given under the weight of the load and the wagon lay half on its side.

Close to a quarter of the wooden crates had spilled on the ground, some broken open but others intact.

Tom's flushed face appeared over the other side of the wagon. 'My father is going to cuss like the dickens. He used to be a sailor so he can cuss like nobody you ever saw.'

Ambrin was impressed to see how quickly Boone and Tom were getting the wagon unloaded, in spite of the fact that it was lying half on its side just beyond the garden gate.

While Marigold led Millie and Frederick to the barn to show them the animals, Ambrin opened boxes.

In one box she found the teapot her mother had allowed her to practice with as a child. It still had a chip on the spout from when she had dropped it.

Her heart felt a little lighter with each familiar treasure coming out of the boxes.

It was as if an echo of home had come along with them.

Seeing her parlour couch being carried inside swelled a lump in her throat.

When she touched the table that had been in her London kitchen it felt as if she was stroking a friend. There was dust from the road on it but she would have that wiped away by dinnertime.

A grateful tear or two did get past her because, one by one some of the furnishings she loved were filling up the space of this unfamiliar house. Many more had to be left behind but she would try not to think of them. Rather she would strive to be happy for what was here.

She started towards the kitchen because people would be getting hungry but then paused to watch while Boone and Tom carried her bed inside.

What a relief it would be to finally sleep in her own bedroom.

Being in intimate quarters with Boone had not been easy on her. Having him so close made her imagine things she should not be imagining. It made her feel things for him that were far too dangerous if she intended to keep her heart separate from his.

Which she did, naturally.

One thing she knew was that she would not fall in love with a man who must have seen her as a lifetime debt to be borne. In spite of the fact that Boone had been nothing but kind and generous to her, she would not be tricked into thinking she was anything but a burden that his partner had left behind.

At least now that she had her own place to sleep she would have some relief from watching him in the night. From wondering what it would be like if she had met him in some other manner. Would he have even given her a second glance? Probably not since they would not have met at all.

Wait, though!

What was this? Boone and Tom were carrying her bed into the room that was intended to be Boone's.

She rushed down the hallway, stood between the bed and further progress into the room.

'You have made a wrong turn.' Perhaps he was getting weary and had not noticed.

'No, darlin'. We will be sharing this one for the time being.'

'No, Boone Rawlins, we will not.'

There were five bedrooms in the house. One for Boone, one for her, one for Marigold. Another for Millie and one for Frederick. It had been agreed upon from the beginning that they would each have their own chamber.

She simply must have her private space, nothing else would do!

What had come over Boone believing that just because she allowed him into the bed meant that she now intended to share his bedroom?

'Son, take a break and go join Marigold in the barn. Get acquainted with the animals.'

'Thank you sir, I will.'

With the enthusiasm of a frisky colt, Tom dashed out of the house. His happy whoops carried in on a breeze through the open window.

'The boy needs a place to sleep. Can't rightly send him home in the wagon.'

Oh, she ought to have thought. It was on her tongue to suggest making him a cozy spot in the barn but no…he was an adolescent boy now in their care, not livestock.

'I shall stay with Marigold in her chamber.'

'That won't work, darlin'. Don't you recall the leaks in the roof of Millie's bedroom? She'll need to stay with Marigold until I get it repaired.'

'It might not rain.'

'Better odds that it will. And do not argue that you will sleep in a wet room.'

How did he know that was exactly what she was about to say?

Neatly boxed in by circumstances there was nothing to do but go along with the turn of events.

Lately, that was how her life had gone. Boxed in at every turn. She'd had no choice of who to wed, where to live and now, where to sleep.

'Very well,' she stated, feeling utterly defeated and wondering if anything would ever happen by her choice again.

She went to the parlour to unpack another box.

The only thing she had power over was how she felt about matters.

Which meant, she was not by any means going to enjoy sharing a chamber with Boone Rawlins.

Chapter Eleven

Boone had no option but to share his chamber with Ambrin. Not unless he wished to sleep with the livestock or out in the parlour on a couch that was too short.

After sleeping on a hard wood floor, as he had been doing, neither of those prospects were appealing.

Now that he had a bed, he meant to use it.

Sharing a room was logical. A natural solution to the solving the bedroom shortage. There was nothing shameful in a married couple sharing a chamber.

Now, here it was in the wee hours and he stood beside the bedroom window watching rain pound hard on the glass. Out in the distance lightning crackled over the hills.

This business of sharing a bedroom was damned harder than he'd figured it would be. Without Marigold acting as a tiny chaperone, it changed things.

When a man had it in mind to be a proper husband

and his wife was asleep in a bed not three feet from his, it made matters uncomfortable.

The fact that Ambrin had no intention of accepting him that way ought to have made it easier to be in close company.

Problem was, every time he looked away from the window, there she was with her hair loose and fanning out over the pillow. One hand peeked out from under the blanket and lay curled beside her cheek. It sure was a sweet sight. A sensual one too.

Worst of it was the blanket did not lie flat on the mattress. It dipped at the little valley between her ribs and her waist, then it rose over the curve of her hip.

He pressed his nose to the glass, doing his damned best not to turn and look at her, his legally wed wife.

How soon could he get the roof fixed? How quickly could he find a blacksmith to repair the wagon?

The sooner he sent young Tom on his way, and Ambrin slept in her own room, the easier he would rest.

He would never force his attentions, but they itched at his insides, nevertheless.

'Well, damn it,' he muttered under his breath.

The plain fact was, it might be easier to sleep apart from her, but it would be lonely.

He reckoned it wouldn't take any time at all to get used to having her close by.

He was a man who liked being married. That is, he liked being married to Ambrin Rawlins.

He liked the way her breathing sounded in the dark.

He liked the soft sighs she made in her sleep for no apparent reason.

And he admired her as much as any person he had ever known. He couldn't say he was in love with her, but he couldn't say it might not happen, either.

There was a connection between them that she apparently did not recognise. He did though and it was a rare thing.

Hopefully someday she would feel the draw. It would be a crime to let it go unexplored. To let it wither and dry up.

For now, it was best to bear in mind that she didn't want him. The only reason she was in the bed beside his, or even in this marriage, was that she had nowhere else to go.

Had she'd been offered reasonable choice of a husband, she would not have wed him.

'Aw, darlin',' he mumbled low.

It seemed like the longer he stood here at the window thinking about it, the more it bothered him. The more he feared that the marriage he hoped for would never happen.

'Come away from the window, Boone.' Ambrin's voice sounded heavy with sleep and worry.

She sat up, motioned for him to move away from the glass where, she must figure, a random bolt of lightning might strike him down. The blanket fell away. Made him imagine what would happen if she was waving him forward instead of sideways.

'The storm seems to be moving away, but I'll sit beside you for a while if you'd like.'

'I'm not an infant to be coddled,' she declared. From where he stood repressing a grin, it was evident she was not. Didn't dare say so though. 'I only wish for you to move safely away from the window.'

Going back to his bed, he lay down, turned on his side then braced up on his elbow to better look at her. The light was dim but he could see her expression. It seemed to be snared somewhere between uneasy at the storm and annoyed at him for inferring that she was an infant. Which he had not done.

If she could see into his mind and known exactly what he thought she'd have another expression altogether. One he probably did not want to see even more than the one he was seeing now.

'Would you like to go to the village with me tomorrow? I need to see what can be done about repairing the wagon and get word to Tom's father that his boy is safe. I'll need more feed for the extra horses, too.'

'Indeed, I would. A visit to Tapperham will be just the thing. We could do with more food in the house now that we have all these people to feed.'

It gave his insides a warm turn to hear her say 'we', even though she probably didn't mean anything by it.

Still though, it gave his heart a tug to be awake in the night like they were, speaking of common little things. Made it feel like marriage the way it was meant to be.

Not all of what it was meant to be, but he would appreciate what she was willing to give.

'Better get some sleep then. We've got a busy day coming up.'

He lay down grinning up at the ceiling thinking that was something husbands and wives were probably saying to one another all over the countryside.

It had been a long time since he'd lain in bed having a quiet conversation with a woman. Made him realise even more how much he had missed being married.

He sent up a silent prayer that one day Ambrin would be glad she was wed to him. That given time, they would have homey conversation face to face in the same bed.

'Sweet dreams, darlin'.'

'Sleep well, Boone.'

Ambrin thought Tapperham was quite lovely. It was a quaint village that was only an hour wagon ride from the farm.

Although it was rural, it was bustling with activity.

Carriages and carts travelled the earthen main street. So far, she had not seen a fancy carriage.

Travelling into the village, they rode past a charming mill with a waterwheel. Continuing, Ambrin spotted several shops she would like to explore. They were not as grand as the establishments in London, but the goods displayed in the windows looked quite finely made.

Boone had told her that their first stop would be the blacksmith, which was at the furthest end of the village. After that they would locate a telegraph office and send word to Tom's father about what had happened, and tell him that his son was safe and would be home with the wagon as soon as possible.

Pray let it not be too long, Ambrin thought. Last night had been difficult. How was a wife to have such an appealing husband and remain distant from him?

What she had reminded herself, during the wee hours, was that he could not possibly want her in the way he had wanted his first wife. Susanna was the wife of his heart. Ambrin was his burden to carry.

'Here we are,' Boone said, drawing her out of the self-pity she was splashing about in.

If she kept that up she was going to be a miserable person making herself, and anyone she encountered, glum. It was time to accept what she no longer had and to be grateful for what she did have.

'Looks like the place is boarded up but I'll have a look around.'

The wagon creaked when Boone climbed down. Ambrin watched him stride to the front door and give it a sharp wrap. There was no response so he walked around a corner towards the back.

It seemed he was gone longer than he ought to be.

Although he was probably perfectly safe, she wondered if she ought to go looking for him. The odds of him being gored by a wandering bull, or having tripped over something and broken a bone were slim.

Really, the man had taken care of himself and Marigold in a place where bears and cougars roamed. The most threatening creature she had seen while riding through the village was a goat that had escaped from its yard and butted a passerby in the rump.

Really, she was not all that worried about his delay in returning. Although, twenty minutes was a rather long time to take walking the perimeter of a building.

Very well, it would not be out of line for a wife to have concern for her husband and go in search of him.

She climbed down from the wagon then straightened her skirt before setting out. Going around the corner of the building she looked at the ground, carefully picking her way around a mud puddle.

All at once she ran smack against Boone's solid, broad chest.

Her balance teetered. Boone kept her from falling backward into the puddle by grasping her arms and pulling her against him.

Oh, but the man had a solid chest. She knew this because it was rising and falling against hers. She ought to do something to step away but how could she? Boone Rawlins had a grin a woman could get lost in.

She could hope that her racing heart had to do with being startled, but of course she would be lying to herself.

Needing a distraction she said, 'Thank you, Boone.

It would have been a very embarrassing day if I had to walk about the village with mud all over my skirt.'

'Reckon so,' he answered but did not let go of her. Rather, his thumbs traced circles on her shoulders.

If he intended his hands to be steadying, he failed. All she felt was lightheaded, in a peculiar way.

'Did you find anything?' She took a step backward and his hands fell away.

She could not deny feeling at a bit of a loss without his supporting touch.

Never mind that, though. They had come to the village for a purpose after all and touching one another was not it.

Would never be it.

'A bit of bad news is all. I spoke with the fellow who owns the feed shop over there. He told me the smithy is gone visiting his grandchildren in another town and doesn't know when the blacksmith shop will reopen. Could be weeks.'

Weeks? Surely not!

'Got some good news, too.' Whatever it was had him grinning and the corners of his eyes crinkling in excitement. 'Turns out the man also knows a fellow who's got a nice herd of cattle to sell.'

Surely not!

While she had not believed that Boone would reconsider selling her London home, she had clung to a slight thread of hope.

Hearing about the cattle for sale drew the inevitable heartbreak nearer.

However, there was no one making an offer now. Boone would have told her.

Boone made a discovery this afternoon.

The way to make his wife smile was to take her shopping.

After having lunch at a place Ambrin called 'cute as a penny', they had spent the following two hours exploring shop after shop.

And to his dismay, there were still two more streets of shops to look at.

Boone wasn't sure what would give out first, his feet from endless walking up and down those streets, or his arms from carrying a stack of packages he could barely see over.

What would not give out was his patience.

For the first time in a while Ambrin seemed more her natural self.

He knew it had nothing to do with his charming company. More she was happy to have a little girl to buy things for.

Every time he shifted from foot to foot, or whenever he set the packages down to give his arms a rest, he imagined how happy Marigold would be when she saw her gifts.

Seeing the frilly, flouncy bows and dresses Ambrin

had picked, he realised he had been lacking when it came to his little girl.

Not having had a sister, or a wife who liked fancy things, he didn't know any better than to purchase only what was practical for farm life.

Ambrin walked in front of him, smiling as bright as the sunshine streaming in through the shop curtains. He couldn't tell how many small dresses she carried in the crook if her arm. They all blended into one colourful heap.

Didn't matter. He was going to buy them all and smile about it. He would do whatever it took to keep Ambrin in cheerful spirits.

What she really needed, he decided, was something pretty for herself. Something she did not need but would make her happy.

A wedding gift.

He hadn't given her one and it was high time he did. There were things he could not yet do as her husband, but other things he could.

When Ambrin finished buying everything he reckoned a little girl could dream of, he carried the goods out of the shop. He wasn't certain how it would all fit in the wagon.

'Come on, darlin'. We're going across the street.'

She gave him a puzzled glance, probably noticing the only establishments on the other side of the street were a boot shop, a bank and a jewellery store.

Although his arms were full, he managed to reach far enough to open the door then follow Ambrin inside.

Sure was a relief to set the packages down beside the door and flex his hands.

'I don't think there is anything in here appropriate for our girl, Boone.'

She'd never said that before. Our girl. It gave him a hopeful feeling that one day they might become the family he envisioned.

Funny, how such a short time ago he hadn't wished to marry. And now? He found he'd missed being wed more than he realised.

He took her hand, lead Ambrin to a glass case with all sorts of pretty jewels in it. The clerk hovered over his goods as if he feared they were thieves who would scoop up his stock and leave him penniless.

Must have been the snakeskin on his hat that made him look like an outlaw, or the side arm he carried. Back where he came from no one would have given him a second glance.

He ought to give some thought to leaving the weapon at home when he went to the village. He doubted that his wife was used to being stared as they had been ever since they'd got to Tapperham.

At least Ambrin looked refined. She outshone any other woman he'd seen strolling along the village paths.

They presented an odd pair and that was a fact.

'We aren't here for Marigold, darlin'.'

'I hope you do not mean to purchase anything for—'

He placed one finger on her lips to stop her protest.

'I haven't given you a proper wedding gift. I'll hear no argument about it.'

'I very well mean to give you an argument.' She took a moment to begin whatever protest came to mind. He reckoned it was because she was giving a sidelong glance at the sparkly things in the case.

'I cannot accept a gift,' she said at last.

After sending him a half-hearted scowl, her glance slid back to the case and lingered on a necklace.

She might be stubborn but he meant to outlast her.

He'd never purchased jewellery, except wedding rings, and had no idea of what the pretty necklace that caught her eye cost. He didn't rightly care either.

He'd spend a great deal to show her how highly he thought of her. How tender his heart was growing.

Saying so with words might make her bristly but that pretty ruby on a gold chain would surely give her an indication.

'Truly, Boone, this isn't necessary.'

Boone tapped the glass, showing the man behind the counter which necklace he would like to have taken out.

Boone held it up to the light streaming in the window. Deep within the gem, the light caught, made it glitter and pulse.

'It is lovely,' she said, touching it with the tip of her finger. 'The way the light reflects makes the heart appear to be beating.'

His was, rapidly. This gift was a personal one. If she took it, to his mind it equated to taking him, in some small way.

If he was wrong about the fanciful thought, it would still give him pleasure to see her wearing it.

It seemed clear that she wanted to accept and was poised right between yes and no.

'It is by far my best piece,' the clerk said, his superior glance suggesting Boone could not afford the necklace.

Practically speaking it was not a wise purchase, not when he needed to invest his funds in a herd. And yet not everything in this life had to do with being practical. There were times when a gift could speak the words that a man could not.

'If you will give us a moment.' He nodded for the shop keeper to move out of hearing range. The fellow complied but kept a narrowed eye on them.

'Darlin', I understand you must have more elegant jewels than this one, but the ruby suits you.'

'I used to have them, of course.' She ran her fingertips lightly over the gold chain dangling from his hand. 'But when my brother failed to send the funds to keep Greycliff afloat, I had to sell most of what I had.'

'I'm sorry for that. If I'd known, things would have been different.'

'I believe you.'

He was relieved to hear her say so, but he doubted

her believing him made a difference in how she felt about him.

'It would please me if you would accept this gift.'

'Oh, Boone. It's so pretty and I appreciate the gesture. But we live on a farm. It is hardly appropriate.'

'This little stone isn't a gesture. It's a promise. A vow to you on my honour that you will never again be in a situation like Grant left you in.'

'You might be the most honourable man I have ever met.' She tapped her bosom right over her heart, which he took as her way of accepting the gift.

So, he set it around her neck then fastened the clasp and sealed the promise.

Her gaze turned soft. The tenderness in her eyes unbalanced him for an instant, made him reckless.

There wasn't much else for a man to do but kiss his wife, so he did.

Although it was only meant to seal a promise, her delighted sigh before she rose to his kiss rocked him to his boot heels.

It was not until Boone helped Ambrin into the wagon that she realised how worn out she had become simply by spending the day shopping.

How long had it been since she indulged in such pleasure? She could not recall.

Browsing shops used to be a delight, until it became a challenge. Having to watch every penny and fear there would not be enough to provide for even a modest living took the joy out of it.

Today Boone had given that joy back to her.

The weight of the ruby nuzzling near her heart was a reminder that those wanting days were gone. He had promised and she had believed him.

It had been proof that no matter how many pretty things she purchased for Marigold, he had not begrudged them by even a glance.

Now, leaving the village, it was well past dark and she was well past weary.

She yawned. How puzzling. One did not yawn in polite company, especially if that company was a gentleman.

Nor did she fall so willingly into his kiss, for all that the said gentleman was her husband.

When her mind was more alert she would give this easy familiarity more thought. She would need to look rather deeply into how one could feel resentful towards a man and easy in his company at the same time.

When she was alert she would think more wisely of kissing someone who had taken her out of obligation, as if she were a stray in need of a home. Indeed, she would be more wary of falling headlong into the kiss of a man who had given her no choice but to marry him.

But no... It was Grant who had left her with no choice. If she thought about it in that light, perhaps her brother had trapped Boone as well. Her thoughts were shifting here and there, making little sense as that tended to happen in the moments before falling asleep. Odd little dream fragments that were ever so confusing flitted through her mind.

She felt her head jerk. She must have nodded off.

Covering yet another yawn with the back of her hand, she listened to the sounds of the night. She was becoming more accustomed to them but still, she did wonder what might be scuttling about in the dark.

Hmmmm… Boone smelled good. She inhaled deep and long to savour his unique scent.

She could not recall when she had been so delightfully tired.

'How long until we get home?' No, not home, she reminded herself. London was that. To the place they lived, she silently corrected.

'Longer than you'll be awake, I reckon.'

'It was a good day. I thoroughly enjoyed myself.' It couldn't hurt anything for him to know it. 'And my necklace. I cannot recall the last time I received a gift.'

Looking back on things, she was sorry she had been stubborn in accepting it. It was only that she feared she was accepting more than a piece of jewellery.

As it turned out she was accepting a promise. Somehow, she did not mind it as much as she thought she would.

Why was that? Here was one more thing she would give thought to when her mind was alert.

There was not much of a moon tonight, which made the road dark and the shadows deep.

'What was that noise in the tree?' she asked.

'Some small creature,' he answered. 'Nothing for you to be afraid of.'

'I'm not. Only curious.'

She was not as alarmed by unfamiliar rustles and sounds as she would have been a week ago. At least, not all the time.

'Lay your head here on my shoulder, darlin'.'

Since she kept nodding off, for all her effort not to, she might as well.

They were wed and she would not really be giving so much of herself away to snuggle close on a dark road. It was not such intimate behavior.

Not like kissing or some of the other more interesting familiarities she had been thinking about lately.

Boone smelled so good.

Boone had never known a person who could fall so deeply asleep while sitting up in a jerky, moving wagon.

He'd like to think it was a sign that she trusted him. That after all the time she'd spent living with her future so uncertain, she now felt secure.

That was the reason he'd married her, to give her that security.

It hadn't been for love, not on either of their parts. But he'd be a fool to deny his heart wasn't gazing down that road and wondering.

The house came into view. The parlour window was

the only one with a lamp glowing inside. Everyone must be sleeping by now.

'Wake up, darlin',' he whispered while setting the wagon brake. 'We're home.'

Speaking the word home gave him a smile inside. Giving his niece a home was the reason he had travelled across the ocean. It is why he had given up everything familiar for what was foreign.

Now that there was Ambrin, the word home had even more meaning.

The imaginary road he'd just gazed down seemed an attractive one. Also, one that a person did not travel alone.

Ambrin did not stir at the sound of his voice. She did not flutter an eye when he jiggled her shoulder.

There was nothing for it but to carry her inside. Keeping one arm on her so she wouldn't topple, he stepped down from the wagon. He eased her down into his arms.

His bride sure was a sound sleeper.

'Wake up, darlin',' he repeated, figuring she would rather walk on her own if she knew.

All he got in response was a huff of warm breath on his cheek.

Sweet breath, which made him aware of the fact that her lips were only inches from his grin.

Inches or miles it was all the same in what he would do about it. Which was not one damn thing.

He was lucky to have gotten the kiss she allowed

out of gratitude. He did not wish to ruin what might be taking root between them by pushing too hard.

Settling her in his arms he went up the steps thinking how her weight felt just right. Not so slight that she seemed frail, but not so heavy that he got winded going up the steps.

The house was quiet so he must have figured right in thinking everyone was asleep.

He carried Ambrin through the parlour and then into the bedroom they were sharing. He lay her down on the bed.

Sitting at the foot of the mattress he unlaced her shoes and pulled them off. Anything more than that would not be right. Not without her awake and consenting.

Gazing down at her though, seeing the way she curled her hand near her cheek, hearing how contented her breathing sounded and then how she gave a smile in a dream… Damn it if he hadn't already put one boot on that path he'd imagined. It felt like quicksand so he yanked his foot back.

Better to keep a friendly relation with his wife and not risk alienating her when she was just warming up to him again.

Someday, maybe. For now, he had a wagon load of purchases to unload and a team of horses to bed down.

At the doorway, he paused and took a glance back. The necklace rose and fell with her breathing. She shifted to her side, then cupped her hand around the ruby all without waking.

Someday…just maybe.

Chapter Twelve

Boone was about to go out the kitchen door to spend an hour working at the woodpile when he heard Millie and Marigold laughing in the parlour.

He turned course thinking whatever was going on in there would be more entertaining than splitting logs.

Turned out he was right.

If Marigold had felt like a princess the night they arrived at the cottage, she must feel properly royal all dressed up in her new frocks.

She laughed in the sweet, infectious way she had while spinning about the parlour.

Millie sat on the couch clapping her hands. Petunia leaned her great hairy shoulder against the elderly housekeeper's knees.

Boone couldn't help himself. He caught Marigold's hand as she twirled past him.

'My lady.' He bowed over her hand and kissed it. 'I am for ever at your service.'

'Then you must be my knight. I will call you Sir Uncle Boone.'

'I will bear the title with honour.'

She stepped on his boots wearing her new slippers and began to hum. Accepting the invitation, he danced her about the parlour.

'Oh my, what a handsome pair!' Millie exclaimed.

When Marigold ended her tune, he lifted her high. She reached her small arms towards the ceiling while he twirled her about.

When he set her down, she looked up at him, swaying and swishing her lacy-edged skirt.

'Sir Uncle Boone, did you know that I am the daughter of a baron? I'm almost royalty.'

'I've known that about you since the day you were born, little darlin'. You've always been a princess to me.'

'But I mean a real one.'

'Oh, but you do look every bit of it,' Millie declared, her eyes alight.

The child gave her impression of a royal curtsy to him, then to Millie and Petunia.

Ambrin's footsteps tapped in the hallway. He had not seen her since last night and couldn't help wondering if, hoping that, she would be wearing the necklace.

'Here is another dress to try on!' she called bustling into the parlour.

Spotting him, she came up short, touched the ruby

hanging halfway between the delicate hollow of her throat and the swell of her bosom. 'Oh, hello Boone.'

He nodded, tipped his hat. 'Darlin'.'

'Ohhhh!' Marigold declared. 'That one is even prettier. I love blue, Auntie.'

Ambrin and Millie helped her into the new dress.

'Why, my word.' Millie pressed her hand to her heart. 'You rival the very queen.'

'Do I get to make commands?'

'Only kind and generous ones,' Ambrin explained. 'It is how a good queen behaves.'

'I will make a fun command.'

'And what would that be?' he asked.

'Sir Uncle Boone, now that I am five years old, I command you to teach me to ride a horse.'

He had promised her that, when she was five, he would begin her lessons. Now that they were settling in at the farm, the time was right.

'Go on, then. Change into your regular gown and we'll go to the barn.'

'But I wish to learn in this one. It is my command.'

'You must change, or your dress will smell like a horse,' he pointed out. 'Pretty dresses are for acting a princess and sturdy dresses are for your everyday life.'

She wrapped her arms about his leg then gazed up at him. Sometimes the plea in her wide brown eyes won him over to her way of thinking.

Not this time.

'But, Uncle Boone, I am a baron's daughter. I must wear fine dresses.'

'You are also a farmer's daughter and must wear what is practical.'

At the start of this journey, crossing the ocean to give them a new life, he had not given any thought to that other part of her heritage. He'd understood that her father was a baron, but that life had seemed so far from the man he knew.

Marigold spun about, dashed for her auntie, then gave her the same pleading look.

'I want to be like you, Auntie. You wear pretty dresses.'

'I did in London. But your uncle is correct. Tomorrow I shall wear a plain dress as is fitting for our life on the farm.'

Marigold's opinion on his decree was made clear when she crossed her arms over her chest and sent Boone a severe frown.

While Ambrin had sided with him, he was not sure how she really felt about his decision. She hid her expression by looking out the window at the sunny afternoon.

He figured she must be hiding how she felt. Not about the clothes, but what trading fancy for practical meant for her life.

There was a ball gown in a trunk in the bedroom. He'd seen Ambrin take it out, hold it to her and twirl once about. Then she'd set it back in the trunk and closed the lid.

That one moment told him things he would rather not have known.

Seeing her longing for her life in London gave him a punch in the gut.

He knew what marriage was supposed to be. It was for bringing one another joy, not heartache. The principle was true, even if the marriage was not founded on a love match.

Guilt nipped his conscience for plucking her from her old life and planting her here. What he had to keep in mind was that there had been no other choice. Ambrin no longer had a life in London.

He must do what he could to help her thrive on the farm and to embrace the joy to be found in living there.

Earlier that morning, Ambrin had watched Marigold sit on a horse. The child had shown no fear or hesitation, only excitement.

In that moment, seeing her niece's complete lack of dread at sitting on the back of a large unpredictable animal, Ambrin had vowed to live her life in a bolder manner.

If the child had no fear, it was only right that her guardian should have none either.

That is why, when Boone invited her to ride about and explore the farm, she accepted.

Not only did she say yes, but she did so with a smile.

This was her life now. The sooner she became accustomed to it, the easier it would be to say goodbye to her old one.

That is also why when Boone brought out a pair of horses for them to ride, she did not scurry back to the house.

She curled her fists within the folds of her skirt, set her resolve and reminded herself that horses were not cows. They did not have scary horns and they did not charge at children hiding in bushes.

Gentleman and ladies of society enjoyed riding horses. There was no reason she should not be one of them.

There had been the issue of the saddle, though. Boone did not own a proper ladies saddle, but why would he?

After a bit of back and forth on the issue, he managed to convince her that she would feel more balanced sitting astride. Since no one from society was likely to come by and see her in the unladylike posture, she agreed to ride this way.

So, here she found herself only an hour into her first excursion on horseback feeling quite accomplished. She no longer feared that she would fall off or that the animal would run away with her as its helpless captive.

Boone had shown her a few tricks which, apparently, Prairie Flower already knew. The horse responded quite agreeably to Ambrin's leading.

Or perhaps the horse was only following the lead of

Boone's well-trained animal. Nevertheless, she found herself enjoying the gentle rock and sway of Prairie Flower's gait while she and Boone rode side by side on this gentle, sunny afternoon.

There could be no doubt that Boone was enjoying their outing.

'Look at that, Ambrin,' he said, turning to look at her with the grin that had been on his face ever since they left the barn. 'I've never seen so many acres of green. And the way it rolls along, so easy like.'

'It must be quite different than what you left behind.' It occurred to her that she was not the only one to have left behind everything that was loved and familiar. 'Was it terribly difficult coming here?'

'In the beginning, yes. I fought the necessity of it as long as I could. I built the house with my own hands. I buried people I loved on the land. I didn't think I could leave my ranch, even though it was in ruins with most of the cattle dead and no way to replace them.'

Now, of course, he did have a way. How long would it be before strangers lived in her home? How long before another woman rocked babies beside the fireplace or played with her children in the garden. How long before another man kissed his wife at the foot of the stairs and then raced her towards the bedroom?

How long before the echo of her family was lost? That house was all she had left of them.

'I reckon you understand why I gave it all up.'

She did of course.

'Marigold, naturally.' Boone was not related to the child by blood, but Ambrin was convinced he loved her as if he were.

'She had her whole life to live and she couldn't very well do it if I gave up on mine.'

The ruby slid against her skin in time with the horse's gait. She wore the necklace under her clothes in order to protect it while she was outdoors. But the ruby heart was not the only one that shifted in the moment.

What he said, about giving up his home, wasn't that a bond they shared?

Both of them had been forced to leave the place they loved. Although, it had to be noted, he had done so more gracefully than she had. At least that is how she saw it.

'I regret that my coming here made a mess of your life,' he went on, his gaze focused on a flock of geese flapping across the clear blue sky.

'My life was a mess already. I just did not know how much of one until you arrived that night.'

'It pained me to have to tell you about Grant. And all the rest.'

It had been wicked, awful news. The thing is, he had not just left her with it. He'd comforted her. Had his arms not supported her in that moment, she might have fallen completely apart.

On that night, although Boone had every legal right to cast her out of his house, he had not done so.

No indeed, what he had done was offer her another life. One that allowed her to raise her niece. To sleep in peace with a roof over her head and his protective presence close by.

How self-absorbed she was, giving such constant thought to what she given up but not much to what Boone had.

Not long ago he was living a life he loved, wed to a woman he loved.

Just now he was looking at the distant hills and the lush valley that rose to meet them. What was he feeling? Regret or delight?

With his attention distracted, she took the moment to have a good long look at the man she had married.

The Stetson shaded his face, but she saw his expression clearly.

Delight. Quite clearly he was giving his heart to this land. Falling in love with it, even as they rode side by side.

She envied him that. It was unlikely she would never feel such affection for the farm. But the man?

If it weren't for the business of him selling her home, she might be more accepting of their marriage and her position as his wife.

Then he turned his smile on her. It was her turn to look at the distant hills. The last thing she wished was for him to read the thought teasing her mind. Which was, in her very secret self, she was beginning to feel wifely in a particular way. A way she did not wish to…did she?

When she felt his gaze turn away from her, she looked back at him.

That was a mistake, because her attention settled on his hands. He held the reins gently, as if in tender communication with the horse.

What, she tried desperately not to wonder is how those fingers would communicate with a lover. With a wife, which she was.

Although in that moment it did not seem to matter if she was a willing one or not. Only that there would be no sin in leaving her bed for his.

As interesting as the idea was, she dare not dwell on the forbidden. Although, it was only forbidden because she had made it so. Had she not chosen this course for her life because too much had happened that she had no control over? In this one thing, she reminded herself, she would stand firm. If she were to be a person she respected, she must stand firm in her resolve.

In order to distract herself from niggling temptation she asked Boone, 'How many cattle will you buy?'

Speaking of cattle ought to help. Nothing was more unpleasant than a cow.

'We'll need a good-sized herd if we are to make a go of the farm. I will speak with the fellow I met in the village and see how many we can afford to purchase.'

'That sounds fine,' she said.

But then he grinned and all of sudden, she meant it.

It was only a shame Boone did not have his sights set on a horse farm. She was becoming strangely attached to the large, but amicable, creature carrying her along.

If one must give up one's home, it would be much easier to do for a horse than for a cow.

Life began early on the farm. More and more, Ambrin found she did not mind.

The first rays of dawn streamed into the bedroom while she dressed. Going to the window, she drew it open, felt cool morning air on her face and listened to the birds welcoming the day.

In the distance she spotted Boone and Tom coming out of the barn. Her husband worked harder than anyone she had ever known. She wondered how her brother had fared with farm work. The image coming to mind of Grant rising early and trying to keep up with Boone made her smile. Did he grumble and frown about the early hours or did he go about his work humming like Boone did? It gave her pause for a moment, realising that she was thinking of her brother with contentment and not a tear. Grief must be easing the grip it had on her heart.

A squirrel chattered close at hand, reminding her that it was time to go about her day.

She fastened her hair in an efficient bun, then tied a yellow ribbon around it to make it look cheerful and pretty. Next, she hurried down the hallway to prepare breakfast. Boone and Tom would be hungry when they came in.

She met Marigold along the way.

'Go change your dress, young lady. After breakfast, it will be time to gather eggs.'

'I like this one,' her niece pleaded, spreading her lace skirt wide before turning back for the bedroom she shared with Millie. 'Maybe this morning there will be chicks.'

Walking into the kitchen she found Millie already at work preparing breakfast.

'It's another beautiful day.' Millie greeted her with a sweetly creased smile.

Millie and Frederick had made the adjustment from town to farm quite easily. She had lost count of how many times they had praised their new home.

She hated to think of what would have become of Millie and Frederick if not for Boone. Even if her brother had not given her home away, how much longer could she have supported them?

Only the Good Lord knew who she would be wed to now if things had been different. Surely not a man as reliable as the one she had married.

Or as handsome, she decided, seeing him stride into the kitchen, flushed and fresh with morning air.

Marigold returned dressed in blue gingham and scuffed brown boots. She dashed to her uncle and gave him a hug.

They all sat together to eat but it was a quick affair since the men had a full day of chores ahead.

So did Ambrin. Now that she had found her role in the household there was much to be done.

Once in a while she thought about her society friends and their lives of leisure. Oddly enough, she envied them less than she used to.

Boone and Tom went back to the barn. Ambrin and Marigold followed them a short time later to gather eggs and hopefully discover that chicks had hatched.

'Look, Auntie!' Marigold held her hand while skipping happily along. 'Lots of butterflies.'

'Aren't they pretty?' Truly they were. London had butterflies to be certain, but not so many and not as brightly hued.

A cool breeze ruffled the hem of her gown. Glancing towards the hills beyond the barn she noticed dark clouds piling one upon another. With luck they would bring no more than gentle rain.

Boone, she knew, appreciated frequent rain. It kept everything green and fresh, he liked to say. Drought was one of the things he'd dreaded back in Montana, as well as the brush fires that came with it.

Given the perils of the American west, she wondered if he were happier in Oxfordshire where life was not so risky.

Or, in spite of snakes and blizzards, would Montana always be the home of his heart?

Home is where the heart is, it had been said. She now understood how true this was.

'I know there will be chicks this time!' Marigold dashed to the last stall where Boone had built a chicken coop large enough for an adult to walk upright in.

Ambrin paused beside Prairie Flower's stall. The horse whickered then lifted her velvety muzzle to be petted. Ever since their first ride together, Ambrin had greeted the animal by stroking her nose and feeding her an apple.

The tack room door was open. It sounded as if Boone was in there with Tom, instructing him on the use of… Well, she did not know what but something that must be to do with the farm.

Tom was fitting in wonderfully well. Boone had even spoken to him about staying on as a farm hand.

He was a good-natured young man and Ambrin would have been glad if he took the job. Except, that would have meant her continuing to share a room with her husband.

That, she decided, was a worry for another time. For tonight. And the night after and the one after that…

Rounding the corner to the chicken stall, Ambrin found Marigold hopping about on her toes, silently pointing at a nest.

'A chick!' she whispered. 'We must be very quiet and move slowly so it does not become frightened.'

'Isn't it adorable?'

Although it was not as adorable as Marigold was

while she was making chirruping noises at a fuzzy yellow head peeking out from under its mother's wing.

Perhaps as the daughter of a baron it would be more fitting for her to practice tea parties but, fitting or not, the child was having a great deal of fun.

Looking back at her own childhood, Ambrin had never cooed over a newly hatched chick. Nor had she ever had a dog to romp with or a cat to cuddle.

Half of her wondered if Boone had been right bringing Marigold up here and not in London.

The other half of her recognised that there were obligations that came along with the privilege of being a member of society.

What a confusing muddle.

Gentle rain splatted on the windows, which Boone was grateful for. Trouble was, it had been doing so for three days without stopping.

Being inside most of the day had made his bones ache for a good stretching.

He put on his Stetson, then his rain slicker. After taking a look at the woodpile, he decided it was too wet to work with.

There was plenty of dry work to do in the barn. Stalls always needed cleaning and tack needed repairing.

Going inside he found the stalls clean enough for a man to sleep in. Young Tom must have beat him to it.

Boone went into the tack room, picked up a broken bridle and then sat on a stool to fix it. After a few minutes of working the leather, he heard the barn door open, giving its usual squeal. Next thing he would do was oil the hinges.

He peeked around the doorway and saw Ambrin shaking out her umbrella. She set it beside the door all the while muttering to herself.

'I shall learn to like you,' Boone thought he heard.

'Very well, like might be a bit much but I will learn to tolerate you.' He did hear the last bit because she spoke it more forcefully.

What was she talking about?

Better not to make himself known if he wanted to find out.

With her back straight and her hands clenched she walked towards the animal stalls, Petunia trotting at her side.

There was a blue ribbon twined in Ambrin's braid that swayed in time with her purposeful stride.

He didn't think she was talking about tolerating the dog. He'd seen his wife sneaking Petunia treats when she thought no one was looking.

This ought to be interesting.

He had to swallow down a laugh when she stopped in front of the cow stall.

'Hello Clarabelle. I have come to learn not to cringe whenever I get close to you.' Ambrin reached her hand towards the milk cow but snatched it back again. 'I suppose you cannot help being smelly and I do enjoy the milk and butter you contribute.'

She reached one finger towards Clarabelle. This time she let it hover a moment before she drew her hand back.

'But the thing is, if I am to live here, I do not wish to go about frightened of you all the time, especially when no one else seems to be. I will admit, your horns are not as wicked looking as the bull that tried to trample me. Although, to be honest I am rather certain it was not intentional since he would not have been aware that I was in the bush. He probably expected to be struck dead by lightning the same as I did.'

The cow gave a long moo. 'At any rate, you have much gentler looking eyes than he did.'

That said, Ambrin turned as if she meant to walk away from the cow, but she stopped and spun back to Clarabelle again.

'Oh drat. I suppose I cannot leave until I touch you. It would be cowardly since that is what I came to do.'

Petunia must have caught his scent because she swung her head in his direction and gave a soft woof. Being absorbed in her mission, Ambrin didn't seem to notice.

To his amazement, Ambrin touched the cow's horn with the tip of one finger.

'It is a pleasure to make your acquaintance,' she said but by the tone of her voice Boone was not convinced she meant it.

Apparently emboldened, Ambrin drew a line between Clarabelle's ears. She traced the spot on the cow's forehead where the hair grew in a swirl. 'The rest of my family believes you are a sweet girl. I shall endeavour to see it.'

Her family? Had he heard her right? Boone's heart roared, tripped up on itself. Had his wife just called them a family?

'I will not, however, milk you. We have made our peace and that will have to do. And thank you for the cheese. You too, Bessie,' Ambrin called, but the other cow was shy and did not come forward for a greeting.

Boone emerged from hiding and crossed the barn. His wife turned, sending him a smile that made him warm and cheery.

'You are a brave woman, Mrs Rawlins. Never figured I'd see the day you faced down a cow.'

Or called them a family. He had been beginning to fear she would never see them that way. Hearing the words gave him hope.

'Yes, well, there is a good solid gate between us. Put me in the open with a bull and I will climb the nearest tree.'

'Didn't know you could climb trees, darlin'.'

'Nor did I but I would learn in a hurry.'

He laughed, wrapped her in a hug. 'Like I said, you are a brave woman.'

She returned his hug briefly then stepped away making the embrace friendly rather than the one he had a mind to explore.

Patience, he reminded himself. They had a lifetime to grow as man and wife, Good Lord willing.

'I am not at all brave and you know it.'

'I don't know it. Even if I didn't see you pet a cow, I would believe you are.'

'Haa,' she laughed. 'You did see me cower at an owl I recall?'

He took her hand, drew her closer but not so close as to embrace her again. 'I'll tell you what I've seen. I've seen a woman enduring hard grief and yet gathering herself so as not to upset a child who had recently lost her father. I've seen a woman who was faced with financial ruin, yet refused to turn out her elderly staff. I saw a woman who could have married a fellow who would fix her problems and yet had the courage to refuse him.'

'Surely you do not mean Willard Dawson? It took no courage whatsoever to say goodbye to him and his mother.'

'He would have given you a home in London and all the money you could ever spend.'

'You know very well he would have made me miserable. It had nothing to do with bravery, Boone.' She shook her head, then whispered, 'I did not have the courage to say no to you.'

'Did you want to, darlin'?'

'I...but of course I did, then.'

'What about now? Would you wish to go back to London if a way presented.'

'That, Boone Rawlins, is not going to happen. It is foolish to discuss.'

Not the answer he wanted to hear, but at least it was honest. And she was right, it was not likely to happen.

Especially since he was expecting Mr Adams to come to the farm and present an offer for the London house.

Within days the process would begin that would result in her losing her lifelong home. Losing the link that connected her to the cultured way of life she loved.

It was only right to tell her before the solicitor arrived. It was what he promised. Too bad the blamed hurtful words got lost between his brain and his mouth.

For all that it was important to Ambrin not to be caught unaware by events, this moment was all wrong for the admission. It would change the course of the moment and where he hoped it was going.

'Do you care for me, Ambrin? Even a little?'

'You are my husband.'

He arched his brows at her, waiting for a real answer.

'Surely you know I do. If it were not for you, I do not know where I would be. Certainly not raising my niece.'

'Or making friends with a cow,' he said giving his voice a playful tone even though he was troubled.

'I am not making friends with a cow. And Boone, I do care for you.'

'I care for you, too.' He kissed her hand.

The truth was, for him, things went deeper than just caring. He'd be a fool to say they didn't. Watching her wrestle down her fear of a milk cow pushed him several steps down that risky path towards love that he'd imagined earlier.

Downright shame that she wasn't on the path with him. But maybe by going slowly, step by step, they might get to where they ought to be.

It couldn't hurt, he reckoned, to lead her down the trail a step or two. See if she was willing to go along.

Lifting her chin, he gave her a peck on her lips. 'In honour of your courage.'

It wasn't really because of that but saying so got his mouth where it wanted to be.

'Oh, well. Perhaps I should find some other brave thing to…' She must have realised her words revealed more than she wished them to for she backed away with her hand clapped over her mouth. '…do. In the house. I have so much to do in the house. I must get back.'

Being a man on the verge of handing over his heart, he wished she had said what she'd intended to.

Picking up the hem of her dress, she rushed for the barn door, drew it open. Rain blew in covering her face in glistening dots.

'Ambrin, there is something else. You called us a family a minute ago.'

She nodded, but did not say more.

'Do you want babies?'

'I…but, Boone, we…' She fell silent again blinking her eyes against the rain.

'I do,' he said. 'I want children.'

Chapter Thirteen

Ambrin lay on her mattress, arms straight and tense at her sides. She stared at the ceiling while listening to Boone's easy snoring. And the wind rattling the bedroom window.

While the rain had finally quit, the weather was unsettled. Which was a fitting match to her mood because ever since her husband had brought up…

A rush of some emotion charged through her limbs. Or more than one emotion, probably, and they were all at war with one another. Otherwise, she would not be this overwrought.

She tossed off her blanket, sat up and bolted off the bed.

Striding the three steps that separated the beds, she stood over Boone, hands braced on her hips.

'Babies?' she mouthed over his prone body. 'You want children?'

He might have mentioned so before she'd wed him!

'Infants?' She did not dare speak and wake him until

she understood the emotions that had her feeling as tense as harp strings. And as quivery. 'How many?'

How could the man have made the leap from seeing her seeming to befriend a cow to him wanting children?

Most likely the idea had not simply occurred to him in the moment.

It made sense that he would have wanted babies with Susanna. He'd loved his first wife.

'You do not love me!' She slashed her hand in the air to express the frustration her voice could not.

Her arm went suddenly limp, flopped to her side.

'Do you?'

Because there had been that kiss, and the few before that, that indicated he might not be indifferent to her.

Heaven help her, she was not indifferent to him.

If she were, she probably would not be wondering if he were wondering what it would be like to conceive said child with her.

She grasped the neck of her nightgown, waved it to cool her chest and throat. It was a wasted effort, so she stopped.

Fanning was useless against heat that pulsed from the inside.

'Of course, I care for you…' She actually whispered this but so softly that she barely heard it herself. 'How could I not?'

He was so handsome that sometimes she simply stared at him while he was unaware. That lock of hair that was in the habit of falling across his brow was simply her undoing.

In the moment she had an irresistible urge to reach down and touch it. To brush it back like a real wife would do.

She did resist because… 'Do you think of me as your real wife?'

Or would his heart always belong to the wife he had taken out of love?

This man had much more to him than being well-formed and having a handsome face. He was both bold and tender. He took his responsibilities to heart, but he could also dance about the parlour with a small girl balanced on his feet.

He could scandalise society by performing a lively dance around a hat at a fancy ball. And did she not feel dizzy with joy in doing it with him?

As much as those things though, Boone Rawlins had the presumption to marry a baron's daughter and remain unflinching in what anyone had to say about it.

'I think you are wonderful,' she mouthed because he was and…well there he was, the blanket drawn down to his hips and his chest bare.

She was his wife. He was her husband.

He wanted children and there was but one way for him to have them.

Some odd, melting heat must have overcome her good sense. The temptation to draw her gown up to her knees and climb onto his bed was overwhelming.

She clutched the soft fabric, inched it up to her shins.

Then he snorted in his sleep and turned onto his side.

Just in time the spell was broken. Good reason hit her like an icy hand on her middle pushing her back.

She got in her bed, but did not lie down. She simply sat and stared at her husband's back while it rose and fell with his breathing.

Whatever made him believe she would agree to have children with a man to whom she was an obligation? No matter how caring Boone seemed, the reason for their marriage had not changed.

Whatever made her entertain the thought for even a moment?

Some mischief of the flesh had caused her to hitch her gown and nearly join him in his bed.

A wary attitude is what she must maintain. She must search out any offending sensation and cast it from her.

The self-admonition might have worked if he had not turned to face her, opened his eyes and said, 'Go back to sleep, darlin'. I won't let the weather harm you.'

Right there with those few words she understood her battle was not with the flesh.

No indeed, the temptation to love him came from her heart.

The three feet of space dividing their beds would do little to prevent it from crossing over.

* * *

There was not much that could keep Ambrin from daydreaming of having children with Boone—the conceiving of them in particular—however a small yellow chick managed to draw her focus away.

Somehow it had escaped from the coop. She dashed about the barn flapping her skirt while attempting to herd it back to where it belonged.

Quick and stubborn, the little creature seemed determined to dash around her and run for the open door.

She herded the chick to within feet of its mother who clucked madly from the inside of the coop. All at once it scurried under her skirt, bumped about her petticoats and then emerged on the side away from the coop.

'You rascal!' she exclaimed waving her arms and dashing after the escapee.

The last thing she wished is to have to tell Marigold that something horrid had befallen her precious chick.

The tiny bird scuttled out the door then made a fast right.

Ambrin gave chase and found it scratching the ground under the canopy of a shady tree.

'Why you little scamp,' she said, walking slowly towards it. 'Your mother is distraught.'

All at once she felt a rush of air, heard the sweep of wings, as a hawk flew past her shoulder. It thumped on the grass missing the chick when it dashed after an insect.

With admirable grace the hawk launched up from the ground and landed on a branch in the tree. Its sharp gaze followed the chick while it pecked about.

'Not so easy to catch, is it?' she said to the hawk. 'Shoo now! Go find something else for your meal!'

Just not a bunny.

She blocked the chick from the hawk's view by spreading her skirt.

'Go away!' She waved one arm at the bird, but it only gave her a considering eye.

In the instant, something hit the tree a few feet from the hawk.

Turning, she spotted Boone grinning at her.

'Rock,' he said with a shrug.

'You missed,' she answered, but really, she ought to have thought about throwing something at the bird to scare it away.

'Nope, hit the tree right where I aimed.'

The brim of his hat shaded Boone's eyes so she could not clearly gage his expression. Just as well since he was no doubt laughing at her.

'Speaking of aim, then,' she gave him an arched brow. 'How do you aim to catch the chick?'

'I aim to finish watching you do it.'

'What do you mean…finish?'

'I was fixing a hammer in the tack room. Looked out just in time or I would have missed the show.'

'The show? I hardly think—' That grin of his would do her in one of these days. How was a lady to hold on to a temper in the face of it? Apparently, she was not. 'I am glad to have kept you entertained.'

Then she laughed at the sight she must have made.

'I propose we team up and catch Miffle before the hawk comes back,' she said.

'Miffle?' He chuckled. The deep, manly timber had her grabbing her heart.

'Marigold named it.'

'Could be for a hen or a rooster I expect,' he pointed out.

'If we don't catch it, it will be called dinner.'

Boone squatted, uncurled his hand and showed her the chicken feed in his fist.

The clucking noises he made were so accurate that the chick must have thought him its mother. Miffle scurried over and pecked feed out of Boone's hand.

The little bird did not flap in distress when he closed his other hand over it.

'Here, darlin', you carry the chick back to the coop since you are the one who rescued it.'

Standing, Boone set Miffle in her hand. She covered it the same as she saw him do.

'You little rascal,' she whispered through the spaces between her fingers. She had never held a chick before. It felt soft, its feet tickled her palm. 'I would have still been chasing it. You get the glory of the rescue, Boone.'

'I'll take whatever glory you want to give me. But this isn't the first chick I've captured. I've been doing it since I was as young as our Marigold.'

Now it was her heart that was tickling. Something in the tone of his voice when he said 'our Marigold' gave Ambrin a sense of them being a real family.

Walking beside him back to the barn, her mind wandered. It presented an image of them holding a baby, each of them with one arm supporting it and Boone saying, our Mary, or our Michael…

'This sure is a wiggly fellow,' she said in order to banish the imaginary Mary or Michael.

Having determined from the first not to become intimate with her husband, she would be wise to stick to it. Just because the reasons escaped her in the moment, they were still valid.

'Your blush looks mighty pretty, wife,' he said while opening the door of the chicken coop.

She set the chick inside then Boone closed the door.

'I am merely flushed with the chase.'

Watching the chick scurry under the hen, probably very relieved to be home, she remembered why she needed to keep her distance from Boone.

Home.

He was selling hers. But it was not even just that. She understood that he needed the money to buy his cattle herd and provide a home for them all. But he had kept his intentions a secret from her and then, all of a sudden, she'd had no choice but to wed him.

Had he been honest about his intentions from the beginning she would have known what she had faced and perhaps she would have chosen him on her own.

'Boone,' she said as they walked side by side from the dim light of the barn and into the sunshine. 'There is something I would like to know.'

Or maybe she would not like to, but now that the thought was in her mind she had to ask.

'What is it, darlin'?' He stopped walking, tugged at the ribbon in her hair and gave her a smile to melt her into the grass.

'Do you regret that you did not inform me you were selling my house from the first?'

'Well, now. There is a time to tell things and a time to keep quiet about them.' He frowned when he said so. 'I hope you understand that I was grieved to have broken your heart with so much bad news all at once. Ambrin, your tears cut me to the quick.'

'It's only… It might have made a difference if you had been honest with me.'

'A difference in what way?'

How could he misunderstand in what way since she was rising on her toes to kiss him?

'I am glad that we settled the business of honesty between us. There is no room for anything else between friends,' she murmured close to his mouth. 'Special friends.'

He opened his mouth as if he meant to speak, or to kiss her.

All of a sudden, a kiss seemed more urgent than words. Her husband was an honourable man. An honest one. And she chose to kiss him, which in no way damaged her determination to keep her heart to herself.

Or maybe it did, but only for this moment. Afterward, she would put it back where it belonged.

'Darlin', there's—'

'There you are, Mr Rawlins!' Tom came rushing from…well she had no idea where from. She had lost track of everything for a moment. She had not even been certain whether her feet were on the grass or dancing in the treetops.

Tom had clearly been in a rush to get to Boone, though. Both he and the horse he led were breathing hard.

'What is it son?' Boone dropped his arms from about her.

'The stream overflowed and washed away a section of stone fence. Now the stones are blocking the water and turning the pasture into a pond.'

'Reckon we'd better get it repaired before it rains again.'

Tom pointed to a mass of black mass clouds mounding in the east. 'Looks like it's coming in fast.'

With that, Boone gave Ambrin a long look and then kissed her cheek.

'Later we'll talk,' he said, glancing over his shoulder while taking a step after Tom. 'And…'

And kiss, she knew he meant. So she caught his hand, went up on her toes and gave him a quick one.

Curiously, the kiss was a mere peck and yet she was

having a difficult time stuffing her heart back into the safe place she always kept it. The fickle thing was dancing about and gleefully taunting her.

She watched Boone and Tom hurry away. When they were out of sight, she walked back to the house.

Along the way she kept a close eye on the clouds. They looked wicked and gave her a shiver.

Perhaps the wind would change and blow them in a different direction.

Anxiety would help nothing, so she forced herself to think about something else.

Oddly enough, her mind turned to her brother and to forgiveness. The thoughts she had of him lately were not bitter ones. It could only mean she must have forgiven him, for everything. If she forgave Grant his sins, then surely she could forgive Boone for keeping secrets from her in the past.

Going into the house and then into her chamber, she sat on her bed puzzling over the matter.

What exactly would forgiving Boone entail?

She stared at the bed he would occupy later tonight.

He wanted her in it. She would be a fool to believe otherwise.

She would be a bigger fool to deny wanting to be in it with him. And yet she had made promises to herself about keeping her heart to herself.

Did forgiving him mean accepting the life he envisioned for them?

Did it mean opening herself to the possibility of loving him?

No.

Yes.

Ambrin flopped back on her mattress, then turned her head to gaze at Boone's bed.

The indentation from his head was still on the pillow from this morning. The blanket lay flat where she had smoothed it with her hand and dreamed of how…

A crash of thunder rolled over the house breaking her train of thought.

Marigold dashed into the room then hopped up on the bed, snuggled close to her.

'Don't worry, Auntie, I'm here.'

Chapter Fourteen

Lightning etched the night sky. Thunder hit hard and fast.

Anxiety crawled under Ambrin's skin. Rubbing her arms did nothing to make the sensation go away.

Still, she did not step back from the window. Even when Millie touched her arm and urged her to come away and have a bite to eat, she remained watching.

Where was Boone? Where was Tom?

If prolonged but easy rain could undermine a stone wall, what would happen in a downpour such as this one when the ground was already saturated? What was normally a friendly stream might wash Boone and Tom away.

Watching rain gush off the eaves like a waterfall made her shiver.

At least the repairs Boone had made to the roof were holding. No one reported leaks as of yet.

'Where are you?' she muttered, her breath making the glass fog.

She wiped it away with her sleeve. Wind lashed tree limbs, flattened bushes and wailed in a way that haunted her.

Still, she did not move from the spot. Although, she could not imagine what help it was to Boone for her to be staring out the window.

How utterly frustrating to be of so little use when any awful thing could have happened.

A movement caught her eye. She touched her nose to the glass, narrowed her eyes to focus her vision on whatever it was.

Boone! She dashed for the front door. She did not know that the movement was him coming safely home, but who else could it be?

Stepping to the edge of the porch she spotted a carriage far out on the road. Poor traveller must have been taken off guard by the storm.

That was not the movement that first caught her attention, though.

The riskiest thing she could do is stand out here in the open and continue looking for whatever had moved.

Chances are, it was only something blown lose in a gust.

Shivering, she hurried back towards the front door.

Thunder rolled overhead but there seemed to be another sound with it. Hand poised on the doorknob she waited for the rumble to pass.

In the next second, she heard a long, mournful sounding low.

A cow wandered in a circle in an open area a distance beyond the front gate.

'Clarabelle!'

Ambrin glanced about praying that Boone would appear and lead the frightened animal back to the barn.

No matter how deeply she peered into the downpour, he did not step out from the tree line or come striding around the corner of the house.

'Oh drat, drat, drat!'

If the animal was to be put inside, she was the one who must do it.

It was her duty. She must act boldly.

Boone would not stand on the porch and let an animal perish because he was afraid to go out in the weather.

He was fearless. She was terrified.

'Here I come, Clarabelle!' she called rushing down the steps before common sense caught up with her.

Electric static lifted the hairs on the back of her neck only an instant before lightning hit a hundred yards or so to her right. Her knees went weak with the need to cower on the ground.

But no, she was no longer a helpless child. Boone needed her to act in his place.

As much as that, this was her home. Hers to protect.

Leaning into the wind, she made her way to Clarabelle.

'Don't worry, I'm here.'

Ambrin touched the cow's wide forehead. It would be helpful if the animal was wearing some sort of tack with which to tow it. How was she to convince the creature to walk back to the barn?

'You remember me, don't you?'

Clarabelle snorted.

'I shall take that to mean that you do.' Ambrin circled her arm under the cow's jaw, urged her along. Being pressed against a cow was not as horrid as she expected it to be. 'Come now, we shall be safe in no time at all.'

To her astonishment Clarabelle moved along with her.

'You must be as frightened as I am, but I promise you when we reach shelter I shall give you whatever it is that Boone feeds you, in celebration of our valour.'

The cow gave a long moo.

'You do not need milking, do you? I have seen it done but…'

Please do not let it be milking time.

Coming to the barn door, she found it blown off one of its hinges.

It was dark inside, but Clarabelle walked without urging towards her stall.

Ambrin lit the lantern that was kept next to the door. By its soft glow she saw that the cows' stall door had also blown open.

Luckily the other cow, Bessie, had maintained the good sense to remain inside the barn.

'That must have been one powerful blast of wind.'

With the danger of being struck by lightning abated, Ambrin's soaked condition began to make itself known. Oh, but it was chilly.

As promised, she gave a bit of whatever was in the feed bags to both cows. She stared at their udders wondering how to tell if they needed to be milked.

Boone always did it shortly before sunset, which had been and gone hours ago.

While she stood debating with herself whether or not it would be cruel to wait for Boone to do the milking when he returned, both cows began to low.

'I shall do my best, then.' It would be a wonder if she gave the animals even the slightest relief.

She could only imagine what her London acquaintances would think if they saw her in this moment. Why, they might faint on the spot, and then awaken to have a good gossip over her fall from society.

Nevertheless, needs were what they were.

She tied both cows to the stall slats as she had seen Boone do. Then she took a stool, sat on it and simply did what she recalled her husband, and yes her young niece, doing.

To her amazement, she soon had a pail full of milk.

Clarabelle and Bessie seemed satisfied. To be honest, she felt rather proud of her accomplishment.

With that challenge met, she then had to make her way back to the house.

'Oh, my word,' she muttered while listening to the barn door flapping in the wind. The storm had not let up but had grown more intense.

She would like to remain here, sheltered with the chickens and the cattle, but the family would be missing her by now.

Under no circumstances must they come looking for her.

She picked up the pail. Boone always brought the milk to the house immediately. She would do the same.

She became soaked again before even going out since rain blew unhindered into the barn.

Gathering every valiant impulse within her, which was not much, she charged headlong into the gusts.

Also, into the arms of a drenched cowboy.

'Boone!' She dropped the bucket. It tipped over. She launched into his arms and hugged him tight. 'Praise the Good Lord you are safe! Where's Tom?'

'He went on to the house. I saw the lamp and came directly here.'

Fearing she might have overstepped in expressing her relief at seeing him safe, she stepped back.

'All is well, then?' she asked.

'With me and Tom it is, but, darlin', look at you. What made you come out in the weather?'

'Clarabelle. You can see what happened to the

barn door and then the stall blew open too and so out she came.'

'And then out you came?'

'Not as easily as all that but, you were not here and so yes. Out I came.'

He gave a glance at the milk pooling around their shoes. 'And you did the milking.'

'Not as well as you and Marigold do, but the cows were ready.'

'My brave wife,' he murmured, and then wrapped her up in an embrace that felt like home. More than walls, or a roof and floors. Boone Rawlins folded her up in security.

'You're shivering. Let's get you back inside,' he murmured, lowering his arms from about her.

Had she been shivering? She hadn't noticed. Now, without his arms around her, she did.

'Perhaps we can wait here until the storm passes.'

'That could be hours and I'm hungry. Better get inside before Tom eats everything.'

Then he slipped one arm about her back, lifted her to her toes and gave her a quick kiss.

'For having courage,' he said after kissing Ambrin.

Now he wished courage for himself.

Seeing his wife stare down her worst fear to go and rescue a cow, to act in his place when he was away, did something to him.

That forbidden road he'd been gazing down? Love

for Ambrin kicked him all the way down to where it ended.

And he stood there alone.

The ache to tell her that he loved her swelled so tight in him he felt like his chest would burst.

Curse him, but he'd been within a breath of pressing her to make a commitment she might not be ready for.

He was ready. Good and ready.

Yet, he would wait and bide his time. The worst thing to do would be to press her for feelings she did not have for him.

Not yet at least. Things were changing between them. He felt it like a tingle in the air. A shift of heart was on the way, sure as he was breathing.

They were making slow progress from the barn to the back door of the house, getting drenched and windblown.

Only yards from the shelter of the back porch, he felt a drag on his hand. Ambrin drew him to a stop.

'Are you hurt, darlin'?' Had she stumbled and he didn't notice? Or maybe she had a stitch in her side from the fast pace he'd set.

'I am not afraid when I am with you. And…' She swiped her face, brushing away the water running into her eyes. '… I do not believe you kissed me for courage. Why did you, Boone?'

He cupped her cheeks then stroked her wet hair. He wanted so desperately to tell her that he loved her.

Hadn't he vowed to be truthful with her? No more secrets or surprises?

'You've thought yourself an obligation to me and who could blame you? I never wooed you or wed you in the way a man ought to. But, darlin', it's not true.'

She closed her eyes and sucked in a breath, looking like she was stuck between believing him and not.

Her cheek was warm. Her skin was slick with rain. So were her lips. He lowered his mouth and kissed her.

No mistaking this for a kiss of courage. It was deep, possessive. And he did not quit until he felt her go soft and responsive in his arms. 'Did that feel like an obligation, darlin'?'

'I don't kn—' She blinked rain out of her eyes.

'It wasn't. That was a man wanting his wife. It was me wanting you.'

Thunder rolled and pounded overhead. Ambrin shivered so he pressed her tight against him. Her heart beat hard. Her breathing came fast.

'I figure you don't feel the same. I shouldn't have pressed you and I won't do it again. But know this, Ambrin Rawlins, you are my wife vowed so before God…' His voice hitched because he suddenly couldn't find it. '…and I love you.'

Damn it if he'd gone and ruined things now. Pushed her away as sure as if he'd shoved her with his hands.

Then again, maybe not. She clutched the soggy lapels of his coat, drew herself up to her toes, sighed against his mouth.

'I think maybe…' She hesitated as if she feared revealing what she thought.

The thing he'd felt shimmering in the air, it hung on what she would say next.

The back door opened.

'Oh, there you are!' Millie exclaimed, relief clear in her tone. 'Come in at once. Mr Adams has arrived.'

Mr Adams? Greycliff's solicitor, here in her house. How curious.

Ambrin quickly changed out of her wet clothing and into a dry gown. She could not get back to the kitchen soon enough to discover why he was here and what could be so urgent to bring him out in the weather?

Whatever his reason, it was at least well-timed. Or ill-timed, she was not quite certain.

Shockingly, she had been within a breath of telling Boone she would share his bed tonight.

Even now, with a bit of time between Boone's confession of love and this moment, her mind was caught in confusing and conflicting emotions.

Was she overjoyed to learn of Boone's love or was she stunned and distressed?

She'd found herself at a crossroads, with a choice to be made at the end of it.

Since she had never intended to have a marriage of the sort Boone wished for, she should not be considering it.

Oh, but she was.

He wanted babies. She wanted babies.

She wanted him.

What would it be like if she allowed herself to follow where her imagination led? Her husband was an appealing man.

They had their whole lives to spend together after all and, just perhaps, it would be better to live those years as a proper married couple.

Sitting on Boone's bed to tie her boots she thought about to her reason for keeping her heart to herself.

Resentment.

That is what it came down to. She had a right to it, she supposed, since at every turn the choices for her future had been taken from her.

Along with that, Boone had kept important truths from her that he ought to have been forthright about.

Matters were different now. He had vowed to be honest with her and she believed him.

When she thought about it, revealing his heart to her had been a way of keeping his vow of honesty.

And the kiss! It went to the deepest part of her heart and there had been no obligation to it.

She had given herself to him in the moment and been so close to telling him so.

The announcement of Mr Adam's arrival could not have been more untimely.

Later tonight they would continue what had been interrupted. She touched her middle to settle the nervousness, understanding that the conversation would have to be with and without words.

Finished with lacing her boots, she smoothed a wrinkle from the blanket on his bed.

For years she'd had her fantasies. Dreamed of the man who would one day speak words of devotion to her.

Now they had been uttered by the man who was her husband. A man whose desire she was free to return.

Boone's admission, the truth so genuine and softly spoken, played over and over in her mind and made her toes dance in her nice, dry boots.

She turned down the lantern then left the bedroom, indulging in a fantasy of what tonight could be like.

Hearing voices in the kitchen, she walked that way.

Somehow, Boone had already changed into dry clothes. His hair still gleamed with moisture, though.

Later, when the house was quiet and put to bed, she would touch his hair, let it tickle and glide through her fingers.

Boone and Mr Adams sat side by side at the kitchen table. Mr Adams pointed to this and that on some sort of document.

'Good evening, Mrs Rawlins!' Mr Adams scraped his chair in rising. He smiled and offered a slight bow as he would have had done had they been in London.

'I hope you did not encounter any problems travelling in the storm,' she said politely, her sense of civility as deeply rooted as his was.

'There were a few tricky times having to do with mud and the wagon wheels slip-sliding. I am happy to have made it through for this appointment. I have very good news indeed.'

Appointment? She did not recall a mention of one.

The solicitor spoke to her and not Boone so her husband must already be aware of this good news.

'Oh?' she asked. Judging by the expression dragging Boone's lips she began to suspect that she might not be as thrilled over the news as Mr Adams was.

'Good news indeed! As I sent word last week, we have an offer for the London House that far exceeds what I had imagined getting for it. All I need is Mr Rawlins's signature and he will have more than what he needs to purchase his cattle herd.'

Last week!

Stricken, she stared at Boone. He was holding a pen in his hand. It was poised over the document.

Here was where she ought to say how wonderful the news was. Boone's dream would be fulfilled.

But she knew that if she opened her mouth that was not the sentiment that would come out.

Once again, she had been caught by surprise. By a secret of vital importance that had been kept from her.

Boone had failed to keep his promise.

What else might be a lie? That he loved her?

Perhaps his vow of love had only been to get her into his bed. How else was he to attain the family he wanted?

It felt as if something clutched her about the throat, choking her voice.

This hurtful news, along with the shock of Boone having likely lied when he declared his love, made her feel as if she had been delivered a blow and a counter punch.

After several trembling breaths, she found her voice. Although it was shaking, she managed to form words.

'You ought to have told me.'

That said, she turned and walked out of the kitchen with all the dignity her brokenness would allow.

'That didn't seem to be welcome news to Mrs Rawlins,' Adams commented, raising his brows while watching her hurry from the kitchen.

'I imagine it wasn't. As you know, she grew up in that house.'

'Yes, and her parents and grandparents before her. I have worked for the family for many years, and I understand what a blow this must be for your wife. I only hope she will adjust to the change.'

The change. Yes, she had been expecting that. But the betrayal… Curse it, but she'd trusted him not to keep secrets from her.

'I have some things to think over, Mr Adams. Would you mind staying the night and sharing a room with young Tom?'

'Not at all. I don't fancy going back out in this weather at any rate.' Adams stood up but Boone remained sitting, didn't know for sure he could trust his legs to hold him up.

'I'll just go the parlour and spend some time by the fireplace before I retire. I wish you luck bringing your wife to terms with all this.'

While Boone appreciated the sentiment, it was going to take more than luck to make this right.

'We will speak again in the morning.'

'Goodnight then,' the solicitor said, and went to the parlour.

Bringing his wife to terms is not what he had in mind. What he needed to do is come to terms with himself.

Earlier, Boone had had it on his tongue to inform Ambrin of the sale. Twice he'd nearly told her. Those moments had been lost. Once by a flooded paddock and then again by the announcement of Adams' arrival.

What he wouldn't give to have the time back and do things differently.

Seeing his wife's stricken expression, the disbelief of his broken promise reflected in her eyes, he'd lost the satisfaction he'd felt when he first saw the generous offer.

It was a plain fact that with that money, he could purchase a fine herd. The bank account would have enough funds to carry them through any misfortune. The whims of nature would no longer leave him in ruin.

His family's financial future would be secure.

But at a cost. The woman he loved was suffering.

In the previous moment, he'd seen any hope that they might have had for building a loving family there on the farm, fade from Ambrin's expression. Watched it die like the light snuffed from a dimming lamp.

He'd confessed his heart, his love. In doing so he'd felt his soul go someplace it could not come back from.

He'd crossed a line and now found himself alone.

What was the point of having his dream, this home and these beautiful acres if the person who mattered so much to him was miserable?

The secrets he'd kept from Ambrin had been well intentioned. To ease the pain of the unjust things happening to her.

What a mistake he'd made.

He hadn't taken a wife only to make her miserable.

Boone tapped the pen on the paper and then set it aside.

A flash of lightning bleached the kitchen. Thunder rolled over the roof and then away leaving behind a steady slap of rain on the window.

Storms, he decided, were a bad omen for him. For the second time one foreshadowed the ruin of his dreams.

With a last glance at the price written on the proposal, he pushed his chair away from the table, stood and went to look for Tom.

Chapter Fifteen

Ambrin felt pressure on her shoulder, fingers gently prodding. What time was it? She cracked open one eye and peered out the window.

Why, it was not yet dawn, although she did hear a lone bird chirruping.

'Wake up. I'm taking you home.'

Home? What was Boone talking about?

She sat up, drew the blanket to her chin and blinked at him, half believing she was in some odd dream.

'Where, precisely, do you imagine me to be?' Perhaps his newfound wealth had gone to his head and left him confused.

'This farm is not your home, darlin'. I'm taking you home to London.'

'I see. And what do you intend to do with me once we get there? Drop me off in some strange place among people I do not know? I might as well stay here and be unhappy.'

She sounded petulant, she knew, but it might be a

while before she felt favourably towards Boone Rawlins. It seemed she could not trust him any more than she could her late brother.

Why, the thought tormented, did he tell her he loved her?

There were only two reasons she could think of.

One was for the children he wanted. The man did seem willing to do whatever necessary to attain his ends, as selling her home would attest to.

The other is that he was not lying to her about loving her. Although, she did not know why she should believe it.

If only she could take back the tender feelings she had entertained for him. From now on she would certainly give it every effort.

'I'm taking you and Marigold to Greycliff. Millie and Frederick have agreed to come with you.'

'For how long? I do not wish to settle back to my life and then have it yanked away again once the new owner takes up residence.'

Boone stood up from her bedside then went to stand in the doorway. He tapped his fingers on the wooden frame.

'I'm not selling your house. You may stay for ever if you wish.'

For ever without him?

It felt like that is what he meant.

She would have asked but he was no longer standing in the doorway.

But she was going home! Leaping out of bed, she plonked her feet on the floor. The wooden planks were hard and cold under her toes. She wasn't dreaming then.

Second by second what he'd told her settled in.

Home. She could nearly hear the comfortable rumble of street traffic beyond Greycliff's walls.

This is what she wanted, beyond anything.

Dressing hastily, she imagined the scent of morning fog whispering over the Greycliff garden.

The sun had set a couple of hours earlier so the streets were dark when they drove into London on the farm wagon.

Ambrin was glad of the shadows, but not for the reason she would have expected.

Weeks ago, when they had departed the city in this very vehicle, she had been sensitive to what people thought. She had dreaded seeing judgement in the gazes of the early risers.

Not so this evening. For some reason, people's opinions did not matter to her like they used to. Let those passing by in their carriages on the way to the opera or a musical think what they might of her return.

The reason she was glad for the darkness is that it hid her husband's expression.

For all that she was attempting to distance herself from tender feelings she did not wish to entertain, it would wound her heart to witness the dejection on Boone's face.

Driving away from the farm earlier, he'd seemed so distant and dejected. His heartache had been plain to see.

There was no indication that he had been angry or resentful, only broken-hearted.

At one point, when they'd crossed the boundary of their farm, he'd patted his coat pocket and squeezed his eyes shut. In the instant, she'd noticed a dried-out lavender flower peeking out.

She was beyond curious to know what it was. Surely it meant something special to him.

Not that she would ask. The easy way they used to have between them had died when she'd discovered he'd withheld the truth from her.

Yet, in spite of everything, she missed how they were together.

Perhaps in time, when her heart had time to heal, they would find their way back to the way it had been when they were friendly. When they had kissed.

Against her better judgement, and within a deep part of her soul which did not judge but only felt, she hoped it would not take terribly long.

Boone had not spoken to her of his intentions once they arrived in the city. But then, he had not spoken of much at all.

Probably, he intended to sell the farm in order to keep Greycliff. It is the only thing that made sense.

What if he did love her and this was his way of proving it?

No, she did not dare hope so. More likely this was his way of easing guilt.

Perhaps once they settled into life at Greycliff, into a daily routine, his good humour would be restored. Surely matters between them would be easier.

A secret part of her longed to hear him call her darlin' again. She did miss the endearment terribly, if she were honest.

Time heals all wounds is what was said. Hopefully that was true. For now, she would simply rejoice in coming back to the home she loved.

Letting go of his dream would not be easy for Boone, she knew. But she prayed that in time her husband would think of this as home as much as he had the farm. To come to love it as she did.

London was such a grand place to live.

What, she had to wonder, would his daily routine be like in the city? What would bring him pleasure?

Try as she might, she could not picture it.

However, society had been drawn to him from the first.

Really there was no reason to worry. Boone Rawlins would fit in quite well with the gentlemen of her acquaintance, even though he held no title but cowboy.

Boone stopped the team in front of beautiful and elegant Greycliff.

'Here we are again,' Millie huffed from her place on the back bench of the wagon.

It did not sound like it, but surely Millie was happy to be home, truly home?

Petunia hopped down then trotted over to sniff the front steps.

Frederick got down from the wagon with a grunt. He and Boone unloaded the few boxes they had brought with them. It was mostly her own personal belongings.

In only a moment she would walk into the hall, light the lamp beside the door. Light would fill the room, overflow with brightness and fill up her heart.

Everything would be as it was before that first night when Boone stood in her doorway looking fearful wearing his gun and his Stetson with the dead snake on it.

That was wrong though. Nothing could ever be as it had been. Grant would never come home.

However, Marigold was here.

Life had gone on and it had changed. There was a ring on her finger reminding her she was a married woman now.

Boone came in behind her carrying Marigold who was asleep. Millie and Frederick came in after, setting the boxes down in the hallway.

What she wanted quite desperately was to tell her husband how grateful she was, how happy he had made her. Now, however, did not seem to be the time.

Although she was beginning to feel better about

what had happened, and the new turn life had taken, Boone clearly did not.

Perhaps tomorrow, in the cheery light of a London morning, his spirits would be restored.

With everything brought in, Boone crossed the parlour. He stood for a moment simply looking at Marigold who he'd placed in an armchair, still fast asleep.

He touched the child's hair, smoothed it from her temple then kissed her forehead.

'I love you, little darlin'. Never forget it.'

Something grabbed Ambrin's chest and squeezed.

There was a quality to Boone's whispered goodnight that seemed wrong. It was almost as if he were saying goodbye.

Surely she misunderstood.

Boone had given up his dream in order for her to have hers. It made sense that he would need time to adjust to the idea. It only made sense that he was not his usual cheery self.

What she wished to do is hug him tight, kiss him and tell him how grateful she was.

Even if the thought that crept into her mind was correct, and he intended to go back and live at the farm until he sold it, that did not mean she would no longer be his wife.

The vows they had recited had been for ever vows. Even though they had been spoken without a bond of love, they were valid, nonetheless.

Nothing would change in that way except for a long

day of travel separating them. And really, by train it would take far less time. Marriages could be satisfactory when the couple did not share a home every day.

Besides, it could not take terribly long to get the farm ready to sell.

But he had not said he was going back and perhaps she was wrong.

No matter what he intended, she still had tonight. Surely they could come to some sort of peace between them. Once she told him that her anger was wearing off and she forgave him, all might be well.

But wait! Had she forgiven him? If so, when exactly had that occurred?

Probably when she'd understood that he'd put her needs ahead of his own. Such behaviour made it difficult to hold a grudge. And made it very easy to want to kiss him again.

But then it was Millie who Boone kissed on the cheek. A tear dripped down her nose. Boone whisked it off with the pad of his thumb.

'It's for the best,' he told her, but Millie shook her head.

'It's a mistake, is what it is.'

What? Millie had to be as happy as Ambrin was to be home.

Next, Boone turned and shook Frederick's hand.

'I'll pray the Good Lord watches over your crossing.' Frederick gave Boone a nod. 'I shall look after things here. And I'll be in touch with Tom as often as I can.'

Crossing? Whatever were they talking about? Probably not the bridge spanning the stream at home, or rather at the farm, she corrected herself.

This was home.

Boone stooped down, wrapped his arms around Petunia's wide hairy neck and hugged tight. 'You be a good dog, now…watch over our girls.'

'Crossing? Boone, what is going on?'

She heard footsteps padding across the tiles as Frederick and Millie walked out of the parlour carrying Marigold.

'I must go back to America.'

'But no, you—'

He held her by the shoulders but did not draw her close. Rather, he held her at a distance, looking her steadily in the eyes.

'I'll need to earn money for my cattle. And to keep up Greycliff.'

He could not possibly mean that.

'If you sold the farm we could—'

'Don't ask that of me.' He dropped his arms then took a step backward, closer to the doorway.

'What about Marigold?' she said scrambling for some reason to keep him in England.

The thought of him being an ocean away was the loneliest thing she could imagine.

'There's no cause for you to worry. It won't be like it was before. I'll send money. It shouldn't take long to begin earning a wage. Ranches always need cowboys.'

'And they pay cowboys enough to buy a cattle herd and send money home too?'

She rather thought not. If only her voice were not quavering. She must sound terribly despairing.

It was not as if she wasn't able to care for herself and the people depending upon her. She had done so before this cowboy charged into her life and turned it upside down. She was capable of doing it again.

Only, the cowboy had charged into her life. He'd swept her up into his own and now… Now nothing would ever be as it was.

'I've left enough money for you to get by until I settle. I'll send word once I do. It could be I'll go to California and make my fortune in oranges.'

'And maybe I will never see you again!'

Greycliff meant everything to her, but the thought of this being the last time she saw her husband cut to the heart.

Once again, he might have told her of his plan. Perhaps she did not forgive him after all. Would there ever be a time when her world was not upended?

All she could do is stare at him in utter disbelief.

'Goodbye, Ambrin,' he whispered then turned towards the door.

'You said you loved me,' she murmured to the back of his leather jacket. 'Was it yet another lie?'

She watched his back expand in a deep breath then his shoulders go rigid. He turned about, his eyes bright with unshed tears.

'I meant it. If I didn't you wouldn't be standing here in your fancy parlour.'

It was the very truth. In the moment she understood that no one had ever loved her more than this man did.

No one ever would. And yet she was allowing him to put an ocean between them. Could she stop him if she tried to?

'Will you kiss me goodbye?' She stepped up close. Felt heat rising from his skin. Breathed the scent of leather and Boone Rawlins in deeply.

She went up on her toes, closed her eyes in anticipation.

Then nothing. No warmth, no strong arms going about her drawing her close and claiming her as his own.

Opening her eyes, she saw him shake his head in one crisp statement of refusal.

'Don't reckon I can. Goodbye, Ambrin.'

With that, he opened the door and walked away into the night.

Rain began to fall. Lightning cracked a few streets away.

Even so, she stood where she was, watching until his shape disappeared into the dark. This is the very way he had come into her life.

Only now he was going out.

As was her custom, Ambrin awoke slowly. Listening to the world come alive beyond her window before she opened her eyes.

Hmmm, where was the cockerel's crow? The bird on the branch outside her window ought to be singing her awake by now.

Sunshine should be streaming in to illuminate Boone's pillow.

How curious she thought, then opened her eyes to look.

All at once she sat up and gasped.

She was home. It was true and not a dream.

What a bright and brilliant day. She got out of the small bed in Grant's old bedchamber. She preferred her own sunny bedchamber but until she managed to have a bed moved there, she would sleep here.

Going to the window, she drew it open to the bright day and cheerful birdsong.

Very well, the day was not bright but foggy. Still, it was not raining and the birds were singing.

Cocking her ear, she listened for the sounds of Mayfair coming awake beyond Greycliff's walls.

Carriage wheels rumbled over the cobbles.

She waited for that familiar clatter to touch her heart. Then she waited and waited.

The wait was interrupted when someone cursed loudly. A carriage driver offended by another driver blocking his way, she supposed.

No matter, what difference did it make that traffic did not sound as soothing as it had before, as long as she was home.

This was going to be a positively brilliant day she decided while rushing for her wardrobe.

Everything here was going to be all the better for having missed it all these weeks.

The few fancy gowns she owned were as lovely as they had ever been and she was anxious to wear them again.

Just wait until she told Marigold that she could now wear her pretty dresses every day.

Dressing quickly, she hurried downstairs all the while thinking of the marvellous things she would show her niece today.

She also thought about Boone, how could she not? If he had travelled all night, he would be home by now. He must be gathering eggs or milking Clarabelle.

She did not think of him for long though, because missing him was too painful. She paused for a moment at the foot of the stairs, looking at the front door and imagining him in the moment she first saw him.

In all her dreaming of coming home, she had never considered it would be without her husband.

Well, he had made his choice and was apparently putting her behind him. Moving on with his life in spite of the fact that he claimed to love her.

And yet, that was not quite right. Moving on with his life meant that he was leaving what was most dear to him, his farm. And he was doing so for her sake.

Giving herself a shake, she pushed away those sorts

of thoughts. There was nothing she could do about the situation even if she wished to.

What she could do is fill her heart with the joy of being home.

She went into the parlour, overwhelmed to be seeing so many of her beloved things just where she had left them. It is as if… It was silly she knew, but it was as if they had been waiting expectantly for her return.

After a few moments of touching this and that beloved item, she noticed something. The room did not look as cheerful as it normally did.

Perhaps she was missing some of her favourite treasures that were still at the farm.

Or perhaps she was missing Boone. Drat, the thought ambushed her from nowhere. She would not think of it now.

Very likely, cheerfulness was missing because she had not lit the fire in the hearth. How quickly she had gotten out of the habit of doing it. At home, at the farm she meant, Boone always lit the fireplace before he went about his predawn chores. She had never woken to a cool, cheerless house.

Not that she meant her parlour at Greycliff was altogether cheerless. No indeed, not.

This is where she grew up. Her memories lived in every nook and corner.

Today was going to be a very good day to become reacquainted with them.

While she began to build the fire, the first memory to come to her mind was of Boone and Marigold sitting on the hearth. Boone had set his bowl of stew on the floor for the dog to lick clean.

The next memory was the way she'd felt when, after he'd given her the news of Grant's death, he'd held her tight to him trying to comfort the awful grief.

Paws padded across the floor, bringing her back to this happy day.

'Good morning, Miss Petunia. I suppose you need to be let outside.'

It was the dog's habit to go out with Boone before daylight. Poor girl must miss him.

'Come then,' she said, ruffling the fur between Petunia's ears the way Boone always did. 'We must make new customs.'

The first afternoon back in London had been quite nice.

Ambrin had let Marigold pick out her favourite gown to wear and they had spent a lovely time visiting shops. They'd had tea and cakes in a quaint tea house then walked in the park.

Truly, it could not have been a lovelier afternoon.

That is until an hour ago when she had discovered her niece curled up on her chamber floor with Petunia, her small fingers entwined in the dog's fur.

'May we go home now, Auntie?'

The question had taken Ambrin aback because this was home.

All of her memories were here and soon Marigold's would be too.

She meant to give her niece the life every little society girl dreamed of.

'We are home now, sweetheart, isn't it wonderful?'

The only answer she got was a shrug, and then, 'When will Uncle Boone come home?'

When indeed?

Not for a long time. She did know that much.

So now she found herself lying on Grant's bed after her first day of enjoying the pleasures to be found in London…and not feeling the glow she'd expected to.

She turned on her side, tucked her hands under her cheek and stared at the empty space where Boone's bed would be if she were back at the farm.

Here she was in the place she'd wanted to be, and only here because her husband was giving up the place he'd wanted to be.

She closed her eyes because the empty space was too hard to look at.

Closed eyes did nothing to help. No indeed, she saw Boone in her mind. The smile he gave her each night before he turned on his side and fell asleep was quite vivid.

All of a sudden, she felt soaked with rain. She wasn't really. It was all just a memory in her head before she was drawn into sleep.

'Ambrin Rawlins, you are my wife, vowed so before God… And I love you.'

The moisture she felt on her lashes, though, was not imagined.

The next morning, Ambrin jolted awake at a harsh sound.

She sat up, pressing her hand to her chest and catching her breath.

What she heard had only been a street vendor shouting and hawking his meat pies.

Although it was not as pleasant sounding as a cockerel's crow, it got her out of bed just the same.

Today would be another lovely day. She would not allow the steady drizzle to convince her otherwise.

Neighbours had noticed her return and she had received invitations to tea. The question was, were they interested in welcoming her home or were they curious as to why her fascinating cowboy husband was not with her?

News that her house had been for sale would surely have been gossiped about.

Venturing out later in the day she suspected it was curiosity more than welcome that garnered the invitations.

Later she was convinced of it. Oh, the tea had been the best she'd tasted in a long time, the cakes pretty and dainty.

However, all anyone one wanted to speak of was her

sudden marriage and how delightfully romantic it was. That is what they said but she knew better. What they wanted to know is what prompted her unusual union and where was her husband?

His whereabouts is the question that was never far from her mind. Was he still at the farm or had he sailed for America?

Very likely Frederick knew but she hesitated to ask. Probably because she took comfort in believing he was still on this side of the ocean. Why was that? She had been perfectly satisfied with her own company before a cowboy burst into her home. All afternoon she'd had the sensation that if she turned quickly, he would be there.

Of course, he never was. What was there, was simply aching disappointment.

She had prepared dinner for her family but eaten little of it herself.

Afterward, everyone retired to their own chambers, leaving her alone in the parlour.

The clock ticked endlessly. The fire popping and crackling in the hearth was not as comforting as it ought to have been. She snapped the book closed that she had been reading.

Pretty, romantic poetry used to make her heart flutter. No longer. It was sitting in front of the hearth with the man who loved her that did that. And listening to him breathe in the night. There was watching him ride across his beloved acres on his horse, too. That was a sight that never failed to catch her attention.

Being downstairs by herself was depressing. It was too early for bed, but she could not bear to remain down here any longer.

As she walked past Marigold's bedroom, Ambrin heard sniffling. She opened the door to find the child, once again on the floor snuggled next to Petunia.

Hurrying across the room, Ambrin knelt beside them.

'What is wrong, sweetheart? Why aren't you in bed?'

'It doesn't feel like my bed. Me and Petunia miss Uncle Boone. May we go home tomorrow?' she sniffled.

The dog gave one slow thump of her tail as if in sorrowful agreement.

Ambrin had it on her tongue to argue that this was home but, in the end, she could not find any convincing words.

Instead, she kissed Marigold on the forehead.

'Tomorrow will be a happy day. Just wait and see.'

Chapter Sixteen

Ambrin awoke on her fourth morning at home smiling because a brilliant idea had come to her in a dream. One that was certain to cheer Marigold up.

Surprisingly she found the idea pleased her as well.

Both she and Marigold were bound to feel more at home if there were a chicken coop in the garden.

The thought jarred her for an instant. What she ought to have thought is that her niece would be the one to feel more at home.

However, what she thought she ought to think is not at all what she actually thought.

Hearing a cockerel crow in the morning would be a sweeter way to greet the day than listening to angry carriage drivers berating their fellows.

Strangely, what used to sound like music now seemed like noise. What used to sound like noise seemed like music.

Boone's voice calling her 'darlin'' had always been music, never noise. She missed hearing it more each day.

Never mind though, now was not the time to dwell on his voice.

And she might not, except that had told her he loved her and how was a woman to forget the sound of those words? She simply could not. His voice in that moment had been poignant, the words softly uttered. They would be for ever embedded in her memory.

Later on that night, in the quiet of her bed, she would have no choice but to dwell on missing her husband. But now it was time to shop for chickens.

Hurrying downstairs, she looked in four rooms before she located Frederick in the garden industriously polishing silver candlesticks.

Something had happened to the house while she'd been away. Impossibly, it seemed to have doubled in size.

'Oh, here you are, Frederick. Why are you working outside?'

'It's a nice morning and I've grown accustomed to working outdoors.' Frederick answered. 'I trust you had a restful night, Mrs Rawlins.'

'Mrs Rawlins? You always call me Ambrin.'

'I like the way it sounds. Wouldn't want to forget it.'

That made no sense whatsoever. No one was likely to forget her name. But perhaps he was not speaking of a name so much as a family position.

In order for there to be a family, a happy one, there must be a husband who loved his wife and a wife who loved her husband at the head of it all.

She did have a husband who loved her. As he said, she would not be living at Greycliff if he did not.

The oddest sort of ache squeezed her heart, clenched her stomach.

Missing Boone hit her harder by the hour. Next, she knew, she might be the one on the floor cuddled up with Petunia and weeping.

What exactly did that mean?

She had always felt she and Boone had a certain connection between them. Oh yes, she had been drawn to him right off.

And yet something had kept her from giving her heart over to him. From allowing herself to fall in love.

'You were looking for me?' Frederick winked at her. 'Looks like you wandered off in your mind.'

'Oh, yes! It is chickens. We ought to have them. I was hoping you might know a place where Marigold and I can go to purchase some.'

'Ah, Fairfield Market. I saw them last time I went to purchase eggs. I will accompany you.'

'Thank you. I'll tell Marigold and we shall go at once.'

Bringing a bit of the farm to Greycliff would be just the thing to cheer the place up.

Wasn't that odd? In the past her home had never required cheering.

Three hours later she, Marigold and Frederick proudly carried home a hen and her six chicks. It seemed rather like they had won a prize since the proprietor of the shop had been hesitant to part with his stock.

Naturally the people passing by would not recognise the value of a hen and her chicks. She imagined her fine neighbours did not often encounter an egg that had not already been cracked and cooked.

What a sight they must seem. Marigold dressed in her prettiest lace dress carrying a box containing noisy chicks while Ambrin, satin ribbons streaming from her bonnet, carried their red feathered mother tucked under her arm.

The hen, clearly distressed by the happenings, made loud, clucking sounds to her babies in the box.

Frederick followed behind carrying supplies to fashion a small coop.

It would not be as nice as the one Boone built.

Nothing was as nice without him.

Ambrin stopped so quickly her skirt twisted around her ankles. This thought, as well as some others she'd had of late, clamped her heart in a fist, squeezed and left her confused. Because if things truly were better with her husband, why was she building a chicken coop in London?

The hen began to squirm under her arm, so she took the box from Marigold and set her inside with her chicks.

'I reckon she wants to live at the farm.' Marigold reached up to pet the hen's soft feathers.

'We shall build her a very nice coop right here in

our garden,' Ambrin said, knowing very well that her niece did not mean the hen, but rather that she, herself, wanted to live at the farm.

There was no way to explain to a young child that even if they went back home, her uncle would not be there and so nothing would be as it had been.

Of course, nothing here was as it had been, either.

'Why! I never in my life!'

She did not need to turn and look to know who uttered the snide remark. Mrs Dawson's censorious tone was one she had heard too many times in the past not to recognise.

Very well, let her be shocked to see a lady parading down the grand avenue with a box of chickens tucked between her arm and her lace trimmed bodice. It would do her good. Ambrin had no sooner closed her front door behind her than a sharp rap pounded on the door.

Ambrin handed the box to Marigold. 'Go along and find a spot in the garden you think they will like.'

Once she was alone in the hall, Ambrin opened the door.

'Good day, Mrs Dawson… Hello, Margaret… How are you, Paulina?'

Naturally, Mrs Dawson had brought her walking companions along with her to witness what could only be the sharp end of her tongue. Which, when she gave it a bit of thought, was the only kind the woman had.

The single reason Ambrin greeted them politely is

because, in spite of what they thought, she was a lady and had been trained in the art since she was a child.

A child who, quite honestly, would have been happier playing with chicks.

'Is something troubling you, ladies?' she asked. 'You look distraught. Perhaps a bit of tea would help.' Ambrin stepped to the side as if she were inviting them to come inside.

'Just look at her, Margaret.' Mrs Dawson said as if Ambrin was not standing right in front of them extending an invitation. 'Imagine a lady of quality shamelessly carrying livestock on our decent streets. I am grateful my boy did not wed that one.'

'Yes, as am I, Mrs Dawson. More grateful than you can imagine.'

Harsh words, a bit uncharitable even, but true, nonetheless. She should not take satisfaction in seeing the woman's chin drop but this was a gesture that fine ladies did not make. Mrs Dawson's true nature was on display.

'Indeed, so that you could marry that cowboy living in your house. Quite the scandal, if you ask me. It is no wonder you had to marry him.' This too was something a lady would never say.

Paulina gave Mrs Dawson a narrowed eye. 'I do not think those words are called for. It was proper to allow Mr Rawlins to live there because of their niece.'

'Be that as it may, I imagine a line was crossed and she found herself in a...position...shall we call it? She was forced to wed that Rawlins man and that is why she could not accept my Willard's courtship. It is the only reason that makes sense.'

All three women's gazes slipped to Ambrin's middle.

A subtle shift had been made inside of her, one she might not have noticed had she not come face to face with Mrs Dawson in this moment.

More and more, though, she wondered if society no longer suited her. Ambrin might have been raised to be a lady, but that is not all she had learned growing up. If the past few years had taught her anything it was to stand stalwartly when trouble came at her.

A gossiping biddy was nothing compared to her brother's death and the financial complications that went with it.

'I have something to say to you, Mrs Dawson. I will only say it this once because I'm certain within the hour everyone will know it. Mr Rawlins was not staying in my house. I was staying in his. Yes, that is right. Me, an unmarried woman, living in a single man's home. My brother gave Greycliff to Mr Rawlins, who, out of respect for my position in society, remained silent about the matter.'

'What? I ask you…' Mrs Dawson pressed her fingers to her throat, glancing back and forth between her companions. 'What has society has come to when a lady openly admits to such wickedness! And just look at her. Clearly, she feels no shame.'

Ambrin was rather stunned that she'd admitted the truth, but shamed by it? Not a whit. She had no reason whatsoever to feel disgraced.

Hot and flustered is what she felt. It was time and past for the truth to be known.

All of the truth, even that that she kept from herself.

In the moment, Petunia trotted across the hall to the front door and slid her wide head under Ambrin's hand, giving her the courage to go on.

The women backed up several steps. No doubt they disapproved of large hairy dogs.

Good girl, Petunia, she thought.

'Think whatever you wish to, Mrs Dawson. Margaret, Pauline, I trust that you will see that what I have to say is reported accurately. But the truth is, I am no longer a lady. What I am is a farmer's wife and grateful to be. My husband loves me and I love him. There is no more compelling reason to wed than that.'

She loved Boone! Had declared it in front of the worst gossip in London.

More, she had declared it to herself.

Her world had not collapsed about her.

Instead of feeling entrapped, she felt liberated. Choosing to love her husband had given her a wonderful sense of freedom and belonging all at one time.

'Good day ladies. I am going home, back to the farm.'

She closed the door in their faces, grinning at the

horrified expressions on two of their faces. Pauline, bless her, offered a smile and a wink.

For too many years Ambrin had been ensnared by choices she did not make.

No longer.

Because of Boone she could live here at Greycliff quite nicely if she wished to.

Or she could go home.

She only wished she had recognised the truth earlier. The truth being that her husband meant more to her than these walls. More than a life in society.

Boone Rawlins meant more to her than anyone ever had.

If she had not been too stubborn to admit she loved him, he would not be on his way to America.

'Please, oh, please, please, please, do not let me be too late,' she murmured dashing after her family.

She caught up with Frederick in the kitchen. Millie and Marigold must have already gone into the garden with the chickens.

'Frederick,' she panted, winded from the run. 'Do you know when my husband plans to leave for America? Is he still here?'

'I cannot say for certain. He told me he would go as soon as he got Tom instructed in everything. The boy is a fast learner. But maybe our Boone is not as quick at teaching.'

She was certain that was not true and yet—

'We are going home.'

'Even if we might find him gone?'

Oh, yes. Even then. Especially then.

'It is where he will find us when he returns. We are going home. It is where we belong. How quickly can you be ready?'

'Right away! I'll inform Millie. She will be so pleased.'

'Let me tell her. I need for you to bring Mr Adams here at once. I have an urgent matter to discuss with him before we go.'

'I'll be back with him within the hour.' With a nod and a grin, he hurried away.

Standing alone in the kitchen, Ambrin glanced about. It all looked like home, but she had been greatly mistaken in believing that the walls held her love and memories.

Boone held her love and she prayed fervently that she would not be too late to tell him.

To show him in the same way he had shown her.

Chapter Seventeen

'Reckon that's it, Tom,' Boone said then shook the boy's hand. 'I know you'll do a fine job looking after the place.'

'No need to worry about anything, Mr Rawlins. I'll make you proud.'

Standing in the centre of the paddock, Boone took a glance at the stable, then at the house.

Only a quick glance though. It was damn painful saying goodbye for the last time. He'd started saying farewell to it when he'd taken Ambrin home to her beloved Greycliff, but this was the last he would see of his acres, maybe for many years.

It hurt him plenty having his dream cleaved near in half. Not put in the grave, though. One day more cattle would graze this land.

Giving Tom a nod, he mounted his horse then turned it towards the road.

It seemed odd that his dog wasn't trotting in place beside him. He couldn't rightly drag Petunia away from Marigold, though. They'd been raised together, frolicked about like both of them were pups. Since he didn't know how long he would be away, it was best to leave the dog with her.

Maybe once he got himself settled someplace and earning money, he'd get another dog.

Not another farm though. This one had gotten under his skin, lodged inside his soul.

Riding along the road, he spotted a tipped fence post.

Dismounting, he set it right. Although he was leaving later in the day than he had planned to, he lingered in saying goodbye.

He got back on his horse and went on a way.

When he came to his property boundary, he had some trouble crossing over, so he dismounted again, tied up his horse to a post and then walked to the tree that marked the edge of his land. It was big and shady with willowy branches that swept the ground. He watched them sway with the grace of dancers doing a waltz.

It wouldn't hurt to sit here one more time. He leaned back against the trunk, same as he'd done many times. Only then he'd been dreaming of how fine it would be when he had his cattle. More often though, he thought of how good life would be when he, Marigold and Ambrin lived here as a true family.

He'd even allowed himself to imagine welcoming new babies into the Rawlins fold. Sure was a foolish thing to do since it wasn't the vision his wife had. Only, he'd hoped that one day… Well, there was no longer a 'one day' for him and Ambrin.

Feeling low about the way things turned out was his own fault. He'd made plenty of mistakes when it came to his wife.

Not being truthful with her was one. He'd promised to and then had betrayed her trust.

Though admitting the truth of his feelings was another mistake. He probably shouldn't have told her he loved her when she wasn't ready to hear it.

Loving her wasn't a mistake though. Even now, knowing how it all ended, he did not regret what he felt for her. Not any more than he'd regretted loving Susanna and losing her.

Loss, he reckoned was the price of love. At some point it had to be paid.

He took off his Stetson, leaned his head back against the bark. It was rough, but soft didn't seem fitting in the moment.

At least, he'd done the right thing by Ambrin in giving back what her brother had taken. Marigold would enjoy growing up to be the proper lady she was born to be, on her father's side at least. It wore on him wondering how much she would change by the time he came home. Children had a way of growing even while a fellow watched.

As much as he regretted it, going away was what he

had to do. He had a home in London to keep up and a dream of his own to fulfil.

But damn it, he was going to miss his wife even more than he would miss his farm.

He reminded himself that forcing Ambrin to continue to live there when she longed to be home, was not loving her. And he did love her. Nothing that had happened to her had been of her choosing. He wasn't sorry for putting that right.

'Better get a move on. The boat won't wait for one miserable cowboy,' he mumbled while reaching for his hat. Mounting up he gave a last, long look at his acres, how they rolled away so green and easy on the eyes.

He aimed to be back one day but life, he'd learned, didn't always turn out the way a fellow planned it to.

The road ahead of Ambrin stretched out ahead, long and empty. She feared she had left the decision to come home for too long. Her stomach was one big, aching knot. This was the only road between the farm and Tapperham. Boone would have to travel along it in order to pass through the village and get to the coast. So far, he was not on the road, which told her nothing, really. Either he was at home, or she had come too late and had missed him.

What would she do if she was too late?

Not shatter. She might wish to fall apart but that would do no one any good.

What she would do was wait.

While she did, she would learn to care for the dozen head of cattle that were crowding the road ahead of her. When Boone returned, he would find the herd he dreamed of grazing his fields.

She and Tom together, along with advice from Hyrum Burnbrow, whom she had purchased the creatures from only hours ago, would learn how to turn this dozen into more.

'I cannot thank you enough Mr Burnbrow. It is kind of you to bring them home for me.'

'Don't mind a bit, Mrs Rawlins. I only hope we make it to the farm in time.'

The man had seemed so father-like and comfortable to speak with that she had told him the whole story, beginning when Boone first stood in her doorway looking like a... Well, he had not been a villain at all. Now when she remembered his appearance in the moment, she recognised him to be her bold and handsome hero.

'They are slow creatures,' she observed thinking that speed did not matter so much. Boone was where he was and there was nothing to be done about it except pray. And that is what she had been doing on and off since she'd left the rest of the family behind in London.

'Hurry now, you cattle,' she urged the plodding herd.

Slow and steady they kept their pace, flicking their tails as they shuffled along.

'Git along, you cow,' she called because that is what Boone always said to their dairy cows.

'Where are you, husband?' she whispered.

* * *

Boone was only halfway to Tapperham and running late. He'd dallied too long saying goodbye to the farm and would need to travel all night to get to the harbour in time to board the ship.

'All we'll get is a quick rest and meal,' he told his horse.

He had a goal to accomplish. He must bear in mind that the good he was doing for his family by going away, was worth the cost.

'What do you suppose our girls are doing right now?' he asked his mount in an attempt to think no further than the moment he was living in.

Dwelling on life in the distant future would only break his heart. With all he'd had to get done in preparation to go away, he'd managed to avoid it.

Now though, riding away from home, it was hard not to.

As far as he could see, the future didn't look bright.

Ambrin would have her life in London. Happy in the society that was so familiar to her.

Boone had no idea where he would be. Back at his farm one day, he hoped.

He sure wouldn't be living there with the family he'd envisioned, though.

Damn it he'd better lasso his thoughts before he got too low-down to press on. He had a ship to get to, an ocean to sail across.

A sound caught his attention. Cattle lowing and on

the move. He couldn't see them around the bend in the road but judging by the clop of hooves on the road, he'd guess there were a dozen or more.

Next time he travelled this road, he would be the one herding cattle, bringing them home. It might take years to happen, but it would happen.

Going around the bend, he shaded his eyes against bright sunshine in order to see who was driving the animals.

A man and a woman as far as he could tell, but he couldn't rightly see them with the light so bright.

The woman screeched.

Funny what a mind could do. It imagined the woman was calling his name. Her voice sounded like his wife's.

Couldn't be, since she was in London, probably buying bows and having tea.

The woman slid off her horse. She shoved her way through the stalled herd, all the while calling his name. Further proof that this was his imagination. Ambrin would never walk through a herd of cattle.

The lady pushed through a patch of shade and then he saw her clearly.

'Ambrin!'

What the blazes? It was her!

He leapt from his horse, snaked his way past one cow after another until he met his wife in the middle of the throng.

'I found you!' She hugged him tight around the middle.

Cattle bumped them from all sides, but Ambrin squeezed his ribs not seeming to care.

'Darlin', what the blazes are you doing standing in the middle of this fellow's herd? Is something wrong? Is Marigold—'

'Nothing is wrong…not any more. I came to tell you I love you.'

'I reckon I fell and hit my head on a rock and this is a vision I'm having.'

That had to be the truth since the last thing the woman he married would do is get this close to dirty, smelly, scary cows.

'Vision? Why, I did not come all this way to be mistaken for a figment.'

Then she grasped the brim of his Stetson, drew his face down close to her lips.

'I love you, Boone. Please, do not go to America.'

Then she kissed him.

She didn't vanish in a puff. Rather, she pressed in tighter. The vivid curves of her form convinced him that this was as real as the cow whose nose just bumped him between the shoulder blades.

'Surely do love to see a happy ending,' the man on the horse declared.

And Boone purely loved the miracle of kissing this woman in the middle of the road. Even with the stranger's cattle pressing on all sides.

'Reckon we ought to let this fellow get on his way

with his herd,' he whispered once he was able to put his mouth to use with speech and not kissing.

'Oh, but this is not Mr Burnbrow's herd, it's yours.'

'What in the great glory blazes do you mean mine?' He took her hand and drew her out from the middle of the cattle where he could hear more clearly. This conversation was not making a lick of sense.

Except that she loved him. Love made sense or she would not be here.

'Unless you want to drive them the rest of the way, young man, I'll take them along to the farm. It looks like you folks have some things to say to one another. I'll get them settled in and then rest awhile. Won't be back this way for a few hours yet.' Grinning, the stranger moved the herd down the road towards the farm.

'Are you certain you do not wish to do it yourself?' Ambrin asked.

With all the goings on, he might slip off his horse if he tried. Besides, something more important than cattle was going on here.

'I reckon we do have some things to say.' Boone grabbed the reins of her horse and his. Seemed like what they had to say would be better communicated while walking, with their feet on good, solid ground.

'I know it's not many for a start,' Ambrin began. 'But once we sell the London house, we can get many more.'

'Whoa there, darlin'. What do you mean sell the London house?'

'Well, now…' She rose on to her toes, hugged him around the neck and kissed him again. 'With all the relief of finding you in time, and with all the kissing, I didn't get a chance to tell you about the house.'

'We'll get to that. But Ambrin, darlin'.' He slipped his arm around her shoulders while gripping both pairs of reins in one hand. He bent his mouth close to her ear. 'First I want to hear more about how you love me.'

'You might not believe it and who would blame you since all I ever said is that…' She frowned, bit her bottom lip while shaking her head. 'I was such a fool thinking that living at Greycliff was all I wanted. That it was home. I missed you so much, Boone. Nothing in that grand place felt like it used to. Without you, no place is home.'

She cupped his cheeks in her both of her hands, maybe thinking she needed to get all of his attention. Truth was, he was not aware of a single thing except her beautiful face and the way she looked at him in the way he'd only dreamed of.

'I love you, husband. Please forgive me.'

His breath caught. His heart tripped. Coming to a prompt halt, he felt hot tears gathering in the corners of his eyes.

'Forgive you? I'm the one who needs forgiving.'

'No, Boone, I only made it seem as if you did. Now I see how you only ever acted out of concern for me.

I blinded myself to… Well to us and to the love we could have.'

'Aw, darlin', feels like I've just been handed a miracle. Do you reckon it's unmanly for a cowboy to weep, because I'm about to.'

'Go ahead, so am I. We…' Her bottom lip quivered, looking moist and glistening in a ray of sunshine. 'We shall do it together.'

And so, they did. She pressed her face to his chest. He dipped his forehead to her shoulder.

Turned out to be joyous weeping and somehow, they were laughing at the end of it.

He lifted his bride off her boot toes then twirled her in a circle.

No one would ever convince him he was not living a miracle.

There was even a dried-out crocus protected inside his saddle bag that had, all along, indicated this moment would happen.

They walked on not speaking for a distance, just feeling each other's presence and giving thanks for their miracle, which this had to be.

There were moments when words were not needed.

Then there were moments when words were needed.

Coming to the edge of their property he tied up the horses then led her to the tree he'd sat under earlier.

He gave her a long, hungry kiss, all the while lowering her to the grass. He lay beside her. Leaned, up on one elbow in order to see the expressions passing over her pretty face.

In a moment or two they would come back to the point where they did not need words to communicate with one another, but now there were things he needed to know.

'Darlin', what did you mean about selling your house?'

'First thing, home is where you are and that is where I will be. I no longer need Greycliff or London.'

She brushed aside the hank of hair falling across his forehead. It was a wifely gesture that made him want to quit conversing in words.

'But I have some very good news. The buyer still wants Greycliff. Mr Adams gave me the contract for you to sign. I also told him to give me the money you left for us so that I could get a start on our herd. Once the house sells, we will have enough for you to have all of your dream.'

Shifting sunlight reflected in her hair where loose strands spilled across the grass.

Damn sure wasn't a contract he was thinking of at that moment. A leaf drifted down from the tree, slowly spinning until it landed on the bodice of her shirt.

He flicked away the leaf but left his hand where it had been. Her heartbeat thrummed against his open palm.

'Having a herd was only the beginning of that

dream, my darlin' Ambrin. Loving you, you loving me, us being a family. That's become the main of it.'

A warm breeze caught the willowy tree branches and swayed them over the grass. Sure did sound like loving whispers.

'I can't imagine what I would have done if you'd already gone away.' Laughter faded from her eyes. She gazed up at him with her love shining in them. 'Truly, I cannot.'

'You'd have thrived. It's what you do, darlin'. When life takes a swing at you, you punch back hard.'

'I would not have thrived. I'd have shrivelled away of a broken heart. You'd have found me in the barn weeping and waiting and milking cows.'

'You'd have waited for me, here? At the farm?'

'Of course,' her smile flashed, her eyes lit up with humour. 'Where else would I have brought our new chickens?'

'We'll discuss chickens later.' He didn't want to know about them just now.

He wanted to know his wife, in the way only a husband did.

'Where's the rest of the family?' he asked, while considering the wonder of how life could take a turn from misery to joy in a moment. In a kiss.

He could scarcely believe they were about to take their marriage from friendly to intimate. Give themselves to one another in a way that would for ever bind them as family.

'They will be here tomorrow. Mr Adams is bringing them.'

'Good then.' He flipped open the bottom three buttons of her blouse.

'What are you doing?'

'What does it seem like I'm doing?'

'Umm, but don't you want to see to the new cattle?'

'I do not. They'll be fine.' That said, he kissed her while freeing two more buttons, these from the top.

Sunshine dappled her face and her throat.

'Never seen a sight prettier than you right now,' he managed to whisper.

'But don't you think we should continue at home…' Her breath came quick so her voice shivered. 'Where there are walls?'

'We are home, darlin'…right here under this tree. Can't you hear the song the land is singing to us?'

She shook her head, smiled.

'Just listen. Hear the grass whispering and the breeze rustling. The branches all sweet and tender?'

'Well yes…now I hear it.'

'So then, with the Good Lord's blessing, I aim to fulfil my wedding vows right here.'

She answered with a wink and a grin.

And he answered back.

The sun was setting when Boone carried her over the threshold of their home.

Never before had they been completely alone in the

house, but now with Mr Burnbrow on his way back to his own farm, Tom gone on an overnight trip to Tapperham to get feed for the new cattle and the rest of the family in London, they were.

The promise of intimacy filled each room he carried her through, as rich and heady as a fine perfume.

Three hours later, with the moon just rising and the promise fulfilled, her husband carried her to the front porch wrapped in a large quilt.

It was a good thing that the man in the moon could not see out of his craterous eyes because Boone was bare to the world…and to her.

Side by side, skin to skin they watched the big white ball rise over the trees. Now that she and Boone had discovered intimate things about one another, it hard to put clothes back on.

Not that she minded one little bit.

'How many cattle shall we have?' she asked, snuggling her head against his shoulder and revelling in his scent, which was quite potent given there was no fabric between him and her nose.

'As many as we can afford, I reckon.' His big hand caressed her shoulder, slid down her arm. 'How many children shall we have?'

'As many as we can love, I suppose.' She wriggled onto his lap, nestled her cheek in his hair.

'Dozens then, I reckon.'

'May I suggest we go back inside and continue inviting them?'

'I suggest we don't bother taking all those steps.'

'Yes, indeed. What is the point in extra steps?' she managed to answer without breaking the kiss she was giving him.

Then there was only Boone and she found her true home.

There were no walls, no roof or floor where her heart lived.

Only Boone.

Ordinarily, the journey from London to the farm took all day by wagon but Adams brought the family home by train, so they were all sitting around the table for the noon meal.

Looking at the faces of the people gathered at his table, Boone gave thanks for each one of them.

There were family. The promise of the lavender crocus had led them here. He would never believe otherwise.

Once they all finished eating, Tom went to the barn. Marigold dashed after him wearing her ruffled, beribboned dress. Petunia bounded after them, her deep bark echoing across the meadow.

Turns out Marigold did not love London, but she did love her frilly frocks. It sure made him smile to look out the window and see her running in the grass, the big blue bow on her dress bouncing and catching winks of sunlight.

When all was said and done, the baron's daughter shined through but the rancher's daughter shined brighter.

He reckoned Grant would be proud to see it.

Adams patted his belly, paying a compliment to Ambrin and Millie for the meal.

After Millie and Frederick left the dining room, Adams brought out the sales contract, placed it on the table where he and Boone sat side by side.

Ambrin stood at his back, her hand on his shoulder, while the solicitor went over the details.

Then it was time to sign his name to the document that would give away the home where generations of his wife's family had lived.

All at once, he was uncertain.

What if this was a mistake that Ambrin might live to regret? What if, once Marigold understood the world was broader than the acres where she ran freely about, she resented him for giving away her heritage?

Adams tapped the paper, indicating the spot for him to sign. Boone set the tip of the pen on the paper. Then he lifted it again, glancing back over his shoulder.

'I wonder if this is a mistake.'

'It isn't.' Ambrin smiled, nodded encouragingly. 'Go ahead and sign it.'

'We need to be certain. You need to be certain.'

'I am, quite.'

Then she covered his hand with hers, guided his hand to the signature line then, together, they signed.

'Congratulations Mr Rawlins, Mrs Rawlins.' Adams

stood, shook both of their hands. 'Be assured that the new buyer is delighted by the purchase. He has a large family and extends his thanks and his promise to love the home as you have.'

'I am glad to hear it. Greycliff deserves a family who will grow and be happy there.' His bride squeezed his shoulder reassuringly. 'The same as we will be here.'

'Well, I must be on my way if I am to make the train back to London. Please call on me if I can be of service to you for any reason.'

Fingers entwined, he and Ambrin escorted Mr Adams to the front porch then watched him ride away in his rented carriage.

'It's done,' Ambrin said.

'No, darlin', it's only beginning.'

Earlier today, he'd put the lavender crocus in his pocket because for some reason it felt fitting that it should be there. He hadn't known why until this moment.

'I've got something for you, a gift, I reckon it is.'

He drew the fragile flower out and placed it in his wife's palm.

'You had this in your pocket before, when you took us to London, didn't you?'

He nodded, smiled. 'I picked it from Susanna's grave on the day I left the ranch. Always imagined it was her way of pointing me on my way. Seems to me like she was pointing me to you. She'd want you to have it.'

'I've never been given a more precious gift.' With

the flower cupped in her hand, she leaned in to hug him. 'I do mean the flower, but more, I mean you.'

'It's a miracle isn't it, darlin'…the journey, I mean. How it led from Susanna's grave to our family here.'

Amber stroked the fragile blossom. 'It is rather incredible that cowboy and a baron's daughter found one another. All I can say is that I'm grateful to whoever had a hand in us standing here on our own front porch.'

And so, they remained, her shoulder leaning against his for a long time, looking out at the land and letting the wonder of the past and hope for the future, wrap them up.

Spring 1891

'It's time,' Boone announced.

'Finally!' Marigold exclaimed, balancing one and a half year old Grant on her small hip. She was nine years old now, but still near a baby herself—in Boone's eyes anyway.

Naturally, his eldest child had quite a different opinion on the matter.

Marigold seemed partial to the youngest family member. He was cute as could be, but Boone figured it might have to do with the boy being named for her father.

'I've been waiting for ever,' Marigold whined.

'Only since last autumn,' Ambrin reminded her.

'Seems like years, Mama,' three-year-old Margarite

complained, taking the side of her cousin as she always did.

Then she lifted her arms for her mother to carry her down the road to the tree that marked the line of their property.

The place where they planted new crocus bulbs each fall.

It had become a tradition to make a family outing of going to see the flowers when they first bloomed.

There was a good-sized patch of them now. Looked as pretty as a lavender carpet this time of year.

Boone swept his daughter up. 'Your mama has enough to carry.'

'Only a piece of wood.' But she hugged him about the neck. 'I like when you carry me too, Papa.'

Ambrin was carrying something made of wood, a surprise she'd told him. She hid it within the folds of her skirt so no one would see.

That however was not the only thing she carried. She rested her hand over the mound of her belly and shot him a smile. Their third child was due any day now.

'Here comes Tom with the wagon,' Millie said. 'Come along Frederick, we will ride.'

Since the family had members from young to elderly, they always took the wagon in case someone needed an easier way home.

He urged Ambrin to ride but she refused, saying the walk would do her good.

So off they went to view the crocus in their glorious first bloom.

Petunia dashed ahead, stopping every once and again to bark at a cow.

The herd was growing right along with the family.

Even Tom had announced he had a special young lady he would like to court and maybe one day add to their number. He was a young man now with his own cottage on the property.

After a cool, damp winter the sun felt warm for the first time.

It was a fine day for the outing.

Seeing the patch of lavender crocuses in the distance, Margarite wriggled out of his arms. The children dashed towards the flower patch together.

Boone put his arm around Ambrin's shoulder.

'There's a sight to warm the heart,' he murmured, feeling grateful to his bones. 'Can't wait to meet this little one. How are you feeling?'

'I'll do for a while.'

'What is it you have hidden in your skirt?'

'You'll know soon.'

As eager as the children were to see the crocuses in bloom, their attention didn't last long so Tom and Frederick loaded them into the wagon, with Millie offering a promise of hot cocoa at the end of the ride.

'Let's sit for a moment,' Ambrin suggested. Boone eased her to the grass.

'It gets prettier every year.' He tipped his wife's chin up, gave her a good long kiss. 'You do too, darlin'.'

'You see beauty in a woman who waddles about like she has a melon within her?'

'I see it especially then. Wonder what this one will be.'

'Loved.' She winced while patting the mound of her belly, which rolled and heaved.

'Cherished.' He placed his open palm on Ambrin's middle. The mass turned firm as rock.

'The miracles just keep coming,' she said with a small gasp.

'Darlin'?' He arched a brow at her.

She nodded. 'It seems I'd better be quick with the surprise.'

Opening the fold of her skirt, she revealed a painted sign.

'I painted it when you were busy with the herd.'

'Oh, Ambrin, darlin'… It's perfect.'

At a loss for words, he spoke with a kiss.

'Susanna's Garden,' he read, feeling a lump swelling in his throat. He set the plaque in place. 'Nothing could be more perfect. Next fall we'll add even more bulbs.'

He got lost in admiring the sign over the crocus blooms.

'Boone.' His attention turned back to his wife when she squeezed his hand. 'Our newest blossom is on the way…now.'

'I'll go fetch the wagon.'

After giving Ambrin a lingering kiss, he leapt up. Dashed after the wagon, waving his arms and leaping for joy.

* * * * *

If you enjoyed this story, be sure to check out these historical romances from Carol Arens:

The Gentleman's Cinderella Bride
Marriage Charade with the Heir
The Truth Behind the Governess

Or let yourself get swept up in her charming The Rivenhall Weddings miniseries

Inherited as the Gentleman's Bride
In Search of a Viscountess
A Family for the Reclusive Baron

MILLS & BOON®

Coming next month

THE MAID'S MASQUERADE
Catherine Tinley

Book 1 in **The Heiress Switch** series

'Why will you never speak of your mother, or our betrothal?' he asked, and her heart was sore at the sincerity in his eyes. 'You must know I wish you to be my wife.'

Marguerite could not help it; she allowed her eyes to show the feelings she must never give voice to.

'Sophia!' he cried, moving to kiss her, but she recoiled, his use of Sophia's name feeling like a slap in the face to Marguerite. 'What is it?' He paused, ever the gentleman.

'No. I—I must not! I am so sorry for leading you to believe...for even suggesting that I might... I cannot!'

'But why?' He took her hands. 'Can you not be honest with me?'

She winced. Honesty was the one gift she was not free to give.

'I have come to know and admire you very well these past weeks,' she began carefully, weighing every word. 'But there are things...there are matters which I am not free to discuss, my lord.'

'You should call me Benedict,' he offered, confusion clear in his expression, but she shook her head.

'It would not be right,' she said firmly. A servant should never, ever make use of the intimate name of a peer of the realm.

'You are a puzzle, Miss Van Bergen!' He ran a hand through his hair. 'A puzzle, and a damn—a *dashed*—paradox, and I know not what to make of you!'

His anger was clear, and suddenly it occurred to her that his own recovery from her betrayal might be expedited if she gave him a disgust of her. So, hardening her tone and lifting her chin, she shrugged. 'It is very simple, my lord. I have done what I needed to do in the pursuit of my own interests.'

Continue reading

THE MAID'S MASQUERADE
Catherine Tinley

Available next month
millsandboon.co.uk

COMING SOON!

We really hope you enjoyed reading this book.
If you're looking for more romance
be sure to head to the shops when
new books are available on

Thursday 20th November

To see which titles are coming soon, please visit

millsandboon.co.uk/nextmonth